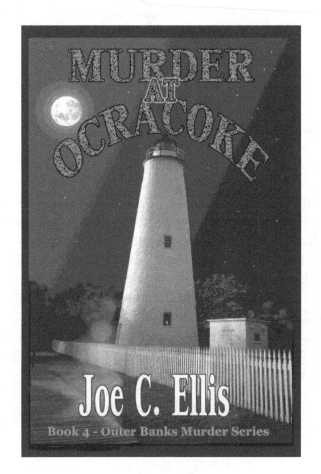

A novel by

Joe C. Ellis

Book 4 – Outer Banks Murder Series

Upper Ohio Valley Books
Joe C. Ellis
71299 Skyview Drive
Martins Ferry, Ohio 43935
Email: **joecellis@comcast.net**
www.joecellis.com

PUBLISHER'S NOTE
   Although this novel, Murder at Ocracoke, is set in actual places, the Outer Banks of North Carolina, various locations in West Virginia, Pennsylvania, and Ohio, it is a work of fiction. The characters, names, and plot are the products of the author's imagination. Any resemblance of these characters to real people is entirely coincidental. Many of the places mentioned in the novel—Buxton Village Books; Manteo, NC; Buxton, NC; Hatteras, NC; Wheeling, WV Suspension Bridge; Youngstown, OH; Martins Ferry; OH, etc., are real locations. However, their involvement in the plot of the story is purely fictional. It is the author's hope that this novel generates great interest in these wonderful regions of the U.S.A., and, as a result, many people will plan a vacation at these locations and experience the beauty of these settings firsthand.

CATALOGING INFORMATION
Ellis, Joe C., 1956-
Murder at Ocracoke by Joe C. Ellis
ISBN 978-0-9796655-7-8
1.Outer Banks—Fiction. 2. Ocracoke, NC—Fiction
3. Mystery—Fiction 4. Suspense—Fiction
5. Martins Ferry, OH—Fiction 6. Youngstown, OH--Fiction
7. Towanda, PA—Fiction 8. Wheeling, WV—Fiction

OUTER BANKS MURDER SERIES
By Joe C. Ellis

The Healing Place--
Prequel to Murder at Whalehead

Murder at Whalehead

Murder at Hatteras

Murder on the Outer Banks

Murder at Ocracoke

All books available in hardcopy and ebook formats.

Chapter 1

"Did you feel that?" Sienna Bryce asked. The tall, middle-aged blonde aimed her camera toward the Pamlico Sound at a spot known as Teach's Hole. The breeze fluttered her nylon windbreaker as she adjusted her camera settings.

"Yes. There *are* spirits among us," her partner, Luna Holiday, said. Luna was much shorter and perhaps ten years younger, with curly black hair that sprang out from under a black ball cap. "Does anyone else feel an odd sensation on the surface of your skin?"

Mee Mee Roberts didn't feel a thing.

"I do," said Adelaide Brackenbury. "Look at my arm." She held her forearm in the swath of her husband's flashlight. "Do you see the goose bumps?"

"Clearly, darling," Rowland Brackenbury said. "You are a ghost detector, maybe even a ghost magnet."

Mee Mee definitely detected a hint of amusement in the

man's voice. She had met Rowland Brackenbury a few months back at her bookstore in Buxton. He was a bald man in his mid-fifties, overweight and red-faced, with a self-important English accent. At his request she organized this ghost hunt.

Standing next to Mee Mee, Achak, a Native American, closed his eyes and tilted his head backwards. His long black hair spilled from his receding hairline and dangled to the middle of his back. Mee Mee figured he was trying to tune in to the spirit realm.

The camera's flash lit the beach, a momentary blaze of white light against the spidery shrubs, sand, and dark waters of the Pamlico Sound. The paranormal investigator held up her camera to inspect the picture displayed on the image viewer. "Look at that!" She gushed. "I see six orbs. Count 'em."

Luna moved closer to inspect the image. She lowered her head, blocking Mee Mee's view. "One, two, three . . . four, five . . . six. You're right. Unbelievable!"

Mee Mee wanted a closer look at what was so unbelievable. When Luna backed away, Mee Mee and Adelaide Brackenbury leaned forward to get a better looksee. The orbs in the photograph appeared to be luminous, floating bubbles against the blue-violet sky. Very weird, Mee Mee thought. She straightened and stared into the darkness. "And what are these orbs supposed to be?"

"Spirit entities," Luna said. "Like a form of energy with personality."

"Ghosts? Why can't I see them with the naked eye?" Mee Mee asked.

Sienna bobbed the camera in her hand. "This photography equipment is much more sensitive to ectoplasmic activity than the human eye."

The photograph seemed to accelerate Adelaide Brackenbury's breathing. She was an attractive woman in her early thirties with mid-length platinum blonde hair and a shapely figure. "Is it possible to identify the spirits who have gathered here with us?"

Achak with his eyes still closed said, "There are three Pamunkey Indians in our midst."

"I knew it," Adelaide Brackenbury said. "I could sense their presence. I feel like I've been here before."

"Maybe in one of your past lives," Rowland Brackenbury chuckled.

"I know you think it's silly, Rowland," Adelaide said, "but it's all so familiar. And these spirits with us . . . I know them. I've been among them."

"All the more reason to proceed with our plans," her husband said.

Achak snapped out of his sky-gazing trance. "What plans?"

Rowland spread his hands. "Developing Ocracoke Island, of course."

Achak grunted. "That would be a grave mistake."

"Ohhhh . . ." Rowland crossed his arms. "I didn't know you were one of *them*."

"One of whom?" Achak barked.

"An extreme preservationist. "

"Hmmmmph." Achak's usual frown doubled in intensity.

Mee Mee stepped forward. "There's nothing wrong with being a preservationist."

"I agree." Rowland held up his finger. "I said 'extreme preservationist' like the ones who control this island. There's a big difference." He turned and faced Achak. "My Native American friend here probably belongs to the Ocracoke Preservation Society, am I right?"

Achak nodded.

Rowland waved his hand. "There you have it: one of the few who limits access of this beautiful island to the many."

"We don't prevent anyone from visiting Ocracoke. We encourage it," Achak protested.

"Hmmmm. Let me clarify." Rowland pointed northward in the direction of the ocean. "Let's say I visited Ocracoke, and I loved it so much that I wanted to buy a parcel of land right out there on the ocean front and build a house."

"Not possible," Achak grunted. "Most of the coast has been designated for preservation. We do not want to see the wildlife or the natural beauty of the land ravaged by greedy developers who are out to get rich through exploiting what does not belong to them."

"You've got me all wrong," Rowland said.

"If you plan to develop this island, then I don't think so," Achak grumbled.

Luna reached and grasped Rowland's elbow. "Your wife drifted over toward the beach. Let's head in that direction. I think she is having a paranormal encounter."

Nice move, Luna, Mee Mee thought. She had invited Achak along because of Adelaide Brackenbury's suggestion to gather spiritually-minded people in hopes of increasing the odds of stirring up a spirit. Achak claimed to be an Algonquin shaman. She never anticipated he would butt heads with Brackenbury. Then again, Mee Mee didn't realize the British diplomat had plans for developing Ocracoke. She assumed his request to organize a ghost hunt was an attempt to placate his otherworldly wife.

Mee Mee followed Luna and Rowland across the sand to the edge of the water where Sienna and Adelaide stood. She heard strange words coming from Adelaide. Was she speaking in tongues? No. It sounded like some kind of Algonquin chant.

"What in the world?" Rowland said.

"Shhhhhhh." Sienna held up her hand and waved her fingers toward Rowland. "She's channeling one of the spirits."

Adelaide's head swung slowly back and forth as the gibberish poured out. Her eyes were half closed with only the whites showing.

Mee Mee wondered if she was having some kind of seizure. "Will she be all right?"

"I think so," Sienna said, grasping Adelaide's arm.

Rowland stepped forward and braced her from the other side.

Adelaide threw her head back and screamed. She lowered her head, and her eyes flashed open, but it appeared as if she was not focusing on anything in front of her. She let out another ear-piercing shriek.

Now Mee Mee felt something—Adelaide's howls sent chills up her spine, the kind one gets at horror movies when the maniac jumps out with a knife and starts slashing.

Rowland shook his wife by the shoulders. "Addy! Are you all right?"

Adelaide went limp in his arms but then quickly stirred back to life, blinking her eyes and catching her breath.

"What happened to you?" Rowland asked.

"I'm not sure," Adelaide said, breathing rapidly.

Luna's eyes grew wide. "You must have tuned in to one of the spirits among us."

Adelaide nodded slowly. "Yes . . . yes, I believe I did. It was an Native American girl. But . . . but . . . she wasn't alone. Someone . . . someone was chasing me. A man wanted to hurt me . . . I mean . . . a man wanted to hurt the girl."

"Can you describe the man?" Sienna asked.

"He was dressed in black and had long dark hair and a beard."

"Sounds like a pirate," Sienna said.

"That's perfect!" Rowland piped.

Everyone glared at Rowland.

"What's so perfect about a Native American girl being attacked?" Achak snapped. "My people have taken enough abuse."

Rowland held his hands in front of him, slowly circling them. "Listen to what I'm saying. This is what I want to recreate here on Ocracoke: history—Native Americans, pirates, settlers. I want to bring what happened centuries ago back to life. It will be Disneyesque and family oriented. I don't want to turn this beautiful island into another Myrtle Beach with surf shops, wax museums, miniature golf courses, and giant Ferris wheels. No way. I want to use the latest technology and creative vision to bring the ghosts of the past into the present."

"An Outer Banks Disneyland? I don't think so." Achak crossed his arms. "It's not going to happen here."

"I didn't say another Disneyland. It would be Disneyesque but on a much smaller scale. Like Disneyland, it would be well done—of the highest quality. Like Disney's best attractions, it will be educational but fun."

Achak uncrossed his arms and put his hands on his hips. "Okay. So you have this great vision of bringing the history of

Ocracoke back to life."

"Exactly."

The Indian's facial muscles relaxed. "How will you do this without developing acres and acres of protected shoreline property? How will you do this without creating massive parking lots?"

"Of course, we'll need land, probably fifty acres or more, but just think about the tourism and the financial blessings this will bring to the people of Ocracoke."

Achak shook his head. "No, Brackenbury, the financial harvest will be reaped by you and your investors. The people of Ocracoke will get only the crumbs."

"You're wrong, Achak. This region and its people will greatly benefit from my plans."

"Not if I can help it. I'll do anything I can to stop that kind of development."

Mee Mee glanced from face to face. Dead silence. You could cut the tension with a sharp tomahawk. She noticed Adelaide's focus drifting off in the direction of the woods.

"You can try to stop me," Rowland said, "but I know all the right people and my pockets are deep."

Achak slipped his hands into the pockets of his fringed leather jacket. "So are mine."

"What's that?" Adelaide shrieked as she pointed.

Everyone turned in the direction of the woods. Above the trees a huge creature hovered. It glowed against the inky night sky. Its wingspan had to be nearly ten feet.

"It's some kind of bird," Sienna gasped, "an eagle."

Mee Mee couldn't believe her eyes. "I've never seen an eagle that big around here. It's not a native bird."

Rowland's eyes grew large. "It's coming this way!"

The winged creature rose on the steady breeze off the ocean, flying in their direction. Then it let out a screech—an ear piercing "Eeeeeeeaaaaaaaaaarrrrrraaaaach!" Mee Mee had never heard anything like it in her life. It glowed like the phosphorescence she had seen in the Gulf Stream at night.

With the huge bird almost directly above them, all heads were tilted skyward. It let out another scream and spiraled downward. As it neared, Mee Mee checked out the size of its talons limned by the full moon.

"Those claws!" Rowland shouted. "It's going to attack us!"

"Run!" Luna yelled.

Mee Mee figured she had three options: take off along the beach and try to outrun the thing, dive into the Pamlico Sound and hope the creature didn't try to fish her out, or head for the cover of the woods. Everyone else sprinted toward the woods. Safety in numbers! She tried to catch up, swatting her hand above her head in an effort to ward off a barrage from above.

The creature screeched and swooped between her and the others, causing the group to break up, each veering off at slightly different angles. With the advantage of seeing the creature in front of her, Mee Mee watched it swerve right in the direction Rowland and Achak had fled. She angled left toward Adelaide and the two paranormal researchers.

She cut between two live oaks and pressed through the undergrowth until she was safely under the canopy of the trees. The screeching continued above the boughs, and the bird's silhouette skimmed over several times, blacking out the stars for brief moments. Mee Mee trudged deeper into the woods, hoping to find thicker cover. She stopped and listened, catching her breath. No more screeching. She panned her surroundings but could barely see anything. Where did everyone go?

Chapter 2

After several minutes of silence, giving her eyes a chance to adjust to the darkness, Mee Mee ventured deeper into the woods. "Can anyone hear me?" She whispered. She heard a cracking noise to her left and halted in her tracks. Peering in that direction, she tried to make out a human form. "Luna? Sienna? Adelaide? Anyone?"

"It's me, Luna."

"Thank God," Mee Mee gasped. She edged in the direction of Luna's voice.

"I'm over here, too."

That sounds like Sienna, Mee Mee thought. As she drew closer, it became easier to differentiate between the trees with their gnarled and twisting branches and the two women.

"Are you two okay?" Mee Mee asked.

"My heart's pounding," Sienna said. "I just need to calm down before I have a heart attack."

"Why did that creature . . . that giant bird attack us?" Luna asked.

Mee Mee shook her head. "I don't know for sure. I've seen hawks attack people when they have approached too near the nest. But that wasn't a hawk. I don't know what kind of bird it was."

"Maybe an osprey," Sienna said.

"No way." Mee Mee rubbed her chin. "Too large to be an osprey or Bald Eagle. My buddy, Lou Browning, spotted a golden eagle once. He's Hatteras Island's bird rehab expert. But he told me that was an incredibly rare sighting. Could have been a big vulture, I guess. But vultures don't attack people."

"Mee Mee! Is that you?," Adelaide called from about twenty yards away.

"We're over here." Mee Mee said.

Adelaide hurried to where they stood. "My heart's pounding."

Mee Mee heard the swish of branches and the crackling of twigs underfoot. Through the convolution of leaves and tree trunks she detected movement. "Who's there?" She called.

"It's me," Achak answered with a low, gruff voice. He moved quickly in their direction.

"Did you see my husband?" Adelaide asked.

Achak grunted and said, "Not a sign of the bastard."

Adelaide's eyes lit with indignation. She took a deep breath, blew it out, cupped her hands around her mouth, and shouted, "Rowland!"

"Shhhhhhhh!" Luna protested. "That bird might still be out there."

"I think we're safe here under the trees," Mee Mee said. "That creature is too big to fly through this thicket."

"Rowland!" Adelaide cried again, her voice edged with anxiety. "Rowland!" She pivoted and peered into the mass of crisscrossing branches. "Rowland!" She clamped her hands over top of her head and raked downward through her platinum tresses. "Why doesn't he answer?"

"Maybe he headed back toward the sound," Mee Mee said.

"Maybe the Animikii got him," Achak grunted.

"The what?" Sienna asked.

"The Animikii—the eagle that chased us, the Thunderbird."

"Thunderbird?" Mee Mee rubbed her chin. "I thought Thunderbirds were mythical. That creature wasn't a phantom, that's for sure. We all saw it and heard it."

Achak nodded. "Yes, we saw it." He tapped his temple with his forefinger. "Up here, with spiritual eyes."

Adelaide stepped forward, her brow tensing. "You're crazy. I could feel the wind from its wings."

Achak extended his arms as if they were wings and let out a loud screech similar to the bird's cry.

Mee Mee and the others stepped back. She felt the chill go up her spine again.

Achak dropped his arms and crowed with laughter but quickly sobered, eyeing the women. "The Animikii opens spiritual eyes. He makes you see him and hear him. He is the servant of the Great Spirit. He comes to warn us."

"Warn us about what?" Mee Mee asked.

Achak closed his eyes and breathed deeply, his arms rising and lowering again. "Clearly, the Great Spirit is not happy with anyone who threatens the balance and beauty of nature. The shadow of the Animikii will come upon him."

Adelaide grasped Mee Mee's arm. "Help me find Rowland. Maybe he wandered deeper into the woods." She drew Mee Mee closer and whispered, "I don't like that man. He gives me the creeps."

Mee Mee glanced at Achak. The moonlight through the trees cast shadows across the deep grooves of his face. His menacing demeanor unnerved her. She shook it off with a shudder of her shoulders and shifted her gaze toward the two paranormal researchers. "Would anyone else like to help us?"

They nodded.

Adelaide pointed her finger at Achak. "Not you. We don't need your help."

Achak grunted, his lower lip protruding like an oversized frog's. "Then I'll be on my way." He trudged off through the shadows toward Springer's Point.

Luna shook her head. "He's an odd one."

"These woods cover quite a few acres," Sienna said. "Do you think Rowland lost his sense of direction and headed north?"

"It's possible," Adelaide said. "He can get lost in Walmart."

"Let's split up into twos," Mee Mee said. "And try not to get out of earshot of one another."

"But how can we see without flashlights?" Luna asked.

"Cell phones," Mee Mee replied. "There's an app for that."

"You're right." Luna reached into her pocket, extracted her cell phone, and activated the flashlight app, beaming it across their faces. "There's an app for everything."

The four women scoured the woods for more than an hour. Mee Mee figured they ventured at least a half mile north of Springer's Point before they turned around and headed back. Trying to inspect the tangled growth and dark paths was problematic with only their cell phone lights. They needed more people and high powered flashlights. When they emerged from the cover of the woods, they walked to the middle of the open field.

"Where could he be?" Adelaide whimpered.

Mee Mee put her arm around her shoulders. "He's out there somewhere. Let's hope and pray he didn't fall and hit his head. If so, he may be lying in a dark ditch. Let me call the Hyde County Sheriff and see if they can send some deputies out to help us."

She poked 911 on the keypad of her phone. After a couple of rings a dispatcher answered. Mee Mee explained their circumstances and the possibility of Rowland Brackenbury being lost or hurt. The dispatcher explained there was not much Hyde County law officers or emergency personal could do without a body to attend to; the wife could file a missing-persons report after twenty-four hours. Then they would organize a crew to find him. The dispatcher assured Mee Mee that Rowland would probably show up within the next twenty minutes or so.

Mee Mee ended the call and shrugged. "They won't send any officers to help us tonight. If he's not back by tomorrow night, they'll form an official search party. I'm sorry."

"Tomorrow night will be too late," Adelaide protested.

Chapter 3

"I don't understand." Dugan Walton pushed up the brim of his Sheriff's hat and blinked. He felt like someone had just thrown a bucket of ice water in his face.

Deputy Marla Easton sat in the passenger's seat of the squad car, a Ford Interceptor, as they waited in the parking lot of Rusty's Surf and Turf in the small town of Buxton. "I need more time, Dugan. I'm just not sure. Marriage is a huge step." She held out the engagement ring, its mid-sized diamond glinting in the glow of the dashboard lights. "Please. Take it back for now."

"But you said you loved me." Dugan felt a huge knot form in his throat. He tried to swallow it, but it resurfaced within seconds. "You said this Christmas we'd have a simple ceremony at the Roanoke Island Presbyterian Church. For God's sake, Marla, Pastor Byron is planning on coming down from Ohio to marry us." Dugan shook his head, refusing to take the ring.

Marla leaned forward, resting her forehead on the heels of her palms. Her ponytail sprang from the back of her black ball cap and trailed halfway down her back. "I'm sorry, Dugan. I'm so sorry, but I'm just not sure we're right for each other."

"There's somebody else."

Marla sat up. "No! I swear to God Almighty there's not another man in my life."

"Then you've simply got cold feet."

"What?"

"You heard me."

She reached and placed the ring into the cup holder between the seats. "Maybe. I don't know. Something doesn't feel right. It's not you, it's, it's . . ."

"Please, Marla. Don't say, 'It's not you, it's me.' You don't need to pacify me. If it's over, I can take it. I'm not a kid anymore. I'm the Sheriff of Dare County, dammit."

Marla opened the car door. "Whatever you say, Sheriff, if that's how you want it, but I'm not trying to treat you like a teenage boy. I'm trying to tell you how I honestly feel."

"Right."

"I'll be back in a few minutes with the food. We're both hungry and tired. Please try to understand how I'm feeling."

Dugan watched her walk to the restaurant entrance. She was a beautiful woman—tall, athletic, well built, with that long, wavy dark brown hair. She reminded Dugan of one of Charlie's Angels, the brunette—too good looking, really, for a guy like Dugan. He glanced at himself in the rearview mirror. Even in the darkness he could see the freckles on his cheeks. He looked like a thirty-something version of Opie Taylor from Mayberry.

For the last year he kept telling himself their engagement was too good to be true. He'd given her plenty of time to get over the loss of her husband, Gabe. But how could he compete with the memory of the seemingly perfect man, her first love? Dead guys don't make mistakes. They stir only good memories; the bad memories fade away like shadows at sunset. No, Dugan was alive and well with all his flaws and faults. Marla finally realized that she couldn't love a guy like him, so far from perfect, average looking, and lacking the creative talents of her late husband.

A knock on the window startled him. A broad-shouldered bald man stared menacingly at him. His heart jumped, but he quickly recovered, recognizing his good friend Sonny Keys. Sonny's grimace transformed into a toothy grin.

Dugan powered down the window. "You just scared the crap out of me!"

A volley of suppressed laughter sputtered from Sonny's round face. "Semper Vigilans, my friend. Semper Vigilans."

"What does that mean?"

"Aren't you the head lawman in this county?"

"Yeah."

"Always vigilant, always alert, the Sheriff should be ready for anything."

"You caught me at a bad time," Dugan said. Marla's sucker punch to the heart had crumpled Dugan to the mat, numbing him to anything outside of his own anguish. "But thanks for pretending to be an escaped axe murderer. I'll try to do better next time. What's going on?"

Sonny pointed to the restaurant. " 'Bout to get me some fish and chips."

Dugan's cell phone erupted, and he slipped it out of his front pocket. "Hang on there a minute, Sonny." He slid his finger across the face of the phone and clapped it to his ear. "Sheriff Walton here."

"Dugan, this is Mee Mee. Are you busy?"

"We're finishing up our shift. Why? What's up?"

"I need a big favor. I'm on Ocracoke at Springer's Point. Could you round up a couple of buddies for a search party and meet me here."

"A search party? Who's missing?"

"Rowland Brackenbury."

"The British diplomat?"

"That's the one."

"What are you doing at Springer's Point?"

"Looking for ghosts."

"You're kidding, right?"

"No. It's a long story. The Hyde County boys won't help us until he's been missing for twenty-four hours. His wife is worried that something terrible has happened."

"Sure. I can help. I just ran into Sonny Keys. Give me a

second." Dugan lowered the phone. "Sonny, you got plans tonight?"

Sonny shrugged. "I'm up for anything." Dugan raised the phone to his ear. "Sonny said he'll help."

"How about Marla?"

"Marla? I don't know." After the Dear-John-it's-not-you-it's me break up, he wanted to get some space between him and Marla. He needed time to recover from the unexpected blow. "I don't think Marla will want to come."

Sonny stepped aside, and Marla lowered her head, peered into Dugan's window, and said, "Marla doesn't want to come where?"

"Uh . . ." Dugan held out the phone. "It's Mee Mee Roberts. She's trying to round up a few people to help look for a missing person on Ocracoke."

"Count me in," Marla said. "Mee Mee's my best friend. Besides, my son won't be home all week. He's back in the Ohio Valley visiting his cousins."

"You heard her," Dugan said into the phone. "I've got my boat hitched to a friend's dock in Hatteras. We'll be there within the hour."

"Please hurry," Mee Mee said. "This has been one of the strangest nights of my life."

"We'll hurry." Dugan glanced up and saw Sonny munching on a fish sandwich. "Where'd you get that?"

"Marla just gave it to me."

"But that's mine!"

"He's hungry, and we're in a hurry," Marla countered. "I'll split mine with you. You'll survive."

I guess I'll have to, Dugan thought as Sonny and Marla climbed into the squad car.

Last summer Dugan had purchased a used Scout 210 Dorado for $45,000 from the same friend who owned a dock in Hatteras. A part of the deal was a free year-round slip for the boat. Pretty good deal, really. It was only a twenty-one footer, but Dugan didn't venture into the ocean that often. Most of the time he used it to fish in the sound or near Hatteras Inlet. It came in handy for trips to Ocracoke, eliminating the need to wait for a ferry at the Hatteras Terminal or even a trip across the Pamlico Sound to the North Carolina mainland.

The fishing boat sported a Yamaha 150 horsepower outboard on it, more than enough power to get Dugan where he wanted to go quickly. Azure blue with a bow rail in front and fold-down table in back, it gave Dugan a great sense of ownership pride. He'd risen in the ranks of law enforcement to the place where he could afford something pricey and fun. With the stress of his job he needed an outlet that gave him a sense of freedom and escape. The boat offered those benefits bountifully, and Dugan felt no buyer's remorse whatsoever. Besides, Marla's son, Gabriel, loved to ride with him out to their favorite fishing spots. Dugan wondered if Gabe knew about his mother's decision to break up with him. He'd bet the Scout Dorado that Gabe was against it.

Hatteras was only about eight miles down Route 12 from Buxton. His buddy, Charlie Cash, lived along Peerless Lane in a modest two-story beach house. Dugan remembered Charlie mentioning that some British diplomat had purchased the big house at the end of the lane. Charlie had also gushed about the diplomat's young wife. He claimed she could pass for Marilyn Monroe's twin sister. Dugan didn't put much stock in Charlie's rantings. The over-the-hill playboy hooked up with some rough looking women over the years. Charlie claimed they were hotties, but Dugan thought most of them looked like roller derby queens who'd taken one too many tumbles.

Dugan parked the cruiser in Charlie's wide driveway. The lights in the house were out. He figured Charlie wouldn't mind if he left the vehicle there and chuckled to himself, thinking Charlie was out trying to pick up one of those roller derby queens. He'd probably bring her home late that night, spot the sheriff's car, and bluster on about being a crime consultant for Dare County.

Dugan thrust the door open. "The dock's right across the street."

"I know where the dock is," Marla said. "I've taken a few rides on that boat."

16

"Maybe Sonny didn't know," Dugan said harshly.

"I do now." Sonny glanced at Dugan with that what's-going-on look in his eyes. He probably had thought Dugan and Marla were the perfect couple, but the ride down from Buxton indicated the waters of their relationship had dropped a few degrees.

A wooden walkway waited on the other side of the road, crossing thirty feet of sandy scrub land to a small platform raised above the brackish sound water. Dugan's boat was secured to one of the thick posts. Sonny helped him remove the cover and then extended his hand to Marla, helping to steady her as she stepped on the edge and down into the front passenger seat. He leaped into the back and stretched out on the wide back seat. Dugan unhitched the boat, climbed into driver's seat and started the engine. It roared to life and settled into a steady rumble.

Sitting just in front of the motor, Sonny shouted, "She sounds like a real tiger! What'd you name her?"

"Lucky Day!" Dugan yelled back. How ironic, Dugan thought. Oh well. The day's not over yet.

The trip from Charlie's dock in Hatteras to the southern end of Ocracoke Island was about eighteen miles. Dugan kept the boat cruising at about 30 mph. Not talking much, he focused on the buoys and dark shoreline. Sonny and Marla had no trouble filling the silence, chatting loudly over the drone of the motor. They had become good friends when she and her late husband had moved into an apartment in Buxton, one of many that Sonny maintained. He was a great guy and a skilled handyman. With Sonny keeping Marla occupied, Dugan could sulk as much as he wanted without anyone noticing. His heart had sunk clear down into his belly.

As the minutes slipped away, Dugan tried to snap himself out of his funk by deeply inhaling the salty air, feeling the breeze on his face, and sensing the rhythmic drubbing of the boat's washboard against the water's surface. He glimpsed the flash from the Ocracoke Lighthouse and his gloom lifted a little more. Rejection had been a big part of his life. This was nothing new. He'd deal with it and move on like always. Just once, though, he'd like to have someone in his life who wanted him, needed him, and couldn't live without him.

He turned the boat to the left to enter Silver Lake Harbor. To his right, the solid white lighthouse stood about 75 feet high, one of the oldest lighthouses on the eastern coast. To the left, he spotted the Visitor's Center where the ferries docked. Dugan guided his boat through the narrow channel and steered to the right towards the docks closest to Springer's Point. Sonny sprang to his feet to help secure the vessel.

"Now who is this missing person?" Marla asked as she climbed out of the boat.

Dugan gathered up the flashlights and leapt onto the dock. "He's a British diplomat by the name of Rowland Brackenbury. Very wealthy. He recently bought a beach house in Hatteras just down the street from Charlie Cash."

Sonny secured the boat, and they walked toward the shore.

"If Brackenbury is a British diplomat, shouldn't there be a Secret Service agent assigned to him?" Marla asked.

"Should be," Dugan said. "But that's whenever he's on official business. If he's vacationing here, I don't think the Feds would be obligated to babysit him."

"Shouldn't they be alerted that he's missing?"

She had a point. Dugan nodded. "We'll give the Secret Service a call if we can't find him. No sense in sounding an alarm yet. He might have just wandered down the beach in the wrong direction."

"Let's hope so," Sonny said. "A missing diplomat would be pretty big news around here."

"Around here?" Marla let out a short whistle. "Sounds like a *London Times* headline to me."

* * *

Dugan gave them each a flashlight, and they briskly walked the half mile from Silver Lake Harbor to Springer's Point, following Creek Road and then turning down Lighthouse Road toward the sound. They cut between a couple houses and made their way to the beach. The water of the Pamlico Sound lapped quietly on the sandy shore, unlike the crashing waves of the Atlantic Ocean on the eastern side of the island.

Dugan spotted the silhouette of four people standing near the point. "There they are." He waved and shouted, "Mee Mee! Is that you?"

She waved back. "It's me! Thank God you're here!"

They picked up their pace, transitioning into a trot. Dugan didn't recognize the three women next to Mee Mee. They squinted as his light scanned across their faces. Dugan immediately picked out Brackenbury's wife by Charlie Cash's description. She definitely could pass for Marilyn Monroe's sister. Knowing everyone, Mee Mee went through the introductions and explained the circumstances.

"How long has Brackenbury been missing?" Marla asked.

Mee Mee glanced at her watch. "Almost two hours now."

"We were hoping he'd show up while we were waiting for you," Addy Brackenbury said, her voice unsteady, "but . . . but he's still out there somewhere."

"Has the eagle or whatever it was reappeared at all?" Dugan asked.

"No," Mee Mee said. "After it chased us into the woods, it took off."

"That is strange." Sonny rubbed his chin. "Kinda spooky. I've seen documentaries about huge birds like that on the Discovery Channel. One guy claimed that a giant eagle actually swooped down and picked him up off the ground when he was a kid."

"Stranger things have happened," Dugan said. "We need to start looking for Brackenbury. We've got three high-powered flashlights. Let's break up into three groups and see if we can scour the woods all the way out to the ocean."

Sonny raised his flashlight. "Who wants to go with me?"

The two paranormal researchers, Sienna and Luna, raised their hands.

Dugan motioned toward the left side of the woods "You three head in that direction." He turned and faced Marla. "Marla, how about you and Mee Mee take the center section?"

Marla glanced at Addy Brackenbury and then refocused on Dugan. "Fine with me if that's what you want."

"Me and Mrs. Brackenbury will cover the right side. Stay together. If anyone finds Mr. Brackenbury, we'll notify each other by cell phone."

As the three groups set out, Dugan noted the irritation in Marla's voice. *She probably assumed that I'd pair up with her. No way. Not now. I'm not in the mood to deal with relationship sore spots when there's work to be done. Besides . . .* Dugan eyed the platinum blonde walking beside him. The full moon's glow lit the curves of Adelaide Brackenbury's form-fitting tank top and yoga pants. *Besides . . . there's a damsel in distress here. It's my job to lend a hand to those in need. Sometimes my job has its benefits.*

Addy reached and touched Dugan's elbow. "Thank you so much for helping. We're desperate. It's been a horrific night."

"I can imagine," Dugan said. He liked her voice. It had a melodic quality. "The bird attack was most unusual. Incredible, really. It may be random, but the timing makes me wonder."

"That creature scared the devil out of me. I never want to encounter that monster again."

As they neared the woods, Dugan asked, "Can you tell me anything about your husband that might help us find him? Was he physically fit? Did he have a good sense of direction?"

Addy let out a sad chuckle. "No and no."

"That's not good."

"My husband enjoys life. He likes to party, but he works hard. Unfortunately, he doesn't like to exercise. I love to work out. He loves to pig out. Recently, we discovered he was a borderline diabetic with high blood pressure problems. Needless to say, he's not in great shape."

"So it's possible that in all the excitement and physical exertion he may have had a heart attack?"

Addy met Dugan's gaze. Her eyes blinked. "I guess it's possible." After several moments of silence she said, "If that's the case, time is of the essence. If he's lost, I'm sure he'll find his way back, but if he had a heart attack, he'll need help . . . if . . . if it's not too late."

* * *

"Is something going on between you and Dugan?" Mee Mee asked. She had noticed that Marla had been unusually quiet as they weaved through the center section of the woods. She had been close friends with Marla for many years and could sense when something was bothering her.

"How could you tell?"

"The way you looked at Addy Brackenbury and then back at Dugan was colder than moonlight on a tombstone."

"That obvious, huh?"

Mee Mee nodded.

"I broke up with Dugan earlier this evening."

"You ended your engagement?"

"For now. We've been dating for a year, and I'm just not head over heels for him. Don't get me wrong. Dugan's a great guy. I love him, but it's not the kind of crazy love I felt for Gabe."

Mee Mee reached and patted her back. "Marla, Marla, Marla. No one is ever going to come close to Gabe. He was your first love. My goodness, you were teenagers when you fell for each other. You can't duplicate that."

"I know. I know. But that's the kind of love I long for. That's the feeling I want to have again with the person I marry."

"Good luck with that. All I can tell you is that things change as you get older. The way you love people changes . . . matures."

"You're saying I'm acting like a goofy teenager."

"Not quite. I'm saying you need to understand the changes you experience in life as you get older. The intensity of feeling isn't the most important part of romantic love."

"Then what is?" Marla's cell phone piped Celine Dion's *If That's What It Takes*. "Hold on a sec." She pulled her phone from her pants pocket and answered. "It's Dugan . . . Where? . . . We'll be right there." She tapped the screen to end the call. "They found Brackenbury."

"Is he okay?"

Marla shook her head. "He didn't say, but the tone of his voice wasn't encouraging."

* * *

21

Marla and Mee Mee arrived at the edge of the ocean and saw Dugan applying chest pumps to a large, unmoving body spread-eagled in the sand. Marla shifted her focus to Adelaide Brackenbury. The platinum blonde, tears streaking her cheeks, hovered over Dugan with a flashlight aimed at her husband's head.

Dugan stopped the chest pumps and leaned closer to Rowland Brackenbury's face, Dugan's ear just above the mouth. "He's still not breathing."

Marla fell to her knees and reached for the big man's wrist. "I can't find a pulse."

Dugan shook his head. "He's gone."

"Please keep trying," Adelaide pleaded.

Dugan fixed his hands on the obese man's chest and continued the rhythmic pumping.

In the flashlight's glow, Marla could see Brackenbury was dead. His face was gray and lifeless. She stood. A distant siren whined like an abandoned dog. "Did you already call 911?"

"Yes," Adelaide said. "We called as soon as we found Rowland."

"Do they know where we are?" Mee Mee asked.

Dugan nodded, sweat pouring down his forehead. "Could you flag them down? They should be coming up the beach from the south."

"Will do," Mee Mee said.

Sonny and the two paranormal researchers arrived. "Anything I can do?" Sonny asked.

Dugan stopped the CPR compressions. "I don't think so, Sonny. It's too late."

Adelaide dropped the flashlight and crumpled to the sand, crying hysterically.

"Be careful where you walk," Dugan said. "This could be a crime scene."

Chapter 4

The paramedics' attempt to revive Brackenbury proved no better than Dugan's. The man was stone dead. Dugan instructed them to wait around until a determination was made as to whether or not it was a crime scene. Ten minutes later, a Hyde County police cruiser arrived, a white Chevy Impala. Sheriff Shawn Calhoon stepped out of the driver's side door, a large imposing man, broad chested with a substantial paunch. He wore a dark blue ball cap and jacket with a gold star embroidered on the left side chest-high. His deputy, a young, well-built guy with a shaved head, sprung from the other door and trotted around the vehicle to join Calhoon.

Dugan knew the Sheriff well. Crime on the Outer Banks had slowly risen over the years as the tourist industry grew. Dugan and Calhoon occasionally traded information about incidents and perpetrators. A few years back they put their heads together to solve a murder case involving a tourist who strangled his wife and dumped her body in the ocean, hoping to make it look like a drowning. Hatteras Inlet, about a mile wide, separated their counties, but boundaries can't contain dirty deeds.

"Good evenin', Sheriff Walton." Calhoon nodded and then eyed the body. "Didn't expect to see you in my neck of the woods this time of night."

"I'm surprised to be here myself," Dugan said, "especially under these circumstances."

The big sheriff thumbed toward the bald guy. "This is my chief deputy, Horace Singleton."

Dugan shook the deputy's hand and introduced Marla and Mee Mee. Luna and Sienna had escorted Adelaide away from her husband's body and down the beach in an attempt to comfort her.

Deputy Singleton aimed a flashlight at the body. "You sure he's dead?"

"Deader than a mackerel," Marla said.

Calhoon kneeled next to the corpse. "I'd say so. He's gray as a December sky. Heart attack?"

Dugan stepped to the other side. "I don't think so. Let's turn him over."

Calhoon raised his eyebrows. "If it's a homicide, we shouldn't move the body."

"I found him on his stomach but flipped him over to do CPR."

"Won't hurt to flip him again, I guess," Calhoon said.

With Dugan handling the legs and Calhoon the shoulders, the two sheriffs carefully rolled the body over.

Dugan pointed to the back of the leather jacket. "See those three slits?"

Calhoon leaned closer. "Yeah." He pulled a penknife from his jacket pocket, opened the blade, and lifted one of the slits in the jacket. "Holy Grandma Moses, look at the blood. This man was stabbed."

"That's what I figured," Dugan said.

Mee Mee stepped forward. "What about the bird?"

"What bird?" Deputy Singleton asked.

"A huge bird chased us into the woods. I think it was some kind of eagle," Mee Mee said.

Sheriff Calhoon raised up. "You think that eagle somehow

24

pierced his back? With what, his beak?"

Mee Mee shrugged and wrung her hands. "I don't know. It had huge talons."

"Hmmmph." Calhoon struggled to his feet and rubbed his chin. "I've never heard of anything like that. I mean, I know birds of prey will attack a person if they feel threatened, especially if you go near a nest."

"Right." Dugan stood. "But can an eagle stab a person deeply enough with its talons to kill him? I don't think so."

Sheriff Calhoon nodded. "Whatever the case may be, I need to call in a CSI team."

"For sure," Dugan said. "And this guy was a British diplomat. He owns a vacation home on Hatteras Island."

"So I've been told," Sheriff Calhoon said. "Got some info about him on the way over here. I'm sure there's an agent assigned to him that needs to be notified."

Deputy Singleton pulled out his cell phone. "Want me to look up the nearest Secret Service field office?"

"Yeah." Calhoon grimaced and shook his head. "This investigation could get ugly. It's international news whenever a foreign official gets killed or even worse . . . murdered." He glanced at Dugan. "What was going on here tonight, anyway?"

"I'll let Mee Mee answer that one."

Mee Mee took a deep breath. "A ghost hunt."

The Sheriff's voice went up two octaves. "A what?"

Marla explained, "Like a séance or a paranormal investigation."

"You sho must be shittin' me."

Mee Mee shook her head. "Mr. Brackenbury asked me to organize a ghost-hunt gathering here at Springer's Point. He figured that I knew a lot of these spiritually-in-tune people. Some of them are regular customers at my bookstore. Brackenbury's wife has extrasensory tendencies. Right now she's with the two paranormal researchers down by the beach. They're trying to calm her down." She turned and pointed in their direction. "Here they come now."

Calhoon peered in their direction. "Who else was a part of this ghost bustin' crew?"

"Achak Rowtag," Mee Mee said.

"The Indian? Where'd he go?"

"He left shortly after we lost Brackenbury."

Calhoon eyed Dugan. "Sounds like he didn't want to join the search party."

Sienna and Luna approached with Adelaide linked between them. Dugan introduced them to the sheriff and his deputy, and Calhoon offered his condolences. Adelaide blinked away tears but somehow held it together.

Deputy Singleton held up his phone. "Here's the number, Sheriff."

The big sheriff took the phone and pressed the dial icon. After explaining the circumstances, he was quickly connected with the agent assigned to Brackenbury. Calhoon relayed that Special Agent Goodwin needed answers to several questions. Mee Mee seemed even more unsettled than before as if someone had just slapped her, but she gathered herself and answered all the questions.

After a lot of yes sirs and nods, Calhoon ended the call. "Special Agent Goodwin plans on getting here tomorrow morning about nine o'clock. He wants all of you to meet him here for questioning. Do you have a place nearby you can stay?"

Adelaide stepped forward. "They can stay at my house on Hatteras Island. I don't want to be alone tonight."

Everyone turned and gazed at her as if surprised by the offer.

"How're we gonna get there?" Sienna asked. "There's not another ferry until tomorrow morning."

"We can take my boat," Dugan said.

"Everybody okay with that?" Calhoon asked.

No one protested.

* * *

Dugan's Scout Dorado, although small compared to most of the charter fishing boats, had no problem transporting seven people across the Pamlico Sound back to Hatteras Island. Adelaide took the seat next to Dugan's captain's chair, Mee Mee and Marla climbed into the front section, while Sonny and the two paranormal researchers settled onto the wide back seat, Sonny bookended between them. Dugan noticed Luna and Sienna had taken a liking to Sonny, and Sonny didn't seem to mind.

As they skimmed across the water, Dugan couldn't help glancing at Addy occasionally. She had wrapped a towel around her legs, and the full moon's light gave the alluring woman an enchanting quality akin to a mermaid or goddess.

Marla and Mee Mee chatted away in the front of the boat, but Dugan couldn't make out much of their conversation. He figured that was a good thing. Marla was probably talking about how she just couldn't love a guy like him enough to marry him. He didn't sweep her off her feet or make the earth move for her. He'd rather not hear about his inadequacies. In the back of the boat Sonny kept the ghost busters entertained, but Dugan couldn't hear much of their conversation either.

He looked at Addy. "You okay?"

She managed a smile. "I think so. It's just . . ."

"Just what?"

"Whenever I leave that island I feel . . . I feel like I'm leaving a part of myself behind."

"On Ocracoke?"

"Yes. It's strange. Something possesses me there. I guess I should say someone possesses me there."

Dugan met her gaze. "Like a past life?"

"That's right. You must think I'm crazy."

"I don't know much about that sort of thing."

"It might be all in my imagination, but when I walk along the beaches at Ocracoke, it seems like I've walked there before. Tonight I felt this spirit enter me, the spirit of a Native American girl."

Dugan didn't give much credence to stories about spirit possession and reasoned that those who did were a little kooky, but Addy seemed sincere. Besides that the moonlight on her face and form captivated him. She was quite beautiful, shapely, and vulnerable. A classic movie fan, Dugan had seen most of the old Marilyn Monroe films. For some reason her appearance brought *Don't Bother to Knock* to mind, a film where Monroe played an unstable woman shaken by the death of her boyfriend. Dugan sympathized with vulnerable people. He came from a broken home, suffering the rejection of his father. He had a sudden urge to comfort her, to reach and clasp her hand but managed to stifle it.

Instead Dugan said, "I can understand how you feel. You've had a tough night. Losing someone you love tears out a piece of your heart."

Addy gave him a weak smile, reached and placed her hand on top of his. "Thanks. I appreciate all you've done."

Dugan turned his hand over and clasped hers. Her skin was warm and moist. He held her hand for what seemed like almost a minute and then gently let go. Glancing to the front of the boat, he wondered if Marla noticed.

* * *

It didn't take long to reach Hatteras Inlet, maybe thirty minutes. From there Dugan followed the buoys to navigate the shallow sound waters to where the ferries docked at the terminal. Then he veered to the left along a channel for fishing boats and pleasure craft which led to the entrance to his slip near Charlie Cash's place. Addy insisted that he park the boat at her dock, about fifty yards farther down the channel.

Her beach house was impressive, three stories high with a rectangular tower that rose another two stories from the third floor. Dugan assumed the tower served as an observation nook, sort of an eagle's nest high above all the other homes in the neighborhood. The house sat on a small peninsula with three sides offering plenty of room to secure boats. Addy instructed Dugan to troll to the back side closest to the house entrance. Sonny quickly leaped onto the dock and lashed the boat to the nearest cleat. Then he extended his muscular arms to Sienna and Luna and pulled them onto the dock. Mee Mee and Marla managed to climb out on their own, but Dugan sprang onto the dock and offered Addy a hand up.

Addy led the way to the entrance as automatic exterior lights flashed on. She rapidly punched the key code into the door lock.

The ornate oak door swung open, and another set of automatic lights brightened the interior. Dugan blinked several times. To his left was a glass elevator. Before him the bottom floor opened up into a combination game and workout room with weights, steppers, stationary bikes, and treadmills on one side, and a pool table, ping pong table, foosball table, and basketball arcade game on the other.

Addy pressed the elevator button and then waved toward the exercise equipment and game tables. "We call this the Fitness and Fun Room." She sniffled. "Rowland would play pool whenever I came down to do a workout." The glass doors of the elevator separated. All seven of them piled in with room to spare. Addy jabbed the 3 button, the doors closed, and the elevator hummed as the second floor whizzed by. "Just a bunch of bedrooms on that floor. You can have your pick. But I thought we'd go up to the great room and get a drink first, something to help take off the edge."

"Sounds like a refreshing idea," Sonny said.

"Yeah," Mee Mee said. "I could use a glass of good wine."

The great room took up most of the third floor with the back section walled off for the master bedroom and bathroom. Most of the beach houses on the Outer Banks adopted this open concept with the kitchen, dining room, and living room separated only by counters or furniture. This one had wide archways with marble columns that gave support to the high vaulted ceilings. The yellow-stucco walls, large windows, huge fireplace, exquisite lamps and chandeliers, and high-end décor and furnishings gave Dugan the sense that he had just entered the dwelling of someone who had way too much money. To his right he spotted another set of steps leading up to the tower.

Addy motioned toward the living room with its two wide burnt-orange couches and comfy-looking recliners. "Have a seat. I'll bring some drinks and snacks over."

"We'll help," Sienna insisted. She and Luna followed Addy into the kitchen area.

Dugan plopped down on the end of the couch across from the fireplace, exhausted from the long day. Sonny sat on the other couch while Mee Mee and Marla slumped into the recliners.

"I could fall asleep right now," Marla sighed.

Mee Mee tugged the handle and reclined her chair. "Me too. This feels like heaven."

The three women returned with bowls of potato chips, corn chips, wine bottles, and glasses. Addy handed a bottle of cabernet sauvignon to Dugan along with a cork screw. He quickly popped it and handed it back to Addy. She then gave him a bottle of chardonnay.

"Who wants red?" Addy asked. All the women raised their hands, and she gracefully poured four glasses and passed them around. "I assume you boys want white?"

Dugan and Sonny nodded as Dugan handed her the opened bottle. She poured three glasses, taking one for herself, and then sat down next to Dugan.

Marla took a sip. "You have a beautiful home here."

"Thanks," Addy said. "We bought it about a year ago. Rowland loved the Outer Banks. He said it was an untamed wonderland, especially the southern end."

"Untamed?" Mee Mee said.

"You know, with the storms and the shifting sands, with all of the natural preservation and undeveloped shoreline."

Mee Mee placed her glass on the lamp table. "Apparently, Rowland planned on taming a part of it—the Island of Ocracoke, anyway."

"Yes." Addy fingered the condensation on her wine glass. "We both had that vision. Like Rowland mentioned tonight at Springer's Point, we wanted to bring the ghosts of Ocracoke back to life. Ever since we vacationed here five years ago, I've felt as if I had roots on that island. But I wasn't sure how far we should go."

Dugan drained his glass and sat it on a coaster on the coffee table. "Do you mean as far as developing the island? What's the right balance of commercialism, tourism, and preservation?"

"Yes. Finding the right balance." Addy reached for the chardonnay and refilled Dugan's glass. Sonny held his out, and she tipped the bottle again, topping off his glass.

Marla cleared her throat. "Is that why you organized a paranormal investigation? To see what the ghosts had to say?"

Addy nodded. "I truly believe in the spirit world. I wanted to get some kind of guidance or sensation from the ghosts that inhabit the island. Do they want us here or not? Do they want more people to discover their history?"

Dugan glanced at Marla and noticed an odd smirk. No doubt she thought Addy was batty.

"The spectral activity was amazing tonight," Luna said. "I've got my camera here. Would anybody like to see the spirit orbs we captured?"

"Sure," Marla said. "I'll take a look."

Luna handed Marla the camera and pointed to the LCD screen.

Marla raised her eyebrows , her mouth twisting slightly. "Those are spirit orbs?"

"Yes," Sienna insisted. "They are spectral entities. They show up as orbs on highly sensitive cameras."

"I see." Marla's odd smile returned. "How do you know they aren't some kind of peculiarity caused by the sensitivity of the camera to any reflective light?"

"We've been at this a while," Luna said. "We know when paranormal activity is being generated. That's when the orbs appear."

Marla nodded. "I see. Sounds highly technical. I guess if you believe, then the ghosts will come." She glanced at Mee Mee. "And you're a witness to all of this paranormal activity, huh Mee Mee?"

Mee Mee lifted her hands, palms up. "I was there, and weird things happened. That's all I know."

"You simply had to be there," Addy said. "I definitely felt the presence of ghosts. One possessed me. I saw the giant bird with my own eyes."

"We all saw the giant bird," Mee Mee said.

Addy placed her wine glass on the coffee table. "But Achak said we saw the eagle with spiritual eyes. What did he call it? . . . the Animikii, the Thunderbird. He told us the Animikii *makes* us see him, that its shadow would come upon anyone who threatened the balance of nature."

Luna leaned forward. "Yes! I remember him saying that. Poor

Mr. Brackenbury may have been the victim of something supernatural."

Marla sat up. "That's bull crap. Rowland Brackenbury was the victim of cold-blooded murder. Forensic science will find the answer to what happened out there, not speculation about a mythical bird that threatens the life of anyone who has questionable designs on a protected island."

Addy crossed her arms. "If you think my husband's designs were questionable, you must not think that highly of me either."

Marla eyed her. "What are you talking about?"

"My husband and I were partners. Now it's up to me whether or not to pursue the development of Ocracoke."

"You can do whatever you want to do," Marla said. "I didn't say *I* questioned your husband's designs. I'm not the judge of what is or isn't responsible development. But clearly, *someone* questioned his plans. And whoever it was responded with lethal force. If you pursue those plans, I'd worry more about the living than the dead."

Addy's eyes ignited. "You don't know everything about the spirit realm."

"That's true." Dugan raised his hand and gently lowered it. "No one knows everything that goes on in the spirit realm. Marla makes a good point, though. We need to look at the facts and be careful to make an excellent forensic investigation. On the other hand, crimes have been solved with the help of paranormal investigators. Science doesn't have all the answers. Who knows what this giant bird could signify."

Mee Mee took a deep breath and blew it out audibly. "I have relatives that live in Point Pleasant, West Virginia."

"What does that have to do with anything?" Marla asked.

Luna leaned forward. "Don't you know what happened in Point Pleasant?"

Marla shook her head.

"The appearance of the Mothman," Sienna said.

Sonny sat up. "Who's the Mothman?"

Mee Mee lowered the recliner. "I was a freshman in high school back then, the fall of 1966. My cousin Mary was with her boyfriend driving along the road that passed by the old World

War II ammunitions plant. A huge bird with red, glowing eyes and a ten-foot wingspan flew toward them. Then it hovered above their car. They took off, and the bird followed them for about a mile. The encounter freaked her out. Whenever she told the story, she would tremble.

"In the next month more than twenty people saw it. These were good, credible people—firemen, local workers, teachers. Some so-called expert said it was an unusually large sandhill crane that had wandered out of its migration route. Other people weren't so sure. They said it had a spiritual quality to it and resembled a flying man. People began to believe it was a bad omen. Others started to have these premonitions that something terrible was about to happen. They believed the appearance of the Mothman was a harbinger of death."

Sonny, eyes wide, leaned forward, his forearms on his knees. "Did anybody actually die?"

Mee Mee nodded. "On December 15, the Point Pleasant Silver Bridge crowded with Christmas traffic collapsed into the Ohio River. Forty-six people died that night."

Chapter 5

When Dugan Walton opened his eyes, the first thing he noticed was the wonderful scent. Was it perfume or some kind of body lotion? Then he felt the pressure on his left shoulder and side. He turned his head slightly, and platinum blonde hair tickled his chin. Sometime during the night Addy had slumped against him on the couch. She seemed to be in a deep slumber, her hand on his knee. The last thing he remembered was listening to Sienna and Luna go on and on about their ghost adventures. One by one everyone had drifted off to sleep on the couches and chairs without bothering to head down to the second floor bedrooms.

Her warmth against him felt incredibly good. She was definitely blessed with all the right parts. He glanced at the recliners. Mee Mee slept soundly, but Marla was stirring. He chuckled to himself, wondering what Marla would think if she saw Addy snuggled against him. Then he realized that wasn't such a good thing. This woman had just lost her husband, and now it may appear that she latched on to him awfully quickly or that he was taking advantage of her vulnerability. How could he create some distance between them without waking her or anyone else up?

He tried sliding out from under her, but his cell phone erupted from his shirt pocket, a classic ringtone. Marla sat up, blinked a couple of times, and then focused on him and Addy. Her eyes widened. Dugan shrugged as Addy pushed against his knee and stretched.

"Oh, Sheriff Walton, I'm sorry," Addy yawned. "I must have nodded off and slid over against you. I apologize."

"No harm done." Dugan put the phone to his ear. "Sheriff Walton here."

"This is Special Agent Russell Goodwin." The voice on the phone reminded Dugan of Gregory Peck's, deep and serious.

"Yes, sir. Sheriff Calhoon told me you would be calling."

"Right. Sheriff Calhoon's CSI team has informed us that Rowland Brackenbury was murdered. His death raises national and international concerns. The Secret Service will be coordinating the investigation with the FBI. Local law enforcement will help out at a secondary level."

"I figured that would be the case. It's out of my jurisdiction anyway. Is there anything I can do to help?"

"Definitely. Could you round up everyone who was at Springer's Point last night and meet me there at 9:00 a.m.?"

Dugan glanced at his watch—7:45. "We should be able to get there on time. However, we're missing one person, Achak Rowtag. He left before I arrived last night."

"Right. Sheriff Calhoon informed me about Rowtag. Well . . . I'll have to hunt him down later. How many people will you be bringing with you?"

Dugan glanced around the room, counting heads. "Seven all together."

"Okay. I'll see you there."

Dugan ended the call. By now everyone had come to life.

Sonny rubbed the top of his shaved head. "What's up, boss?"

"That was Special Agent Goodwin."

Mee Mee straightened up. "Special Agent Goodwin?"

"That's right. He works for the Secret Service. They will be assisting the FBI with the investigation. He wants us back at Springer's Point by 9:00 o' clock. That doesn't give us much time."

"I'm starved," Luna said.

"Me too," Sienna chimed in.

Addy stood and waved toward the kitchen. "We can grab a bowl of cereal. Got about any brand you might like."

"How about some coffee?" Dugan asked.

"No problem." Addy headed toward the kitchen. "I'll get a full pot brewing."

Dugan had a hard time getting started in the morning without his coffee. "Sounds good. Let's get a quick bite to eat and then head out."

* * *

Dugan led the way from the dock, down Creek Road toward Lighthouse Road. Addy kept pace beside him, and Sonny and the paranormals followed slightly behind them. Bringing up the rear, Marla and Mee Mee conversed in quiet tones as if they didn't want others to know what they were saying. Dugan figured they were talking about how he and Addy had suddenly become an item. He didn't care. He knew he hadn't done anything wrong. The poor girl had lost her husband, and he offered his help and comfort as best he could. Once this meeting with Goodwin was over, he would never see her again. He wondered if the Feds would need his help or even access to Dare County's accommodations or resources, but he would graciously offer them just in case.

As they cut between a couple of houses and headed toward the sandy strip along the Pamlico Sound, Addy said, "It's chilly this morning,"

"Yeah," Dugan said. "The sun can't find its way through those clouds, and the breeze makes it worse."

"Do you think my husband's body is still on the beach?"

"I doubt it. They probably completed their investigation last night."

"Would they have taken him to the hospital?"

"Yes, the Outer Banks Hospital in Nags Head. They'll want to do an autopsy. I'm sure they'll bring you up to date this morning on all that's happening."

"I see." Addy sniffled. "Well . . . whatever needs to be done, I'll gladly cooperate."

"I know it's difficult to think about, but an autopsy could definitely help the investigation."

"Will they be able to determine exactly how my husband died?"

"Yes. They'll discover what caused the bodily injuries and whether or not foul play was involved."

"Good. If it was murder, I want the sonovabitch caught."

Dugan looked up to see a tall man standing near where Springer's Point jutted into the sound. The breeze rustled the sea oats at his feet. He had close-cropped, almost white hair, wore a black suit with a gray tie, and sported dark sunglasses.

"That's Russell Goodwin," Mee Mee said. "He hasn't changed much except for his hair. It used to be jet black."

Dugan glanced over his shoulder. "You know him?"

Mee Mee smiled. "It's been a while, but yeah, I know him."

Dugan sensed an odd buoyancy in Mee Mee's voice and wondered how in the world she had a connection with a secret service agent. I shouldn't be surprised, Dugan thought. That's Mee Mee.

Dugan nodded toward the man. "Special Agent Goodwin, I presume."

The agent extended his hand. "Yes, Russell Goodwin."

Dugan matched his firm grip. He appeared to be in his late fifties and stood about six feet three inches tall. He was slim but well built. When Dugan stepped to the side to introduce the others, he noticed Goodwin's eyes grow wide."

Goodwin leaned slightly. "Mee Mee Roberts?" He seemed to hold himself back.

"It's me," Mee Mee beamed.

Dugan wondered if she would spring into his arms, but she took a deep breath and stood her ground.

Goodwin straightened. "I was hoping to meet up with you

37

sometime while I was down here, but I never dreamed it would be this morning. Were you here with the ghost hunters last night?"

Mee Mee's face flushed, and she slowly nodded. "Yes. I'm the one who organized the gathering."

Goodwin tilted his head, his eyebrows rising. "Interesting."

Dugan introduced the rest of the party, identifying those who attended the paranormal session, and apprised him of Achak Rowtag's early departure. He explained that Marla, Sonny, and he had volunteered to help with the manhunt and arrived about two hours after Brackenbury had disappeared.

Goodwin informed the group he wanted to interview them individually and started with Addy. He led her about thirty yards down the beach, just out of earshot, and extracted a small notebook and pen from the inside of his jacket. After talking to her for about ten minutes and taking extensive notes, he sent her back to their huddle.

When she rejoined the group, she informed Mee Mee that he wanted to talk to her next. Mee Mee headed over with a spring in her step. Dugan noticed they talked like old friends, occasionally touching each other on the arm or shoulder.

"What's their connection?" Dugan asked Marla.

"They go way back. It was one of those vacation romances. Russell walked into her bookstore back in the early eighties looking for books about Blackbeard. It didn't take long for sparks to fly. They had a week together before he had to return to Georgia for specialized training. They both became incredibly busy after that and drifted apart."

Dugan chuckled. "I thought Mee Mee looked a little stunned last night when she heard his name mentioned. Must have been some week."

Marla smiled. "Most people go through those kinds of romances when they're younger. What better place for it to happen than the Outer Banks. Didn't you ever experience a vacation romance?"

Dugan thought for a few seconds. "Yes, I did. When I was twelve, my aunt and uncle took me on vacation right here on the Outer Banks, up north to Corolla. I met a girl named Janey. To my surprise, she had a crush on me, even gave me my first kiss. How about you?"

Marla shook her head. "I fell in love with Gabe in junior high. I had no desire to chase after boys when my family went on vacation. I guess he was everything I wanted back then."

I'm sorry I asked, Dugan thought. Another dart to take the air out of my courtship balloon. He drifted over toward Addy as she stood talking with the two paranormal researchers.

"What did he ask you?" Dugan said.

"Real basic stuff," Addy said. "You know, what happened and how long we searched and where we looked. He seemed especially interested in the giant bird."

"Really? Hmmm." Dugan wondered if Goodwin thought she was exaggerating about the creature. Maybe he knew something they didn't know.

"He's taking me to the Outer Banks Hospital after this to sign the autopsy papers. He's got his own plane."

"Wow." Dugan glanced over his shoulder toward the small airstrip several hundred yards away near the ocean side. He couldn't spot a plane but figured the trees and dunes blocked his sightline.

Goodwin sent Mee Mee back and asked to see Luna. She took her camera with her. Dugan figured she wanted to show the Secret Service agent her proof of the afterlife—those strange spirit orbs. Then he interviewed Sienna. After he questioned her, it didn't take him long to interview Marla and then Sonny.

Finally, he called Dugan over. "Everyone gives very similar accounts. The paranormal researchers and Mrs. Brackenbury are definitely . . . enthusiasts when it comes to describing the otherworldly encounters they believe they had last night. Mee Mee Roberts was more of a skeptic. All of them mentioned the argument between Achak Rowtag and Mr. Brackenbury over the development of Ocracoke. Then there's the giant bird attack, which I find fascinating."

Dugan nodded. "Yes sir, that was extremely unusual."

"After that they fled into woods, they eventually regrouped and had a confrontation with Rowtag, then he left. Is that what they reported to you?"

"That's pretty much it. Then they contacted the Hyde County Sheriff's Department, but they couldn't send anybody out until a missing person's report was filed after twenty-four hours. They figured he'd come wandering in sooner or later. So the four women went looking for him on their own but couldn't find him. That's when they called me."

"How long did it take you and Mrs. Brackenbury to find him?"

Dugan rubbed his chin. "About an hour. After he'd been stabbed, he somehow made it all the way to ocean-side beach before he died. Perhaps the perpetrator chased him in that direction before finishing him off. He probably crawled part of the way. Maybe he didn't have a good sense of direction. Whatever the case, we never expected him to be that far from the woods."

Goodwin jotted a few notes onto his pad. "So you think he was stabbed?"

"That's my guess considering the slits on the back of his jacket and all the blood."

"Who do you think did it?"

"I don't know. I suppose the prime subject is Achak Rowtag."

"You sure it wasn't the giant bird?"

Dugan eyed Goodwin's expression to see if he was serious. He didn't detect any hint of sarcasm. "No. I don't think a giant bird could have done that, even if it was trained."

"Do you mind if I call Mee Mee and your deputy over here?"

"Certainly not."

Goodwin turned and waved toward the group. "Mee Mee! Deputy Easton! Could you please join us over here for a few minutes?"

The two women walked briskly toward them. Dugan wondered why Goodwin wanted a powwow with the four of them. Did he discover something in the interviews that they could help him clarify, perhaps something that required putting their heads together?

"Thank you for joining us, ladies," Goodwin said. "I've already mentioned this to Mee Mee." He glanced at Marla and then Dugan. "The reason I find this bird attack so interesting is because it is not an isolated incident. Recently, we've had similar

40

reports from hydraulic fracturing sites in Towanda, Pennsylvania, and Youngstown, Ohio. In each case where the bird has appeared there have been accidents, tragedies, and unusual occurrences."

"No kidding," Dugan said. "That's odd."

"Very odd," Marla said.

"It reminds me of the Mothman phenomenon," Mee Mee said.

"Similar perhaps." Goodwin slid his notebook back into the inside of his suit jacket. "More than likely it's coincidence. The bird makes its appearance, and something bad happens. We haven't been able to tie any of these incidents specifically to one person who may have trained this bird. We're baffled. Now we have to add the Outer Banks into the mix of locations."

"So you think there's a mastermind behind all of this?" Marla asked. "Someone is traveling to locations that are environmentally threatened and setting this bird loose to wreak havoc."

Goodwin waggled his hand in front of them. "It's possible. Another commonality is that the locations were once inhabited by Native Americans. It all seems like a combination of design and chance, fact and fiction: Someone trains a large eagle, sets it loose at these locations, and then lets the imagination of the eyewitnesses go wild—it's a good recipe to create a legend. Anyway, Mee Mee informed me that she occasionally writes articles for the *Island Free Press*." Goodwin reached and rested his hand on Mee Mee's shoulder. "Could you tell them what you plan on doing?"

Mee Mee cleared her throat. "Sure. Originally, I planned on heading back to my old stomping grounds in West Virginia tomorrow. A Marcellus shale fracturing company has made a lease offer to my mother on the land she owns, and she wanted me there to look over the contract before she signs it. When Russell told me the giant bird has appeared in the tri-state area near fracking sites, I knew I had to write an article about it for the newspaper. Since I've seen the thing firsthand, I wanted to interview the eyewitnesses in Ohio and Pennsylvania who have also seen it. To me it's a fascinating story, especially considering the tragedies that seem to accompany the appearance of the bird. Now it's become an Outer Banks story."

Goodwin shook his head. "I don't recommend this journalistic adventure. I think there's danger involved, but I know how strong willed Mee Mee can be. However, since she insists on going, she may come up with some information or revelations that could help this investigation. But I don't want her to go by herself."

Marla raised her hand. "I'll go with her."

Dugan stiffened and eyed Marla.

"That is, of course, if you approve, Sheriff Walton," Marla said.

Dugan thought about Marla's son, Gabriel, but remembered that he was visiting his cousins for a week up in Ohio. "I guess we can get along without you for a few days."

"Excellent." Goodwin said. "I feel better knowing an officer will be accompanying Mee Mee. I recommend taking your gun with you, Deputy Easton. Like I said, several deaths have been connected with this bird, and Mee Mee may be stepping on the wrong toes when she conducts these interviews."

Mee Mee put her arm around Marla's waist. "Don't worry, Russell. We're a dynamic duo."

Goodwin managed a grim smile. "I hope so." He then eyed Dugan. "Sheriff Walton, I'd like to recruit your help on this case too."

"Sure. Whatever you need."

"I'm flying Mrs. Brackenbury up to the hospital in Nags Head to take care of the paperwork for the autopsy. Could you pick her up in a few hours and drive her back home?"

"No problem."

"She seems pretty shaken up. I'd like you to keep your eye on her. She resides in your county. Besides that, she and her husband were partners. It's possible that she could also be a target."

"I'll make sure she's safe." Dugan glanced at Marla and noticed her eyes narrowing.

"And another thing—on your way up to Nags Head could you stop by Achak Rowtag's place and see if he's there. If he is, tell him to stay put until I get a chance to question him. If he gives you any guff, inform him Rowland Brackenbury was murdered, and he is a person of interest. Tell him I'll stop by later this evening. By order of the U.S. government, he is not to leave town."

Chapter 6

Luna and Sienna headed to the ferry terminal to pick up their car and catch a ride on the ferry back to Hatteras Island. Marla figured she would ride back with Mee Mee so they headed to the terminal parking lot also. They planned on driving to West Virginia as soon as they could get packed. That left Dugan and Sonny. They climbed into Dugan's Scout Dorado which was docked across from the terminal. Sonny unhitched the boat while Dugan started the engine. Within minutes they were cruising north on the Pamlico Sound back to Hatteras Island.

Achak lived in Frisco which was on the way to Buxton. Sonny's car was parked at Rusty's Surf and Turf in Buxton. Dugan steered the boat between the buoys marking the channel that led to his dock at Charlie Cash's beach house. "Hope you don't mind stopping in Frisco to pay a visit to Achak."

"No problem," Sonny said. "I'll be your backup."

"My backup? Okay. You can unofficially be my backup. Do you know Achak?"

"Yeah, I know him. We've talked a few times. He's a strange bird."

Dugan chuckled. "That's a good way to describe him. Do you think he's ruthless enough to kill someone?"

Sonny leaned back in the passenger's seat and cupped his hands behind his head. "Good question. He reminds me of one of those people who might just cross that boundary but not because he's ruthless or evil or greedy or anything like that."

"What do you mean?"

"Well, if he murdered somebody, there would be a good reason. He wouldn't take another person's life unless he felt it was serving a higher purpose. "

"So you're saying he might kill Rowland Brackenbury if that act promoted a greater good."

"That's right. He's a very spiritual man, an Algonquin shaman. Besides that, he's dedicated to his heritage and the environment."

Dugan turned into the inlet that led to his slip. "You mean to tell me you think he'd kill someone in cold blood just because that person insulted his heritage or threatened the environment?"

"I think it's possible. You and I would call it murder, but he'd call it duty."

It didn't take them long to secure the boat and walk over to the Ford Interceptor parked in Charlie Cash's driveway. The gray skies had cleared, the sun's rays warming the cool morning. Dugan opened the car door but then turned and eyed Addy Brackenbury's beach house. Two seagulls glided past the tower, their lilting calls like random musical notes. The sense of her warm body against him as they reclined on the couch rushed through him. He shook it off, thinking it wasn't a good idea to dwell on that memory. He took a deep breath, blew it out, and climbed into the Interceptor.

When he started the engine, he noticed Charlie's black Cougar parked under the deck. He wondered if Charlie had company last night, some wrinkled, honky-tonk angel long past her prime. He felt tempted to blow the horn to see if his friend would come out onto the deck and shoot the breeze a little, but he knew time was in short supply. Instead, he backed out and headed down Peerless Lane toward Route 12.

Frisco was about five miles up the road from Hatteras. Achak Rowtag lived in small house at the end of Timber Trail. The lane was narrow with a lot of loblolly pines, live oaks, and overgrown shrubbery and brush encroaching on its edges. Two posts stood on each side of his driveway, which snaked back about fifty yards to his house. Both posts had NO TRESPASSING signs nailed to them. The shadows of tall pines darkened the drab brown house which was mounted on eight-foot pilings. The parking area under the house was empty. Wooden steps on the right side ascended to the main floor. Dugan and Sonny climbed the steps.

Dugan pounded on the door. The frenzied barking of a dog exploded from the back of the property. Dugan eyed Sonny. "Hope he's tied up."

Sonny pointed at Dugan's holster. "Glad you got your gun with you."

Dugan patted his Smith and Wesson revolver. "Hope I don't have to use it." He pounded the door again.

Sonny peered into the window next to the door. "That's interesting."

"What do you see?"

"Above the fireplace is a painting of a Thunderbird, and I don't mean a Ford."

Dugan scooted over, cupped his hands above his eyes and leaned against the window. The image was composed of flowing red, white, and black lines and shapes, simplistic yet striking. The creature had a large beak and talons. Its body was composed of an angry, abstracted face with black eyes, a red nose, and white fangs. Its wings were large, stretching across the wide canvas.

Dugan leaned back. "Hmmmph. Not your typical beach art. Let's head around back."

"Fine. You first. Dogs don't like me." Sonny waved his hand in front of him. "I told you I'd be your backup."

Dugan smiled and trotted down the steps. The dog's barking intensified. When they turned the corner they spotted the large black hound thrusting against a six-foot chain-link fence. To Dugan the canine looked to be part lab and part pit bull. As it bayed and snarled, slobber dripped and twirled from its mouth. The fence enclosed the backyard in a rectangle about sixty feet long and forty feet wide. A fire pit, about four feet high and made of natural stone, rose from the center. A few old live oaks overhung the fence, and beyond it Dugan could see the Pamlico Sound and a rickety dock with a small boat. Near the back of the property was a tall pole with primitive faces carved on it, a totem. On the top of the pole someone had secured a wooden box which contained branches and straw—some kind of nest, perhaps an osprey's nest, but Dugan didn't see any birds.

"What kind of vehicle does Achak drive?" Dugan asked.

Sonny tilted his head. "I think it's one of those old Chevy vans."

"Well, obviously it's not here, so I'm guessing he's not here."

"Good guess."

They walked back to the front of the house. Dugan glanced around the front yard but didn't see anything unusual. "No sense wasting any more time here."

"Yeah," Sonny said. "I've got work to do today."

They climbed into the Interceptor, and Dugan backed it into the yard so that he could pull forward down the driveway. As he turned on to Timber Trail he noticed a neighbor forty yards ahead checking his mail. Dugan beeped his horn and pulled up beside the neighbor, an obese man wearing black-framed glasses, a wrinkled white dress shirt, and gray pants.

Dugan powered down the window. "Good morning, We're looking for Achak Rowtag. Have you seen him lately?"

The man shook his head. "Not today." He held up a handful of mail. "But I did get a note from him."

"A note?"

"Yeah. Sometimes Achak goes on these trips. He'll be gone three or four days." He plucked a small square of paper from between a couple of letters. "Here it is."

"Could I take a peek at it?"

The man hesitated, giving Dugan a quizzical look. "I . . . I guess it wouldn't hurt." He handed Dugan the slip of paper.

The hand writing was rough, heavily scrawled in pencil. He printed his letters like a kid in grade school and used thick underlines under certain words : HENRY, I'LL BE GONE FOR A FEW DAYS. COULD YOU PLEASE LOOK AFTER BEAR. A NEW BAG OF DOG FOOD IS IN THE CLOSET NEXT TO THE REFRIGERATOR. THE KEY IS IN THE USUAL PLACE. THANKS, ACHAK.

Dugan handed the paper back to the heavyset man. "Do you have any idea where he went?"

"No idea. Achak is a private man. We've been neighbors for years. Get along okay. Whenever I leave for a few days he looks after my cats. If he takes off, I'm more than happy to feed Bear. That's the big dog out back."

"We've met him. Does Achak own any birds?"

"Birds? Do you mean like a parakeet?"

"No. More along the lines of an eagle or a big hawk."

"Not that I know of. He's got an osprey nest out back, but he wouldn't claim that he owns them. He just lets them nest there. I think he likes to watch them raise their young."

"Nothing wrong with bird watching I guess."

"Is Achak in trouble?"

"He's wanted for questioning."

"Questioning?"

"That's right. No warrants or anything like that. We just need to ask him a few questions."

"I see. Well, I'll tell him you stopped by when he gets home. Sheriff Walton, right?"

"That's right."

"I voted for you last election."

"Thanks."

As Dugan pulled away he powered up the window. "I wonder where Achak hides that key."

"What key?" Sonny asked.

"The note mentioned a key hidden somewhere."

"Something in particular you'd like to find in his house?"

"Sure. The murder weapon—a knife. And maybe there's a cage in there somewhere with a big bird."

"A Thunderbird?"

"That's right, a Thunderbird."

Chapter 7

After dropping Sonny off in Buxton, Dugan drove another five miles up the road to Avon and stopped at Burger Burger to get a hamburger, fries, and a large coffee. Without the coffee he'd fall asleep at the wheel on the fifty minute drive to Nags Head. It had been a long night, and he definitely didn't sleep well stretched out on Addy's couch.

The coffee helped, but he still had to shake himself awake several times before he pulled into the hospital parking lot. The Outer Banks Hospital was a modern facility that offered a wide variety of services to the growing local population. The tourist industry had boomed over the last twenty years, which increased the number of year-round residents. Its location in Nags Head offered the long stretch of barrier islands a centrally located healthcare facility.

To his surprise, Addy was standing in front by the entrance to the main building, basking in the bright sunshine. She wore the same clothes she had on the night before, a formfitting red tank top and black yoga pants. Her platinum blonde hair blazed almost white, and her sultry eyes with their long lashes were half closed against the sun's light. Dugan couldn't help admiring her figure, blessed with curves in all the right places and definitely fit.

He stopped the vehicle in front of her and powered down the window. "Been waiting long?"

She smiled, her teeth bright white against those red lips. "Not really. The sunshine felt so good I just want to stand here and let it warm me up."

"The way the day started I figured it would be dreary most of the afternoon."

She walked around the car and opened the passenger door. "Don't become a weatherman. It's a beautiful day. Stick to your day job."

Once Addy got in, Dugan drove to the parking lot exit and turned south on Route 158. It would take about an hour to drive back down to Hatteras.

She reached and gently touched his arm. "Thanks for picking me up."

"No problem. Did you get something to eat yet?"

"Yeah, I ordered a turkey sandwich at the hospital cafeteria. How about you?"

"Hamburger and fries at Burger Burger."

"You're not that health conscious are you?"

"Not really. I'm single. I eat a lot of junk food when I'm on duty, but I work out."

"I can tell."

He glanced at her, and she winked at him.

"How was your flight up with Agent Goodwin?"

"Okay. He's a good pilot, but I don't like those small planes. He asked a lot of questions."

"I figured he would. What kind of questions?"

"He wanted to know if Rowland had any enemies. I told him he had a few. Rowland liked to get his way when it came to projects he was passionate about. Ocracoke was one of his obsessions. Once news leaked out about his development ideas for the island, we received a few threatening letters."

"How threatening?"

"Very—a couple death threats and one that was more of a veiled threat."

"Did you keep the letters?"

"Of course. They're at the beach house."

"Do you mind if I take a look at them?"

"Not at all. You can deliver them to Agent Goodwin if you'd like. He said he needed them for the investigation."

Dugan figured he'd talk to Goodwin later that day to update him on Achak. "No problem. I'll make sure he gets them. Where is Agent Goodwin now?"

"He had to fly to the field office in Richmond to coordinate the investigation with the FBI. He said he'd be back later today."

"Was he worried about your safety?"

"Yes, especially after I told him that Rowland and I were business partners. It's now up to me to proceed with the development plans. But I'm not worried."

"Why not?"

She reached and grasped his hand which was resting on the divider between the seats. "Because he said you agreed to look after me. Is that true?"

"Yes." Dugan squeezed her hand. "I'll do the best I can."

She released his hand and folded her hands in her lap. "Then I'm not worried. I trust you."

"How far along were you and Rowland with these development ideas?"

"We had a meeting set up in two weeks with some North Carolina lawmakers and investors. We're not the only ones who believe the public has been deprived of Ocracoke's beauty and availability because of a few environmental extremists. There are people with money and power who are very willing to listen to our plans."

"With what has happened, do you think you'll go through with the meeting?"

Addy crossed her arms. "I don't know. It depends."

"On what?"

"You might think I'm crazy, but I want to do some more paranormal investigation. I truly believe the spirits on the island have a say in this. I feel connected to them. I've talked with Sienna and Luna about another meeting. Who knows? Maybe we'll discover some clues that could help with the investigation."

Dugan didn't know what to think about Addy's fixation on the netherworld. Was she unstable? Or was she more sensitive to the spirit realm than he? Dugan believed in God and heaven. He believed every person had an eternal soul, but did those spirits return to earth after death to haunt houses or even barrier islands? He didn't think so. Then again the words of the Apostle Paul came to mind: *For now we see through a mirror darkly. Then we shall see face to face.* That scripture reminded him that there were some things you just won't know until you pass from this world to the next.

"So you think these ghosts on Ocracoke may *want* the island to be developed?"

"Hmmmm. I wouldn't put it that way. I think they want people to know their lives meant something. When I think of our vision for Ocracoke, money gained through development isn't even a factor. Yes, the shoreline would be divided into plots and sold to people for vacation homes, but what's wrong with that? There's nothing more beautiful than waking up in the morning, walking out onto your deck, and seeing the sunrise above the Atlantic. Why deprive people of that?"

"The environmentalists would say we need to preserve that shoreline to protect the natural habitat, the wildlife, and the sea life."

"But that shoreline goes on for miles and miles. Besides, building houses along it wouldn't damage the environment to any great degree. But more than that, I want to see the history of Ocracoke presented to the world through the best possible technologies and facilities. Wouldn't it be fun to walk through a hologram village and witness their daily lives? Imagine a tour where the ghosts of Ocracoke—Indians, pirates and settlers actually appear and interact with the people about life in those days. A special pirate exhibition could be constructed where tourists would meet Blackbeard and his crew and witness a 3-D reenactment of Queen Anne's Revenge attacking and plundering another ship."

"It sounds like fun."

"Oh yes! But more than fun, it would be educational. I want people to know about the lives of the Pamunkey Indians, settlers, fishermen, and even the pirates. It's fascinating. These people lived and loved and survived and died in a difficult and demanding environment."

"I agree. But why would these . . . spirits be concerned about presenting their past lives to the living?"

Addy turned to Dugan and placed her hand on his shoulder. "Because their lives counted. They want us to know that. The sacrifices they made and the ground they broke and settled here on the Outer Banks has meaning for us today. The living can benefit from knowing the price that was paid by those who came before us." She sat back in her seat, rested her hands on her knees, and breathed deeply.

"You're very passionate about this, aren't you?"

"Yes. I guess I feel so personally involved because . . . because I once lived on the island."

"Do you mean when you were a kid?"

"No. I mean in a past life."

"Oh." Here we go, Dugan thought.

"It's hard for people who aren't sensitive to these sorts of things to understand."

"Try me."

"Well, whenever I'm on the island, I sense it the most. It's a young Native American girl. If I open myself to the spirit world, she comes to me and enters me. Then it becomes clear. I go back in time and everything is familiar. I feel alive and free when she possesses me. But sometimes it's scary."

"Why? What happens?"

She leaned forward and placed her hands on the dash. "There was an incident in her life that traumatized her. These anxious images speed through my mind. I'm running across the beach and through trees. This man with long hair and a beard is chasing me. He's dressed in black. I stumble and fall and get up again and run, but I can't get away. He catches up and tackles me, and then he . . . he . . . overpowers me."

"I see."

54

"Usually that's when she releases me, and I come back to the present." Addy sat back on the seat and stretched. "Do you think I'm some kind of wacko?"

"Of course not. I'm familiar with crimes that have been solved with the help of paranormal investigators. There's no scientific explanation, but science doesn't have all the answers. Don't get me wrong. I'm not a clairvoyant enthusiast, but I'm open to the possibilities."

"Your deputy isn't."

"Who? Marla?"

"Yes. She said that forensic science would uncover the identity of my husband's murderer rather any kind of hocus pocus."

"You're right. Marla had a brush with someone in the past who claimed to be possessed by the spirit of her deceased husband. It was a scam the guy used to try to take advantage of her. Ever since, she has become the ultimate skeptic."

"That's too bad. Frauds have given spiritualists a bad reputation. Now your deputy is completely closed off to even the possibility of the spirit realm. Can I ask you a personal question?"

Dugan shrugged. "Sure."

"Are you in love with her?"

Dugan took a quick peek at Addy. She had angled toward him, those entrancing eyes with their long lashes locked on to him. "What makes you ask?"

"I can feel something between you two. I'm good at that sort of thing."

Dugan gripped the wheel tighter. "We were engaged. She recently broke it off."

Addy reached and gently touched his shoulder. "I thought so. I'm so sorry."

"Well . . . I'll live. It's not the first time I've been rejected by someone."

"Marla is a fool. You're a good man. She'll regret it."

"Thanks. Do you mind if I asked you a personal question?"

"Go ahead."

"I noticed your husband looked a lot older than you, fifteen or twenty years."

"That's right."

"You're a beautiful lady. Why did you marry an older man?" Dugan caught a glimpse of a smile.

"First of all, thank you for the compliment. Rowland didn't seem that old ten years ago when he was in his mid-forties. A lot of his friends accused me of being a gold digger back then, but I really loved him. We had a lot of things in common. Being a British diplomat, he was a world traveler, and I loved to travel. Neither of us wanted kids. He was a powerful man, yet he respected me and my ideas. That's why he made me an equal partner in all his development endeavors. When he turned fifty, his health began to slide." She tapped her fist against his thigh. "Like you, he enjoyed his junk food. He ended up with diabetes and heart problems. For the last five years he's been impotent. No libido whatsoever."

"Sorry to hear that."

She chuckled. "You think you're sorry. Anyway, our relationship transitioned from being lovers into a good friendship. A lot of men have come on to me over the years, but I didn't stray. I was faithful to our wedding vows—till death do us part. But now he's . . . he's gone."

The rest of the way home their conversation drifted from their past lives to future hopes, occasionally touching on something deeper or somewhat guarded. Dugan enjoyed Addy's company. He hadn't had a lot of luck with women over the years, but she was one of the few with whom he could easily talk. Before he knew it, they had reached her beach house in Hatteras. He went through the bottom floor with her and checked in every closet. Then he checked the alarm system to make sure it was working properly. They worked their way up through every room and ended up on the top floor in the kitchen.

Addy leaned against the marble-topped island. "Thanks so much for checking the house for me."

"You're welcome. You look exhausted."

"I need a shower and a good sleep."

"I'm not far away. I live in Buxton, about ten miles up Route 12." Dugan took out his wallet and withdrew his sheriff's information card and handed it to her. "My cell number's on there."

She examined the information card "Dugan Walton – Dare County Sheriff. 'Serving with Integrity, Honor, and Commitment.' Very noble."

He shrugged. "Yeah, noble but not easy. I try to do my best."

"I don't doubt that at all."

"Before I forget, could you please get me those letters you were talking about—the ones that threatened your husband."

"Sure thing. I'll be right back." She cut across the great room and opened the master bedroom door. It only took her about a minute to find the letters and return. "Of course there's no return address on any of them." She handed Dugan the first envelope.

He slid out the letter. The message resembled something a serial killer might send to a newspaper composed with a variety of cutout fonts from various magazines: DON'T EVEN THINK ABOUT VIOLATING OCRACOKE OR YOU WILL DIE. Dugan checked the envelope's postmark—Kitty Hawk, NC. "This one's local."

"So is this one." Addy handed him the second envelope.

It was postmarked Nags Head, NC. Dugan extracted the paper, unfolded it, and noticed it had probably been printed from a home computer using a common font—Courier: *We heard a rumor that you are pursuing a dangerous objective—the development of Ocracoke. We advise that you immediately cease and desist this course of action. We guarantee that it will lead to your demise. Sincerely, the Guardians of Ocracoke.*

Dugan lifted the letter. "Interesting. They seem to be a bit more elegant in their threats."

Addy handed him the third envelope. "This one's the most recent. It's from Ohio."

"Ohio?" Dugan checked the postmark—Youngstown, OH. As soon as he opened it, the scrawled, heavy printing startled him: IT IS NOT WISE TO TREAD ON SACRED GROUND. Below the words was a primitive sketch of a skull and crossbones. The handwriting was rough, heavily scrawled in pencil. The writer printed his letters like a kid in grade school and used thick underlines under certain words. Dugan knew immediately who sent the letter. But why was it sent from Ohio?

Chapter 8

The trek from Buxton, North Carolina to Star City, West Virginia took about nine hours. Marla and Mee Mee decided to take Mee Mee's Jeep Grand Cherokee and share driving duties. One caught up on some sleep when the other handled the wheel. Star City was a quaint little town just north of Morgantown along the Monongahela River. Mee Mee's mother, Eudora Roberts, a former school bus driver, lived in a small house on the outskirts of town along Baker's Ridge Road.

They sat around Eudora's kitchen table at eight o'clock in the evening sipping homemade iced tea. The mid-September sun had gone down an hour ago, and darkness was extinguishing the fading twilight through the window over the sink. The room had simple furnishings, a yellow Formica-topped table with chrome legs, pine cabinets and a black and white checkerboard linoleum floor. To Mee Mee everything felt familiar and comfortable.

At eighty-five years old, Eudora was still as sharp as a tack. A petite woman, just over five feet tall and weighing about one hundred pounds, she kept a summer garden and drove a '95 Chevy Lumina.

Eudora slid the contract across the table toward Mee Mee. "Take a look. See what you think."

Mee Mee scanned the first page. "I'm sure this is very similar to what your neighbors have received." She took a few minutes to go through the pages. "These oil and gas leases are all pretty standard. It looks like they want to give you $5500 dollars per acre for a five-year lease."

"I've got ten acres. So if my math is right, that's $55,000 dollars."

"That's correct," Mee Mee assured her.

Eudora sat back in her chair and crossed her arms. "Why wouldn't anyone sign this? $55,000 is a lot of money. I could buy a new car."

Mee Mee finished off her iced tea. "Some people are worried about what hydraulic fracturing will do to the environment. This industry isn't regulated as closely as other industries."

"Why not?"

"I've done some reading on it," Marla said. "The industry has recently swept into the Ohio Valley, my old stomping grounds. Because they offer America the possibility of energy independence, the government doesn't closely monitor their methods. For example, they don't have to reveal what chemicals they are injecting into the ground."

Eurdora leaned forward. "That's how they get the gas and oil, by injecting chemicals into the ground?"

"Of course," Mee Mee said. "It's pretty much a chemical cocktail shot deep into the earth to fracture layers of rock. That allows the gas or petroleum to flow freely back up their pipes."

"What's the worst that could happen?" Eudora asked.

Marla held up her glass. "Water contamination, both ground water and surface water. I've also read that this deep fracturing of rocks can stimulate earthquakes."

Mee Mee pushed the contract back toward her mother. "From what I hear they don't hire too many locals to do the work, so you've got a lot of strangers moving into town, and the rents go up. With all the construction comes noise and truck traffic. The roads will get beat up, and they'll be putting pipelines in all over the place. Vermont and New York have outlawed fracking."

Eudora slid the contract to the middle of the table. "Then I'm not gonna sign it."

Mee Mee shook her head. "You might as well."

"Why?"

"Because they're going to take the oil and gas from underneath your property whether you sign it or not."

"You're kidding?"

"No, " Mee Mee said. "What's to stop them? If they put a well in a half mile from here, the oil or gas under your land will get sucked up with everyone else's."

"There's been a lot of problems with fracking in Pennsyvania and Ohio," Marla said. "People are up in arms about it."

"That's another reason I drove up here today, Mom. I'm writing a story on it for the *Island Free Press*."

Eudora's eyes grew wide. "They're gonna start fracking on the Outer Banks?"

Marla couldn't help smiling. "They wouldn't have much luck fracking on the Outer Banks. There are no Marcellus shale deposits there. But we do have an environmental issue—the threat of development of protected lands."

"That reminds me," Mee Mee said. "Has anyone reported seeing a giant bird around here?"

"Giant bird?" Eudora pointed to the window. "I've seen some turkey vultures in those trees across the way."

"No. I'm talking about a really big bird. Ten-foot wingspan. Has kind of a glow to it. Chases people."

"It glows?" Eudora laughed. "That sounds like the Mothman from Point Pleasant with its glowing eyes. Are there some crazy people saying that some giant bird has been swooping down on them?"

Mee Mee raised her hand. "Yes, Mom, in particular—me."

"You've seen the Mothman?"

Mee Mee let out a loud sigh. "No, not the Mothman. But I swear to sweet Moses that a giant bird swept down on me and my friends last night on Ocracoke Island. There are similar sightings in Pennsylvania and Ohio. Wherever the bird shows up, bad things happen."

"Did something bad happen last night?"

"Yes, indeed. A man was killed, possibly murdered. He was the very man who wanted to develop the protected shores of Ocracoke."

Eudora sat back, her head slowly bobbing. "That is weird. Was he your friend?"

"I guess he would be better described as an acquaintance. You'll probably hear about it on the news. He was a British diplomat."

"What were you doing hanging out with a British diplomat on Ocracoke Island?"

"It's a long story." Mee Mee tried to condense the details of the night before into a concise narrative, but her mother kept asking questions. It took about a half hour, but finally Eudora seemed satisfied with the account.

"And you say this giant eagle has appeared near here?" Eudora asked.

"Not yet. Tomorrow morning we're heading up to Towanda, Pennsylvania, about five hours northeast of here. The bird made several appearances there and also in Youngstown, Ohio, a few hours north of here. I'm going to interview the people who saw the bird."

"So you've become an investigative journalist for the *Island Free Press?*"

Mee Mee nodded. "Yes. I'm very excited about writing this story."

"Then who in the world is running your bookstore in Buxton?"

"That's taken care of, Mom. Jamie Leighton, a good friend of mine, runs things whenever I'm gone."

"I hope so. You need to keep your bookstore business. Journalism doesn't pay much unless you write for one of the big magazines."

Marla chuckled. "Who knows, Eudora? Your daughter just might knock it out of the park with this story."

* * *

With Marla at the wheel, they reached Towanda, Pennsylvania about noon the next day. Main Street resembled ten thousand other Main Streets in this part of the country. Many older buildings from the 1800's still stood and served the community as family-owned shops, banks, bars, and offices. Newer brick buildings had been constructed between the older ones with no gaps between, creating an interesting mix of styles. They passed the *Daily Review*, a three-story, green and white edifice that housed Towanda's hometown newspaper. The familiar chain store, Ben Franklin, came up on the left, and a block after that the colonial-styled Bradford County Courthouse appeared with its statues of Civil War soldiers guarding the entrance. Then a series of red and beige and white brick buildings scrolled by on either side.

"This is interesting," Mee Mee said as she gazed at her iPhone. "It says here that Towanda is an Algonquin Indian term for sacred burial ground."

Marla stole a quick glance at her. "That is an odd coincidence. The Outer Banks were inhabited by Algonquin Indians."

"That's true. And Achak Rowtag claimed that Ocracoke was a sacred place for the Algonquin peoples. The name of the island is supposedly a derivative of some Algonquin word meaning protected area."

"There's the link for your story—sacred Algonquin Indian grounds that are environmentally threatened."

"Yeah. Maybe an *important* link."

"You getting hungry?"

"Starved."

"Let's find a good old mom-and-pop restaurant and get some chow."

Mee Mee patted her stomach. "I'm all for that. Keep your eyes open."

Marla noticed a print shop on the right and then another law office. On the left she could see a big red brick building with the words "Keystone Theater" running vertically along its edge and a marquee in front announcing the latest Cohen Brothers' movie.

"Bingo!" Mee Mee pointed to the right. "The Red Rose Diner! And there's a parking space right in front."

Marla whipped the Jeep Cherokee towards the curb and pulled into the open parking space. The diner looked like an old fashioned train car that had been lifted off the tracks and plopped down in the middle of Towanda long ago. It was white with red trim and had an arched, barrel-style roof. Three small stained-glass windows graced the front, and a large pot of pink petunias sat next to the entrance. Patriotic bunting draped the railing along the front stoop. The diner's logo was painted to the right of the door—a red rose between two green leaves.

As they approached the door, Mee Mee pointed upward. "Take a look there."

Marla noticed a couple of words painted just below the roofline—LADIES INVITED. "Guess that means us."

The place was small, but filled with friendly faces. Marla and Mee Mee took their seats at the counter. The only other option was two small tables along the other wall, but they were occupied. The walls offered numerous old photos and signs to check out, and shelves near the ceiling held old mugs, lanterns, and vases.

The waitress, a plump gal in her forties with long brown hair piled up in a hairnet, counted money at the register. A signboard on the wall behind them advertised today's special—a bowl of homemade vegetable soup and chicken quesadillas for $7.95. When the waitress greeted them, they both ordered the special and a large glass of lemonade.

A young blond guy wearing a red flannel shirt sat a couple stools down next to an older gentleman with thick gray hair and wire-rimmed glasses. The young guy complained about all the truck traffic rumbling down his road because of the installation of a new horizontal gas well not far from his house.

The old man slammed his fist on the counter. "One of those damn trucks near ran me off the road the other day. They don't care one iota about us. Just so we get the hell out of their way. So what if we've lived here all our lives. Don't matter to them. They're only here for the money."

Mee Mee glanced at Marla and raised her eyebrows.

The waitress delivered two tall glasses of lemonade. "You ladies from out of town?"

"Yes, we are," Marla said. "North Carolina."

"What part?"

"The Outer Banks."

"Oh, heaven bless us. I love the Outer Banks—Kitty Hawk. Nags Head. My family has been vacationing down there for years. What brings you up here?"

Mee Mee cleared her throat. "I'm writing an article for an Outer Banks newspaper. We hope to interview some people up here."

The waitress tilted her head. "What's the article about?"

"This might sound odd, but it's about a giant bird people have reported in this area."

"Oh no, Honey. Not odd at all. I've heard about the bird."

The young man in the red flannel shirt turned on his stool and faced Mee Mee. "I've seen it." He hadn't shaved for a couple of days and had a deep dimple on his chin.

"Is that right?" Mee Mee said. "Do you mind if I ask some questions and take some notes?"

"Not at all."

"What did the bird look like?"

"It was huge, like one of those condors. It had big talons and it screeched like a banshee. It had this strange aura like someone spilled glow-in-the-dark paint on it."

"Where did you see it?"

"Up along Sugar Creek where I live, near a new fracking well."

The old man leaned on the counter and peered in their direction. "Have you seen it?"

Mee Mee nodded. "Last night it showed up on Ocracoke Island. I was there. It swooped down on a bunch of us and chased us into the woods."

"Yeah," the young guy said. "It's aggressive."

A girl at the table behind them stood and approached. She had long blonde hair and looked to be in her late twenties. She wore Daisy Duke shorts and a blue T-shirt with a Jamboree in the Hills logo on it. "I've got a friend who was attacked by the bird one night about two months ago."

Mee Mee turned toward her with pen and notepad in hand. "What happened?"

"Jessie and her boyfriend, Jimmy Warren, were parked out on Kokopelli Lane in Jimmy's Mustang convertible about a mile from the golf course. They were just, you know . . . they were . . ."

Marla smiled. "Doing what young couples do in parked cars on country roads."

"Right," the blonde said. "Suddenly this huge bird swoops down on them. Jessie screamed, and Jimmy managed to get the car started. The bird soared back up into the sky and began to circle back. Jessie said it was easy to see the creature because it sorta glowed. Jimmy pulled the Mustang out onto the road, but the thing swooped down again. That's when Jimmy floored it. He panicked. Going around the next turn, he lost control and hit a tree. Jessie ended up with a broken leg and cuts on her face and arms. Jimmy got a concussion from the airbag. It was terrible."

"What happened to the bird?" Mee Mee asked.

"It disappeared. Took off. They kept thinking they were sitting ducks, but it never came back."

"Wow," Mee Mee said. "I'm sorry to hear about your friends' injuries. From what we've heard, bad things happen whenever the bird shows up."

The old man leaned closer. "Did something bad happen last night on that island?"

"Yes," Marla said. "A man died."

"Did he kill himself?"

"No. We believe he was murdered. Why would you ask if he killed himself?"

"I have a lady friend who saw the bird. She ended up taking her own life."

Mee Mee gasped. "Why did she commit suicide?"

The old man slowly shook his head and blinked his eyes several times. "She was a goat farmer with more than a hundred head. About a year ago she spotted the bird shortly after two new fracking sites had been constructed near her property. She said the creature was a harbinger of doom. It wasn't long before her goats began to die, and her drinking water went bad. She contacted the EPA, but they blamed it on a faulty well. The eagle kept appearing at night every couple months. It wasn't long before most of the herd died. She started having other health problems—nose bleeds and fibromyalgia. When one of the truckers hauling water up to the drill site ran over her collie, she had enough—shot herself right in the temple."

Marla swallowed a gulp of lemonade. "I'm so sorry to hear that."

The old man straightened up. "Some of her neighbors said that eagle was a death angel, but I don't blame the bird. I blame the oil and gas companies. They destroyed her life by defiling the land."

"They're destroying my family's life too," the young man said.

"How's that?" Mee Mee asked.

"We live along Sugar Creek. Not far from us atop a nearby hill is a fracking well. As soon as they started construction about a year ago the bird showed up at night screeching louder than a demon from Hell. The first time I heard it I went outside to see what was going on. There it was circling high above me all aglow. Strangest thing I ever saw. Once they started drilling the well, things began to happen. I noticed this nasty red liquid oozing out of the ground across the creek from our house. That's when my family started getting sick—nosebleeds, headaches, rashes, and boils. Then our well water started tasting funny. Found out it had been contaminated. They said it was a faulty well just like the goat lady's. Then I found out all those chemicals they pump into the ground are carcinogens. My family was being poisoned by cancer-causing agents."

"Did the drilling company make any kind of restitution?" Marla asked.

The young man shook his head. "It's all a big legal mess right now. Course we can't drink from our well anymore, and the doctor bills are killing us. What's worse is the chemicals are literally killing us."

"I'm so sorry to hear that," Mee Mee said.

The waitress delivered the soup and quesadillas and refilled their lemonade glasses.

Mee Mee nudged Marla, shook her lemonade glass, and quietly said, "Let's hope this water's good."

The diner grew quiet as they ate their lunch. Marla thought the homemade vegetable soup was delicious, and the quesadilla hit the spot. She wiped her mouth with a napkin and said, "Where to next?"

"I've got an idea." Mee Mee tilted her head toward the young guy. "I want to go see the polluted creek firsthand."

Mee Mee leaned toward the young guy. "Sir, would you mind showing us that creek you were talking about? You know, the one with the red sludge oozing out?

The young guy nodded. "Yeah, I could do that. It's not far from here. Are you ready to head out now?"

"We're ready to go."

Marla met the waitress at the register to pay the bill and thanked her for the good service and food. Mee Mee thanked the patrons for sharing their stories with her.

The old man pulled her aside. "Listen, you need to be careful who you talk to."

"Why's that?"

"These fracking companies don't like bad press. You could end up being a target. I've seen bad things happen to people who try to stand up against them."

"I'll be careful," Mee Mee assured him.

"I'm parked around the corner," the young guy said. "The old Ford pickup truck. By the way, my name's Harold Perkins."

Mee Mee introduced Marla and herself and then pointed out the glass front door. "We're driving that Grand Cherokee. I'll follow you."

* * *

Mee Mee drove as they followed Harold Perkins's old red pickup down a couple of back streets. Finding eyewitnesses so quickly excited her. Could it possibly be the same bird? If so, someone was orchestrating these encounters. Mr. Perkins turned right on York Avenue. The blocks of stores and offices ended, replaced by residential neighborhoods with modest, older homes. Within minutes the surroundings became more rural, and they made a sharp left onto Sugar Creek Road, a narrow asphalt road in need of resurfacing. About a half mile down the road they reached the Perkins house, a small frame structure with white siding and a red brick chimney. An American flag waved on a tall pole in front, and in the back on the left was a carport.

Mr. Perkins parked under the carport. Mee Mee stopped in the driveway, and Marla and she stepped out of the car. He climbed out of the pickup and pointed across a narrow strip of hayfield to a large hill. "The fracking site is on top of that hill."

Mee Mee shaded her eyes and gazed at the top of the hill. She could see the blue framework of the drilling rig above the trees.

"Where's the stream?" Marla asked.

"Follow me." Mr. Perkins walked across the recently cut hayfield and stopped under the shade of a maple tree at the top of the creek bank. The stream looked to be about thirty feet wide. He pointed across the water to the side of the hill. "See that?"

The opening in the ground and the red sludge oozing out of it was hard to miss. The odd color tinted the steam and smelled like insecticide or some kind of weed killer.

Mr. Perkins shuffled down the bank, stood at the edge of the water, and pointed to something several feet out in the stream. "Check that out."

Mee Mee and Marla joined him at the water's edge. The water was bubbling where Mr. Perkins had pointed.

"What in the world is causing the water to bubble like that?" Marla asked.

"Methane gas," Mr. Perkins said. "It never did this before they began drilling. All those chemicals they pumped into the ground has forced the gas to the surface. And you can see what's happening across the stream. It's like giving the earth an enema. The crap has to come out somewhere."

Mee Mee shook her head. "No wonder you're concerned for your family's welfare."

Mr. Perkins rolled up his sleeve and held out his forearm. A nasty rash covered his skin from his wrist to his bicep. "I've never had these kinds of problems either until the frackers showed up. The kids and wife are sick all the time. We can't use the well water any more. It's awful."

"I sure hope your lawyers can get you a good settlement," Marla said.

Mr. Perkins let out a sad sigh. "Yeah, if we don't end up dying or in the poor house first." He pointed back toward his house. "I've got one more thing to show you before you leave."

They walked back across the field to his back porch. "Come on into the kitchen. You're not going to believe this."

The kitchen was small with white-painted cabinets and a refrigerator covered with family photos and children's artwork. Everything was tidy but modest.

He leaned on the counter by the sink. "My wife and kids went to her mother's house for the day over in East Smithfield. Sometimes you just have to get away from here. Anyway, this is what I wanted to show you." He lifted the handle on the faucet, and water poured out. Then he reached into his pocket and pulled out a Bic lighter. "Watch this." He struck the lighter. "Stand back." After Mee Mee and Marla took a step back he reached toward the flow of water with the lighter, and with a sudden whoosh, a flame engulfed the flow, burned for few seconds and then went out. He did it again with the same results, and then turned off the faucet.

"I've never seen anything like that," Mee Mee gasped.

"Isn't that dangerous?" Marla asked.

"Sure," Mr. Perkins said. "This water line comes directly from my well. Methane gas is coming up through the line just like it's bubbling over in that stream. Oh well. The fracking companies claim the methane has always been there. No kidding. But the fracking forces it to the surface and into our well water."

"That is just wrong," Marla said.

Mee Mee put her hands on her hips. "It's criminal."

"Yeah," Mr. Perkins said, "They're raping Mother Earth and getting away with it."

They walked out onto the back porch, and Mee Mee pointed to the fracking tower on top of the hill. "I'd like to go up there and interview the guy in charge. What's the best way to get there?"

"It's only a couple hundred yards from here if you walk, but that's a tough climb up the hill, and through the woods and weeds. To get there by car, head back the way we came, make a right on York Avenue and then another right on Braxton Boulevard. Braxton will take you straight to the fracking well."

* * *

Braxton Boulevard was a newly paved road, but Marla saw very few houses on either side. She noticed an onramp to State Route 220 on the right just before they passed under the busy highway. Then the asphalt abruptly ended, replaced by gravel. To the right she spied a yellow sign warning drivers of the presence of overhead power lines. That's odd, Marla thought. Then she realized the warning applied to large trucks. The next sign had the word ELEVATION on it and the word CHESAPEAKE, but that's all she could make out. A large white gate composed of welded steel poles had been swung open, and just beyond it stood a blue port-a-potty.

"Are you sure we're allowed to drive right up to this fracking well?" Marla asked.

Mee Mee gripped the steering wheel with both hands and leaned forward. "They left the gate wide open, and I don't see any NO TRESPASSING signs."

They drove past a huge pile of sand and around a slight turn. The narrow road cut through a wooded area with tall trees on both sides, but then they entered a clearing and saw the fracking site. Mee Mee pulled off to the side and parked out of the way in a grassy area. Marla could see lots of trucks, storage tanks, machinery, and the framework of a large blue tower on the back of the site, the same tower they had seen from Harold Perkins's backyard. It was all situated on a large rectangular area of crushed gravel. Workers wearing yellow hardhats and coveralls squatted and scrambled among the pipes and fittings. Several men stood talking next to a row of water tank trucks. One of the men, a beefy guy with a white hard hat, noticed them standing there and immediately headed in their direction.

"Uh oh," Marla said. "Here comes the boss."

"Let me do the talking."

71

Marla chuckled. "You're the one writing the article. I'm just the bodyguard."

"Get your deputy I.D. ready."

"My deputy I.D.?"

The guy had a broad face, narrow, dark eyes, and a full brown beard. He approached with quick, rigid steps. "Are you ladies lost?"

"No sir," Mee Mee said brusquely. "My name is Mee Mee Roberts. This is Deputy Marla Easton."

Marla flashed her I.D. and quickly slid it back into her jacket pocket.

Mee Mee continued. "We are part of an investigative team in partnership with the Secret Service and FBI under the direction of Special Agent Russell Goodwin."

The man's eyebrows tensed. "The Secret Service? What's this about?"

"We'd like to ask you a few questions."

"I guess so, but what . . . what . . ."

Mee Mee pulled out her notepad. "Name please and position."

"John Scarbrough. I'm the operations manager here."

Mee Mee wrote the name. "I see. How long have you been the operations manager at this facility?"

"About a year. Ever since the well was installed."

"Have you received any kind of threats lately?"

"Threats?" He shrugged. "Not so many lately."

"But you have received threats?"

He waved his hand back toward Braxton Boulevard. "Some of the townspeople aren't happy with us, but that's fairly normal."

"Has there been any threats of physical violence?"

"I can't recall anything lately, but it happens. You know how people are. They blame us for everything that goes wrong around here. They get a hangnail and blame it on the oil and gas companies."

"Yes. We're well aware of that. There have been a lot of environmental issues with the locals since the wells have been drilled. For example, right over the hill here along Sugar Creek a fissure has appeared along the bank from which chemicals are pouring into the stream."

"Well . . ." the big man cleared his throat. "That may be, but there has not been any clear evidence proving the seepage down there is direct result of this operation."

"The creek also has an excessive amount of methane gas bubbling up through the water, far above normal levels. Besides that, many of the local residents' wells have been contaminated."

"Listen. I've heard this all before. Methane has been bubbling up along these creeks and streams for thousands of years. People need to understand that the ground in a Marcellus shale region is full of methane. And most of these property owners' wells go bad because they're old and unsound."

Mee Mee peered over her wire rim glasses. "But you do agree that these kinds of problems increase in areas where hydraulic fracturing has been operating?"

"Wherever major industries operate there is going to be occasional problems and accidents. Do you realize what the steel industry did to our rivers over the last hundred years? Do you know how many lives have been lost in the coal industry? Yeah, occasionally the oil and gas industry has been guilty of various violations, but we are empowering America. This industry is moving our country in the direction of energy independence. Do you want our future to be controlled by some Middle Eastern country which has the market cornered on oil?"

Marla glanced at Mee Mee and wondered how she would answer that question.

Mee Mee cleared her throat. "Well, Mr. Scarbrough, let me get to the point of this investigation."

"Yes. Please do."

"We have reason to believe there may be a threat against your industry and those who work in this region. Specifically, we are convinced that an environmental extremist may be planning some kind of nefarious act to draw attention to his viewpoint."

"What kind of act? Some type of terrorist attack?"

"Along those lines, yes. Last night a man was murdered in North Carolina. He was a developer and considered a threat to protected lands along the coast. His death has been linked to the sighting of a large bird that has also been reported in this area."

Scarbrough rubbed his chin. "No kidding. Two of my workers

claimed to have seen that bird. Said it was huge. You're saying that a guy was murdered by environmental extremists at the same time this bird showed up?"

"That's correct."

"And you think that I might be in danger?"

"We're not sure who might be in danger. All we know is that bad things happen when this bird shows up. We're trying to find out why things happen and who's behind it."

A loud boom erupted behind them.

"Whoa! That was close." Scarbrough turned in the direction of the explosion. "Could that be a bomb?"

Marla pointed toward Sugar Creek. "Right over the hill there."

"I see smoke . . . and flames," Mee Mee said. "That's down near where Harold Perkins lives."

Marla shielded her eyes and gazed at the smoke. "I just heard someone scream."

"We better check it out."

Marla said, "That's only a couple hundred yards from here down through the woods. It'll take ten minutes to get back there by car."

"Let's go!" Mee Mee took off running toward the woods.

Chapter 9

Marla knew Mee Mee kept fit by doing a lot of walking on the trails and beaches around Buxton, but the added adrenaline supercharged the sixty-two year-old bookstore owner. Marla kept up as best she could, descending the hillside, weaving between trees, climbing over fallen branches, and tramping down thick growth. Finally they reached the creek and got a better view.

"It's the house down from the Perkins's place!" Mee Mee shouted.

"How are we going to get across the creek?"

Mee Mee bolted into the water. "C'mon! It's not deep!"

Marla waded in, the shock of the cold stream sending jolts up her spine. She stepped carefully, trying to avoid large rocks. Halfway across, the water rose almost to her crotch but quickly became shallower as she neared the bank. Mee Mee had already tromped into the hayfield on a diagonal path towards the burning house.

They approached the house from the back. It was one of those split-levels with beige siding and brown shutters. Flames shot out of the windows and roof on the right side, which Marla guessed to be the kitchen and dining area. She figured the left side where the split level was located probably housed the bedrooms. She hoped no one was in the kitchen. The smell of smoke and crackling of burning wood sent a wave of panic through her, but she managed to keep focused.

Mee Mee rushed up the few back steps and tried the door. "It's locked!"

Marla could hear muffled screams. She charged up the steps, pulled out her Magnum pistol and broke the nearest window with the gun handle. She knocked the shards away from the frame. Gray smoke billowed out of the top of the window.

"Give me a hand up," Mee Mee said.

"You can't go in there." Marla placed the pistol back into her holster under her jacket.

"I'll stay low. I heard a kid screaming. I've got to try. Now link your hands so I can step up into the window."

Marla thought this was a bad idea but knew Mee Mee wouldn't take no for an answer. She linked her hands, and as Mee Mee placed her foot on her intersecting fingers, she heaved upward to thrust her toward the opening.

Mee Mee leapt inside, landed with a thump, turned, and yelled, "Call 911!"

Marla fumbled for her phone. Her hand was shaking, but she managed to dial the numbers and report the fire. The seconds passed interminably. She kept looking into the window, trying to make out anything in the smoky interior. Then she heard footsteps and coughing. A smudged face appeared—a little girl with blonde hair.

"Take her!" Mee Mee shouted as she sprung into view and lifted the kid to the opening.

Marla reached up, clasped the child's waist, and lowered her to the porch. The girl clung to her, choking and sobbing.

"I'm going back after her mother."

"Be careful!" Marla could hear louder popping and crackling noises from the right side of the house, and the smoke thickened as it poured out the window. She lifted the girl and carried her down into the yard. The kid kept coughing and crying. Marla guessed she was about eight or nine years old.

Harold Perkins came running around the corner of the house, keeping his distance from the flames. "Is everyone okay!" he shouted.

"Keep your eye on the girl. I'm going in after Mee Mee." Marla dashed to the porch and gripped the ledge of the window. The roar of the fire had become so loud she couldn't hear any footsteps or voices. She jumped and pressed herself up to the window. The smoke engulfed her head, and she couldn't breathe. Choking, she pushed off and landed on the porch. After getting some good gulps of air, she jumped again, this time trying to shoot into the opening. Her stomach and hips landed on the ledge, and she precariously tottered there like an off-balance gymnast.

"Get out of the way!" Mee Mee ordered.

Marla managed to edge her weight back toward her legs and lowered herself onto the porch. She peered up and saw an unfamiliar woman's face. She had short sandy blonde hair and wide blue eyes.

Between coughs Mee Mee managed to say, "Help her down."

Marla reached, pulled the woman through, and fell to the porch with her. The blonde struggled to breathe, gasping and hacking.

Mee Mee dropped down from the window. "Grab her arm. Let's get her away from the house."

They gripped her arms and lifted as the woman struggled to her feet. The woman clasped her arms around their shoulders and they helped her descend the steps.

"Where's George?" Mr. Perkins asked.

Marla glanced at him. "Who's George?"

"My father," the woman said between coughs. "I told him not to smoke in the kitchen."

"Oh no," Mr. Perkins said.

Mee Mee eyed Mr. Perkins. "What's the matter?"

"Methane gas builds up in the kitchen, especially if the faucet leaks."

Marla gazed at the right side of the house. The flames had completely engulfed it.

The blonde woman tried to stand on her own but needed to hold tightly onto Marla's arm to keep her balance. "I have to go back in after my dad."

"No way are you going back in there," Marla said.

"I have to," she wailed.

Marla pointed to the raging fire. "Ma'am, if he lit a cigarette in the kitchen and ignited that gas, he didn't survive."

The woman crumpled to the ground, sobbing, and the young girl embraced her.

In the distance Marla could hear a siren.

Harold Perkins shook his head. "Poor George. What a way to go. I knew that guy most of my life. Nice man."

Mee Mee placed her hand on Harold's shoulder. "I'm so sorry. You and your family have suffered, and now your neighbors are facing a terrible tragedy."

"Ever since the frackers and that big damn bird showed up . . ." He swallowed and blinked his eyes. ". . . the strangest things have happened in this town."

Chapter 10

Dugan Walton sat in his office at the Dare County Sheriff's Department in Manteo. Agent Goodwin was stopping by later that day to pick up the death-threat letters. Dugan wanted to provide him with a thorough report from what he had discovered so far. Who knows? Dugan had always wanted to be become a federal agent. Even when he was a kid he had dreamed about it. Maybe Russell Goodwin would offer some guidance and possibly help open a door some day.

His stomach growled, and he glanced at his watch—almost noon. He had just completed a background check on Achak Rowtag. He scrolled down the computer screen noting several arrests. In October of 2000 in Denver, Colorado, Rowtag had been arrested with numerous other Native Americans who protested the Columbus Day parade by pouring buckets of red paint onto the street, splashing the parade participants. According to the report the protesters claimed the red paint represented Native American blood spilled by Christopher

Columbus and his Italian armed forces.

There were several other similar arrests over the years. The latest occurred in Lancaster County, Pennsylvania, where a proposed natural gas pipeline cut right across sacred Indian grounds. Rowtag and several of his fellow protesters marched up to the drilling rig and demanded the workers stop the machinery, remove their equipment, and leave the area immediately. They positioned themselves around the site to block normal workday activity. The project manager called the local sheriff and arrests were made. Clearly, Rowtag was not afraid to take extreme measures to prevent what he considered a violation of Native American rights.

Dugan picked up the three letters that Addy had given him, and looked carefully at each again. Because they differed so much in style, he reasoned they had been sent by three separate individuals. However, that didn't rule out a group effort. The one with Rowtag's handwriting had been sent from Ohio. Why? Considering his arrest report, Dugan reasoned that he definitely traveled to where the action flared up. There was probably some kind of perceived trespass upon sacred ground near Youngstown, Ohio that sparked his activist impulse. Didn't Goodwin mention that the large eagle had been spotted near there? He wondered if Marla and Mee Mee were stopping in Youngstown to interview eyewitnesses. He'd call Mee Mee later that afternoon.

His stomach growled again, and he decided to head over to Darrell's Restaurant on Route 64 and grab some kind of seafood salad for lunch. Addy would approve—much better than a greasy hamburger and fries. He caught himself thinking about her when he wasn't occupied with work—her bright smile and those lips, her perfect skin and enchanting eyes, and that knock-out body. Suddenly, it occurred to him that he was thinking more about Addy than Marla. He knew why. When he thought about Marla heaviness settled upon him, the heaviness of rejection and relationship failure. Thinking about Addy had the opposite effect: Being with her made him feel more lighthearted and better about himself. He knew he was still in love with Marla, but Addy needed him, and he enjoyed being with her although she was a little kooky.

As he scooted his chair out, the phone rang. "Sheriff Walton here."

"Dugan, this is Addy."

"Is everything okay?"

"Yes. Fine. I just wanted to let you know about the séance."

"What séance?"

"Tomorrow night at the Ocracoke Lighthouse. Can you believe it? Sienna and Luna got permission to conduct the session at the *Ocracoke Lighthouse*! It's one of the most spiritually energized spots on the island. I want you to come."

Dugan tried to wrap his mind around the investigative possibilities of attending a séance. Would it be worth his time? "Who's going to be there?"

"Sienna and Luna of course, but you're not going to believe who they are bringing with them."

"Who?"

"Darrin Brownstone."

The name didn't ring a bell. "Who's Darrin Brownstone?"

"He's one of the most famous mediums of our time. He specializes in channeling the dead. Just think of the possibilities."

Dugan racked his brain. "I know you want to communicate with the ghosts of the past on Ocracoke—Native Americans, settlers, pirates . . ."

"Right. And we'll try to get a feel for what they think about our plans for the island, but that's not all. Brownstone could channel Rowland. He might be able to reveal who the killer is."

Dugan closed his eyes and grimaced. This was too bizarre for him. Then he wondered why such a famous medium would want to become involved in solving a murder. Publicity? Money? Maybe it wouldn't be a waste of time. "So you think this Darrin Brownstone could be a channel for your husband to tell us what he knows about the attacker."

"Yes. I have no doubt. I've seen Mr. Brownstone in action. He has helped to solve several murders. When Sienna and Luna contacted him and told him about my husband and the way he was murdered, he seemed very interested."

"Is he doing this pro bono?"

"Yes. No charge. That's unusual. He often commands twenty thousand dollars per séance."

That struck Dugan as odd. Brownstone must've known about Brackenbury's political position as a diplomat and no doubt heard about his incredible wealth. Dugan needed to go to this paranormal powwow just to make sure Addy wasn't fleeced through some kind of ghost conjuring racket—the first one is free but then the stakes go up. "We can take my boat over to the island. What time do you want me to pick you up?"

"The séance begins at midnight. Could you pick me up at 11:30?"

"I'll be there. See ya tomorrow night."

"Great. I'm looking forward to seeing you again. Bye."

Dugan couldn't help feeling elated after hearing those last few words. He shook off the feeling, though, knowing he had to keep things on a professional level during the investigation. He couldn't imagine a long term relationship with a woman like Adelaide Brackenbury—rich, beautiful, powerful, and a little off kilter. She was more of a fantasy girlfriend than one with whom he would want to build a long life together. Then again, the one he wanted for a lifetime didn't want him.

Dugan's stomach reminded him it was lunchtime. He stood and headed for the door. In the parking lot a crimson Lincoln MKC pulled into an open space. As Dugan opened the door to the Ford Interceptor, he heard a horn beep. Russell Goodwin stepped out of the Lincoln carrying a briefcase. He waved and headed in Dugan's direction.

"I was hoping you'd still be here." Goodwin raised his briefcase. "I've got the results of the autopsy. Do you have time to talk?"

"Have you had lunch yet?"

"No."

"You like seafood?"

"Sure."

"I know a great place. I'll drive, but let me run back in and get the evidence I've collected."

Goodwin gave him a thumbs-up and said, "Hurry up. I'm hungry."

* * *

Darrell's Seafood Restaurant on Route 64 had been a popular lunch spot in Manteo since the early sixties. The storefront was surfaced with cedar shingles, and striped awnings shaded the windows. Below the windows white flower boxes overflowed with zinnias. Dugan loved their seafood and appreciated the reasonable prices. They sat in a back corner booth munching on crab balls. Dugan ordered a Ceasar salad with fried oysters, Goodwin went for the flounder. Dugan couldn't help gobbling the first few bites to kill the hunger pains.

Goodwin placed his briefcase on the table and popped the snaps. "The autopsy provided an incredible break."

Dugan nodded, trying to talk through a mouthful of food. "What do ya got?"

Goodwin withdrew a photograph of a triangular white stone-like substance, very sharp at the point. "That is a close-up of the very tip of the murder weapon."

Dugan took the photograph and focused on the object. "Some kind of knife point?"

"Yes. It's made of animal bone. Very sharp. Of course, the photograph is blown up. It's only about a sixteenth of an inch. The killer may not even have noticed the point had been broken off."

"So the murder weapon was a knife made out of animal bone?"

"That's my conclusion. Brackenbury was stabbed three times in the back. One punctured his lung. A second jabbed the lower section of his heart. The third ricocheted off a rib. That's what broke the tip of the knife."

"I see. I'm guessing he didn't get a good look at his attacker. Not that it matters. Dead men don't say much."

"I figured it took a while for him to die. With one lung punctured and an injured heart, he didn't have the capacity to call for help with much volume. He was probably disoriented, but he managed to crawl out of the woods. Problem was he went in the wrong direction and ended up near the ocean side instead of the sound side."

Dugan swallowed his last bite and wiped his mouth with a napkin. "But now we have a piece of the puzzle."

Goodwin picked up the photograph. "All we have to do is find the matching piece."

"You might want to get a search warrant to check Achak Rowtag's place."

Goodwin leaned forward. "Do you have enough evidence for me to convince a judge to sign a warrant?"

Dugan placed the folder with the death-threat letters and printouts of Achak Rowtag's arrest record. He slid the arrest records across the table.

Goodwin scanned them. "I see he's been in trouble a few times. Looks like he's a regular at Native American protests."

"He's not afraid to make big moves if he perceives Indian rights have been violated or sacred grounds have been defiled."

"I agree, but would he make the ultimate move and take someone's life over these issues?"

Dugan picked up the envelope with the Youngstown postmark. "Check this out."

Goodwin quickly extracted the letter and read the contents. "You think Rowtag wrote this?"

"No doubt. Before I picked up Addy at the hospital, I stopped at Rowtag's house. No one was home. I asked his neighbor if he knew Rowtag's whereabouts. The neighbor produced a note Rowtag had left asking the neighbor to care for his dog for a few days. When we got to Addy's place and I saw the letters, I recognized the handwriting immediately."

"You're sure?"

"Yes—the thick, scrawled lettering, the childlike way he made each letter. There's no mistaking it. Achak Rowtag wrote that letter."

"Hmmm. If we could get that note from the neighbor for comparison, I'm sure a judge would grant a search warrant. Could you stop by the neighbor's house and ask to see the note again?"

"Yeah. I could do that right now."

"Take a photograph of the note with your phone and email it

to me. Tell the guy the note is needed for evidence in a murder case. Hopefully, he'll give it to you."

"If not, I'll inform him that his refusal could be deemed as tampering of evidence with intent to interfere with an investigation, and then I'll threaten to arrest him."

Goodwin smiled. "That usually works. In the meantime, I'll contact a local judge and get the ball rolling. Make sure you send me that photograph. As soon as I get it, I'll send it on to the judge. I'm sure he'll issue a search warrant immediately when he hears the evidence and compares the handwriting."

Dugan stood. "Let's go. I'll drop you back off at your car and then head on down to Frisco to talk to the neighbor."

On the way back to the Dare County Sheriff's Office, Dugan remembered the question he wanted to ask Goodwin. "Didn't you mention that the giant bird had been sighted in Youngstown, Ohio?"

"Yes. And lots of strange things have happened there including a murder and several earthquakes."

"Whoa. That is alarming. Do the people blame it on the bird?"

"No. They blame it on the hydraulic fracturing companies. There are different opinions about the bird. Mee Mee and Marla are heading to Youngstown today. Maybe they can come up with some information that may shed some light. Any commonality helps to connect the dots."

"That death-threat letter was postmarked in Youngstown. Achak must have been there recently."

"That's possible. Did you see any evidence that he may be keeping or training a large bird on his property?"

"There was a big osprey nest out back in a box mounted on a totem pole. His neighbor said he just enjoys watching them raise their young. Other than that I didn't see anything."

"Well, we'll find out if we get a search warrant. Have you been keeping your eye on Mrs. Brackenbury?"

"Yes. I checked her house thoroughly when I dropped her off the other day. We talked earlier on the phone. Addy invited me to a séance tomorrow night."

Goodwin chuckled. "Really. That's interesting."

Dugan put on his blinker and turned into the headquarter's

parking lot. "Some famous medium is supposed to conduct it. I think his name is Brownstone. She thinks he will be able to channel her husband and perhaps reveal who the killer is."

"Right." Goodwin chuckled. "That would save us a lot of man hours. What do you think about the possibilities of using mediums to solve crimes?"

Dugan pulled into his parking space. "Like I said before, dead men can't say much. It all sounds a little suspect to me. Addy's somewhat vulnerable when it comes to this otherworldly stuff, but I'll watch out for her."

Goodwin opened the car door. "Sheriff Walton, do you mind if I give you some advice?"

"Not at all."

"I've noticed you've been calling Mrs. Brackenbury by her first name—Addy. I appreciate you keeping an eye on her but don't let your eyes linger too long. She's a beauty, and you're on duty."

Dugan felt his face flush. Goodwin definitely had a point, and he even made it rhyme.

Chapter 11

Late that afternoon Marla and Mee Mee left Towanda and headed south on State Route 220 to catch Interstate 80 West to Youngstown, Ohio. Marla estimated the trip would take about five hours. She volunteered to drive, knowing Mee Mee had expended so much energy rescuing the young girl and her mother. They'd stop somewhere along the way, maybe at an Olive Garden or Bob Evans, and get a good meal.

Mee Mee conked out once they got on the interstate. Much of the drive was through rural areas and small towns with names like Turkey City, Riddle Crossroads, and Barkeyville. The countryside reminded her of the Ohio Valley where she grew up. Maple trees, beech trees, and oaks covered the rolling hills interspersed with white and mountain pines. In another month the hillsides would be alive with colors of fall, crimsons, oranges, and yellows.

Everything changes, Marla thought. Nothing stays the same. Her husband, Gabe, had been dead now for almost seven years, a victim of a brutal murder. Dugan was a Dare County deputy at the time and helped solve the crime. Then he became a shoulder to cry on and a father figure for her son, Gabriel. Back then she worked for Mee Mee at Buxton Village Books. Spending time with Dugan convinced her to go into law enforcement. He was so passionate about his job. As the years passed she and Dugan grew closer and became a couple.

Why couldn't she fall deeply in love with him like she did with Gabe? Mee Mee had told her you only fall that hard once. Maybe Mee Mee was right. Maybe she needed to grow up and give up those adolescent dreams of some prince who would sweep her off her feet. She definitely had feelings for Dugan.

When she saw Adelaide Brackenbury slumped against his shoulder sound asleep like some teenager at an all-night party, she wanted to thump him. How could he let a strange woman use him as a pillow? What was he thinking? Her husband had just died. Fortunately, Marla lassoed her tongue and reined it in before words escaped that she would have regretted. Perhaps the bleach blonde was exhausted, and Dugan found himself unexpectedly in an awkward situation. He didn't seem too uncomfortable, though. Was she jealous? Definitely. Does that mean she needed to recommit to the relationship? Maybe. Those pangs of jealousy confirmed some kind of passion for Dugan flared within her. But was it enough?

Mee Mee stirred and stretched her arms. "Where are we?"

"About two hours east of Youngstown."

"You're kidding? I've been dozing that long?"

"Like a grizzly in January."

"How are you hanging? I can drive."

"I'm fine. My mind's been shuffling through problems and possibilities."

"Been thinking about Dugan?"

"A little. Why?"

"Breaking off an engagement tends to trigger all kinds of rationales and doubts."

"Yeah." Marla shifted in her seat to relieve her numbed rear. "I've definitely wrestled with my reasons. Do you think jealousy is a sign of love?"

"No. It's a sign of insecurity."

"Well, then I guess I'm insecure."

Mee Mee sat up. "Who are you jealous of?"

"Adelaide Brackenbury. For a woman recently widowed, she sure snuggled up to Dugan in a hurry."

"She does possess that air of sensuality. You know, one of those women who can't help but stir up testosterone when they get around men."

"Dugan was definitely stirred."

"Dugan is flesh and blood like any other man. But she's not his kind of gal. You're the one who gets to him at the deeper level."

Marla sighed. "You may be right, but sometimes a man isn't looking for that deeper level. Dugan feels rejected. He's looking for comfort. She's the type that just might accommodate him. If he tumbles into her bed, I don't think I could forgive him."

"Now you're not making sense. You're the one who broke off the engagement. Do you want him to save himself for you even though you're not sure you want him?"

"Quit asking hard questions."

"No one said love is easy."

Marla snickered. "What about you?"

"What about me?"

"I saw that sparkle in your eyes the other day."

"What sparkle?"

"I guess I'd call it the Russell Goodman sparkle."

"Oh . . . that sparkle." Mee Mee grinned. "I must admit, seeing him again stirred the coals."

Marla smiled. "Yeah, that stirring must be contagious."

"You must admit, Russell is quite a handsome man."

"I won't argue that."

"I'll never forget that week he vacationed on Hatteras Island back in the early eighties. He would stop in the bookstore in the late afternoon and pick up a book on Outer Banks history. He loved to read about Blackbeard. Then he would hang around until the store closed, and we would go out and eat at some seafood place."

"Sounds like you hit it off instantly."

"We did. My favorite memories are the beach walks. After dinner we'd head for the beach, take off our shoes, and walk for hours. It was a wonderful week in my life. One day we went to Ocracoke and spent the day scouring Springer's Point for any clues of Blackbeard's buried treasure."

Marla sighed. "That sounds incredibly romantic. Why didn't you ever reconnect with him?"

"I always hoped we would, but life and careers got in the way. We were both determined to succeed at what we did. Sometimes that determination overcomes nature's impulses." Mee Mee sat up and straightened her wrinkled sweatshirt. "But you never know. There's still time. We may not be young and restless anymore, but we're not over the hill either."

"Of course not. They say sixty is the new forty."

"If that's true, then we have another forty or so years to explore the possibilities."

"I guess Dugan and I have time too."

"Sure . . . unless . . ."

"Unless what?"

"Unless Adelaide Brackenbury stirs him up too much."

Marla gritted her teeth. Certainly Dugan wouldn't jump into bed with her on a moment's notice. At least she hoped he wouldn't. Maybe she should call him and tell him they need to talk when she gets back, try to plant a seed of expectation in his mind to keep him from temptation. No. Manipulation wasn't the answer. She'd just have to trust him. There wasn't anything she could do about it now. She needed to stop thinking about it.

"Hey, I'm hungry. You?" Marla asked.

"Famished. Look, there's a Cracker Barrel."

Nothing like a big plate of fried chicken, mashed potatoes, and green beans to get your mind off your problems, Marla thought.

* * *

They reached downtown Youngstown about six o'clock that evening. On Federal Plaza East they found a coffee shop, Joe Maxx Coffee Company, and stopped in to get recharged. The walls in the place were a bright yellow-orange contrasting with dark brown trim and table tops. Mee Mee noticed the customers were young and hip, the generation that loved their specialty coffees. Youngstown State University was only a few blocks away. That also accounted for the youthful crowd.

They found a corner booth and looked over the menu. Mee Mee read the story about Joe Maxx on the sidebar of the menu. Apparently, he was a famous World War Two pilot who went into the coffee cargo business after the war. In 1952, he was flying a heavy load of the finest coffee Costa Rica produced when his plane lost power near Myrtle Beach, South Carolina. He managed to crash land the plane on Ocean Highway. Although the plane was crippled, he realized he had 1400 pounds of the finest coffee in the world. Right there along Ocean Highway the fuselage of the plane became the home of the Joe Maxx Coffee Company. Mee Mee loved the story, realizing old Joe Maxx was a lot like her—someone who flew by the seat of his pants.

Mee Mee overheard a couple of college kids in the booth across from them talking about the latest earthquake. She motioned Marla to be quiet by tilting her head toward them. They listened.

"Oh yeah," one of them said, the one with long brown hair, an unruly beard, and a mustache. "I definitely felt it. Had to be at least 4.0 on the Richter scale. A couple of my history books fell off the shelf."

The other guy was clean shaven with short black hair. He wore a red T-shirt with a YSU logo on it. "It's gotta be the fracking. I read an article in *Scientific American* that said the drilling doesn't cause it, but rather pumping the waste water back down into the sandstone is what triggers the tremors. Man, that is crazy. We are living on unstable ground here."

"Excuse me," Mee Mee said.

The two young men glanced in her direction.

"I overheard you talking about a recent earthquake. I'm writing an article about what's happening up here for a newspaper down in North Carolina."

"Are they fracking down there too?" the bearded guy asked.

Mee Mee scooted to the end of the booth to get closer to

91

them. "Not in our area, but the environment is definitely being threatened and strange things are happening."

"What kind of strange things?" the short-haired guy asked.

Mee Mee smiled. "I know this sounds weird, but a giant bird has been spotted in the threatened areas. I saw it myself."

The long-haired guy's eyes grew wide. "It's been spotted up here too. My landlady saw it a couple of times. It really messed with her mind."

Marla scooted to the end of her booth seat. "We're traveling around to places where the bird has been spotted to find out if there is a connection. Does your landlady live near here? We'd like to talk to her."

"Yeah, about two miles from here up on Dearborn Street right off of Route 422. Me and my girlfriend live in the upstairs apartment. She lives downstairs."

"Tell me," Mee Mee said. "What do people think about the sightings?"

The bearded guy shook his head. "People think the bird is some kinda omen. You know, what's it called . . . a harbinger of bad things to come. Everybody is worried about these earthquakes and all the crap we have to put up with now that the oil and gas industry has taken over. The bird spooks people."

"People are just superstitious," the other young man said. "No damn bird is going to cause an earthquake or pollute the air and water."

"I didn't say that," the other guy argued. "Irresponsible industries do the damage, but people believe the bird is calling down doom upon this area. They may be right."

"Bullshit. We doom ourselves by allowing these guys to come in here."

A waitress, thin, cute, and blonde, arrived at their table and took their orders. Marla asked for a Joe Mocha Maxx, which promised a double dose of chocolate and caffeine, and Mee Mee tried the Black and Tan, a rich mocha steamed with creamy peanut butter. As they waited, they could still hear the two young guys debating the bird's significance.

It didn't take long for the coffee to arrive. Mee Mee took a sip of her Black and Tan. "Ohhhh . . . that's heaven."

Marla tried hers. "Yummmm—chocolate dynamite. We hit a homerun coming to this place—good coffee and connections."

"When we get done here, I'd like to talk to the guy's landlady."

Marla checked her watch. "It's 6:45. Plenty of time before it gets dark. We need to find a hotel too."

"That shouldn't be a problem." Mee Mee withdrew a pen and some paper from her purse. She turned and faced the young guys. "Gentlemen, forgive me for interrupting, but would it be possible to get your landlady's address and directions to her house?"

"No problem." The bearded guy took the pen and paper. "She might be in a riled up mood tonight."

"Why's that?" Marla's asked.

"Tomorrow's the big protest, and she's one of the organizers."

"What kind of protest?" Mee Mee asked.

"I don't know all the details, but she's upset because the frackers are at it again. Tomorrow they plan on dumping the waste water back down into those deep wells. She says if they do, there'll be hell to pay."

* * *

Dearborn Street traveled through a working class neighborhood on the north side of Youngstown. The houses seemed tired and old, most probably built in the 1930s or 40s. Mrs. Stratton lived in a peach-colored, two story frame house with a small front porch and a detached garage in the back. Mee Mee steered into the driveway, narrowly missing two large green trashcans filed with recently trimmed branches and weeds. They exited the car and walked to the front porch.

To Mee Mee's surprise, Mrs. Stratton stood at the screen door. She looked to be in her early seventies, a slight woman with silver hair tied up in a bun

"You two the reporters?" Her voice was gravelly.

"Yes. I'm Mee Mee Roberts, and this is Marla Easton. Are you Mrs. Stratton?"

"That's right." She opened the screen and waved them in. "But you can call me Katie. Jesus told me you were coming."

Mee Mee's and Marla's eyes met, and Mee Mee could sense the look of uncertainty in Marla's expression.

"Don't worry. I'm not crazy. That's what I call Jimmy Jamison, the guy with the long hair and beard. He rang me on his cell phone and told me you were coming to interview me."

Mee Mee smiled. "Well, thanks for welcoming a couple of strangers into your home."

Mrs. Stratton led the way through the foyer toward the back of the house. "You might be strangers, but you don't look too scary. Believe me, there are much scarier things happening around here."

They sat down at the kitchen table, an old pine table with a distressed surface from years of use. The cabinets looked to be made of the same knotty wood with the same wear.

"Where's my manners? Can I get you something to drink?"

"Oh no," Marla said. "We just finished up a couple of large coffees."

Mrs. Stratton leaned on her elbows, her hands cupped in front of her. "Jesus tells me you want to know about the big bird I saw a couple of times."

Mee Mee pulled her notepad and pen from her jacket pocket. "Yes. A large bird has been sighted in several places in the eastern part of the country where the environment has been threatened. We're trying to discover if there are commonalities with the sightings."

"You think it might be the same bird?"

"Possibly."

"Well, it was the biggest bird I've ever seen, like one of those giant eagles that can pick up a mountain goat and carry it off."

Mee Mee nodded. "Did you spot it in the daytime or nighttime?"

"Nighttime. But it glowed. Flew right over this house screeching like a cat on fire. Almost pissed myself."

"Did it have big talons?"

"Huge. The first time I saw it, I couldn't believe my eyes. Thought maybe I was going crazy. That's when the earthquakes started. Then it came back again a few months later, and the earthquakes got stronger. I realized what it might be—a sign, an omen, you know, like a warning you just can't ignore. That's when I began organizing protests against the oil and gas companies."

"I see." Mee Mee rolled her pen between her finger and thumb. "So the eagle inspired you to take action?"

"That's right. I was upset about all the problems with the frackers, but when I saw the eagle it was like seeing a vision from God. I knew deep in my heart I had to do something."

"Kind of like Moses when he saw the burning bush," Marla said.

"That's right. Once you see that kind of thing, you can't sit still and do nothing. The next day I typed up a petition to stop the waste water injection. They do it at the well about a half mile from here. The seismologists concluded that the epicenter of the quakes could be traced to that well."

"What did you do with the petition?" Mee Mee asked.

"First I got all the women in my bridge club to help me. They felt the same as I did: it was time to do something. I made copies, and we divided up the neighborhoods. It wasn't hard getting signatures, especially after all the earthquakes that we've had."

"How many signatures did you get?" Marla asked.

"Over ten thousand. That was a little over a year ago. We succeeded in getting a moratorium on the injection of waste water into that particular well. State officials couldn't ignore the public outrage any longer. Any fool could see the fracking was causing the earthquakes. When their frequency and intensity increased, everyone around here had enough. They just needed someone to spark the flame.

Marla spread her hands, palms up. "If the waste water disposal was halted, why is there a protest planned for tomorrow?"

Mrs. Stratton knotted her brow. "Because the moratorium has ended. The scientists the state hired said they couldn't find a clear connection. The energy companies have a lot of power when it comes to politics. Without concrete proof of the exact cause of the quakes, the frackers demanded that they resume business as usual. A couple of days ago the trucks started to arrive at the well again to dump the brine and poisoned water back into the well."

"What's going to happen tomorrow at the protest?" Mee Mee asked.

Mrs. Stratton put her hands flat on the table and leaned forward. "I'll tell you what's going to happen: We're gonna stop them again."

Chapter 12

They decided to stay at the Quality Inn on Belmont Avenue about two miles north of Mrs. Stratton's house. The place was clean, inexpensive, and offered a free continental breakfast. Marla figured that's three for three as far as she was concerned. Besides, the hotel was only five minutes away from the disposal well.

Although they were exhausted from traveling, they arose early, about 6:30, so that they could shower, eat, and be out the door before 7:30. Mrs. Stratton informed them the protest would begin about 8:00 in the morning. She also promised to introduce them to a few more people who spotted the giant bird.

Marla drove as Mee Mee finished off a container of strawberry yogurt she had snatched from the cooler at the breakfast bar. It was a bright and sunny mid-September day with a briskness in the air that snapped Marla into full wakefulness. The trip had been eventful, too action-packed for her tastes. She wondered what this day held in store.

At the stoplight Marla made a right onto Gypsy Lane. "It's interesting how the bird affects people in different ways."

Mee Mee swallowed a bite of yogurt. "I'd say so. Mrs. Stratton sees the eagle as some kind of inspiration. "

"Yeah. Seeing the bird convinced her she had a divine calling. Once she saw it, she became a woman on a mission."

"Right. But other people are terrified by the bird. They see it as some kind of freak of nature or even a supernatural phenomenon."

"So what do you think it is?"

Mee Mee scratched her head. "It scared me to death. The way it glowed gave it an unearthly aspect. Because it was dark and so frightening, my imagination may have gotten carried away. Now that I've talked to several people who've seen it, I'm leaning toward believing the creature is part of a plot."

"What do you mean? Like a story someone is trying to create?"

"That's one way of putting it. It's a story that writes itself. The bird makes its appearances, and the witnesses write the story. We create the legend and discover the significance. That's exactly what the bird's trainer wants to happen."

"Interesting. I guess you could say the plot thickens with every appearance." At the end of Gypsy Lane, Marla turned left onto Martin Luther King Jr. Boulevard. "But, of course, the bird's trainer, if he exists, has staged the story by releasing the creature where the environment it threatened."

"That's correct. Those who see the bird connect its appearance with the exploitation of Mother Earth. The trainer doesn't have complete control over our interpretation but knows the probable direction. Speaking of direction, I think you better turn here onto Division Street." Mee Mee pointed to the right. "The disposal well is that way." The road cut through several industrial parks with expansive metal buildings, various types of machinery, and a few train cars stationed near loading ramps. Marla noticed workers' parking lots on the other side of the road. Youngstown had a substantial blue collar bedrock. They drove beneath a couple overpasses, passed an old crumbling building that appeared as if it had been bombed long ago, and then crossed a small bridge, its blue-painted framework corroded with rust.

"That's the Mahoning River below us," Marla said. "We must be near the well. Mrs. Stratton said it was on the other side of the river."

"Look!" Mee Mee said. "I see people with signs."

Marla spied a line of cars parked along the road ahead. To her left was another industrial park enclosed by a tall chain-linked fence. The protesters had managed to get through the gate and set up a human wall across the entrance road. Several workers in hardhats stood off to the side, pointing and shouting at the protesters. A few reporters and cameramen stood nearby, getting ready to cover the demonstration. On the back of the property loomed three gray cylinder-towers, each connected by pipes. Another pipe extended from the third cylinder into some kind of pump-like contraption. She figured that was the injection well.

Marla pulled off the road and parked behind a blue Ford Ranger. She and Mee Mee quickly exited the Grand Cherokee and headed toward the protest line. As she neared, she read some of the signs: SAVE OUR WATER – NO FRACKING; BAN FRACKING NOW; NO DRILL NO SPILL; FRACKING CAUSES CANCER; DON'T FRACK WITH MY FUTURE. She noticed a variety of people, ages, and sizes. Clearly, the conviction to stand up to the energy companies crossed educational, economic, racial, and gender lines.

Mee Mee waved, and Marla saw a hand go up toward the end of the wall of people. It was Mrs. Stratton. They headed in her direction. Next to her stood a tall, thin man, probably in his mid-thirties with tawny skin and jet-black hair that hung just above his shoulders. He wore frayed jeans and a blue T-shirt with an odd design. Marla discerned it to be some kind of abstract eagle.

"Good morning, ladies. Glad you could make it," Mrs. Stratton said.

Mee Mee stepped up to her. "We didn't miss anything yet, did we?"

Mrs. Stratton shook her head. "No. We just formed the protest line. No trucks have arrived yet." She pointed to the guys in the hardhats standing near the fence. "The workers have been shouting out profanities and insults, but we figured they would try to intimidate us. The news guys will probably begin interviewing people soon."

"Do you expect any violence?" Marla asked.

"Who knows? Nobody wants violence, but the citizens of Youngstown are tired of being pushed around by these big corporations. We're not going to allow it to continue."

"That's for sure," said the tawny-skinned man. "Those waste-water trucks will have to run me over. I ain't moving."

Mrs. Stratton placed her hand on the man's shoulder. "This is Raven Powaw. He's one of the organizers. Raven, this is Mee Mee and Marla. They're reporters from down South."

Raven nodded toward them.

Marla smiled. "Mee Mee is the reporter. I guess you could say I'm her body guard. I work for the sheriff's department in Dare County, North Carolina."

"Raven, are you a Native American?" Mee Mee asked.

Raven chuckled. "Does my name give it away?"

Mee Mee nodded. "Your name and your appearance."

"Yes. I'm a Shawnee. I work for a software company that started up here a few years ago. Moved here from Oklahoma, but I wanted to come to this area because my people hunted these lands for centuries before the Europeans arrived."

"So these are historically sacred lands?" Marla asked.

"Yes. Mahoning Valley offered an abundance of wildlife and fish to the Shawnee for centuries. It was a happy hunting ground that provided sustenance. Now look what's happening to it."

"Raven saw the eagle too," Mrs. Stratton motioned toward the image on his shirt. "He called it a Thunderbird."

Marla glanced at Mee Mee and then back to Raven. "So you think the bird is some kind of spiritual entity?"

"Yes. An Animikii. The bird comes as a warning. Those who see it must bring its message to the world before it's too late."

Mee Mee raised her hands as if holding an invisible object. "But don't you believe it was an actual physical creature?"

"Perhaps," Raven said, "but it captured my mind and heart. When that happened I saw something supernatural. It glowed and cried out like a restless spirit seeking justice and retribution." He touched his chest near the eagle's head. "And that kind of perception can only come from an inner vision."

"I saw the bird too," Mee Mee said, "down in North Carolina on the Outer Banks. That's one reason why I'm writing this story. But to me it was definitely not a spirit bird. It was huge, scary, and aggressive. It swooped down on me, and I could feel the beating of its wings. Its screech hurt my ears. I don't think a spiritual entity could do that."

Raven grinned. "Then you don't know the power of the spirit realm. Have you ever dreamed a dream so real that you woke up and wondered if it actually happened?"

"Well . . . yes. I've had a few of those kinds of dreams. Sometimes they're frightening."

"What seemed real happened up here." Raven touched his temple. "Am I right or wrong?"

"You're right, but . . . but . . ."

"Listen." He lowered his head, his dark eyes intensifying. "You would be amazed at the places the spiritual realm can take you. What you see on those journeys deepens your understanding of the meaning of life."

Marla glanced at Mee Mee. All this talk about the spirit realm seemed bizarre, perhaps even a bit absurd. She refused to let these metaphysical meanderings persuade her. She had encountered too many cons in her life to be taken in. The rumbling of a large truck turned her attention to the left where the road entered the facility. A reporter near the gate began his coverage, microphone in hand, talking as he gazed at the cameraman.

At the middle of the line a thin, bald man wearing black-rimmed glasses yelled, "Get Ready! Here comes a truck!"

The line straightened, and everyone linked arms. Marla and Mee Mee took a few steps back to watch the spectacle unfold. The vehicle was bright red, the front end resembling a regular semi cab. The back consisted of a flatbed with a huge red metal cylinder mounted on it. The words LIQUID WASTE MANAGEMENT AND CONTROLLED WASTE were printed on the side of the cylinder. The brakes squealed, and the truck jolted to a stop inches from the wall of people.

"Get the hell outta the way!" one of the workers hollered. He marched toward the line raising a large fist. Marla estimated he weighed nearly 300 pounds. Two other workers followed him. They were dressed in dark blue coveralls and wore white hardhats. They looked to be about half the size of the big guy.

"I'm calling the cops." Mee Mee withdrew her cell phone from the back pocket of her jeans.

"Surely the police knew about this protest. I'm surprised they're not here," Marla said.

The big man strode right up to the middle of the line where the thin, bald guy stood. He plowed into him, breaking the link in the human chain. The older man fell backwards, his glasses flipping off his face and clinking onto the asphalt. The other two workers moved in, shoving the people where the line had been broken. The truck inched forward, threatening to run over the poor bald guy.

Marla reached inside her jacket and patted her Magnum pistol just to make sure it was handy.

The bald guy rolled away from the truck and scrambled to his feet. He seemed a lot quicker for his age than Marla expected. His eyes widened as he glared at the truck driver. The truck rumbled forward and stopped a foot from him. By now the wall of people had been broken apart, and everyone watched the bald man as he faced down the truck.

The driver poked his head out the window and shouted to the big worker, "Get that geezer out of my way before I flatten him."

The bald man ripped apart the front of his red flannel shirt, popping the buttons. Marla could see a large handgun strapped to his chest.

"He's got a gun!" one of the blue-clad workers barked.

"That's right!" The bald guy unsnapped the holster and pulled out his pistol. He raised it with both hands and aimed it at the driver. "I'm ready to die. Are you?"

"Hold on there, old man." The big guy raised his hand plaintively. "Don't do anything stupid."

The bald guy whirled and directed the barrel at the big

worker. "You shut up! Don't call me stupid. Last year your boss got arrested for dumping brine water into the Mahoning River. Now that's stupid. In the last six months we've had ten earthquakes because of that disposal well over there." He waved his head in the direction of the well. "Now that's stupid." He shifted the gun back to the driver. "If that truck moves one more inch, I'll show you stupid."

From her peripheral vision Marla caught a glimpse of the other blue-clad worker slinking off toward a pickup truck parked by the fence. The guy opened the door, reached behind the seat, and pulled out a rifle. Marla fumbled inside of her jacket to unsnap her holster.

The worker raised the rifle in the bald guy's direction. "Put the gun down you old fart! I swear, I'll shoot you."

The bald guy whirled and fired. People screamed. The worker fell backwards, his rifle clattering on the ground.

The big guy charged the old man, but he pivoted and fired again. The bullet took off the big guy's hardhat, splitting his skull and splattering blood and brains. He collapsed with a loud thud at the man's feet.

Marla managed to free her pistol. She whipped it from her jacket and aimed it at the bald guy. "Put the gun down!"

He spun, eyes wide and searching. When he spotted Marla, he whipped the gun in her direction.

She fired before he could get off a shot. The bullet struck him right in the chest. He fell backwards, dropping the pistol. In the distance Marla heard sirens.

Chapter 13

Occasionally, Dugan drove by the Cape Hatteras Lighthouse as he made his rounds through Buxton. The black-and-white-striped tower was one of Dare County's biggest tourist attractions and the most historically significant lighthouse in the United States. Today he decided to carry his lunch, his usual hamburger and fries from Burger Burger, up the 268 steps to the top and enjoy the view. It was a great place to do some thinking. His mind had been addled lately. Women and crime had muddied the mental waters.

The breeze blew briskly off the ocean, probably thirty knots or more. He tugged his black sheriff's ball cap down snuggly on his head to keep it from flying off. Just offshore of Cape Hatteras he could see the warm Gulf Stream current colliding with the much colder Labrador Current. This collision of currents often created conditions for devastating ocean storms and sea swells. Here the infamous Diamond Shoals had doomed hundreds of ships as they ran aground on its shifting sandbars. Somewhere below the surface the U.S.S. Monitor, an ironclad Civil War ship, had sunk to its final resting place. The area became known as the Graveyard of the Atlantic.

As Dugan eyed the choppy waters where the currents clashed, he thought about Marla and Addy. Their personalities clashed as much as the currents. Marla was sensible, down to earth, and somewhat skeptical of anything that smacked of mystical. Addy was mysterious, enchanting, and otherworldly. Marla was the woman he wanted to marry. Addy was the woman he wanted to bed. He knew that kind of longing was wrong, but her sexual appeal wouldn't be as tempting to him if Marla hadn't ended their engagement. He had loved Marla so much he ached at night lying in bed thinking about her and their future together. When she dashed those dreams she created a void in his soul. Addy's beauty, sensuality, and strangeness quickly filled that space.

Dugan wondered if he so easily succumbed to Addy's allure to buffer the pain of Marla's rejection. What if Marla changed her mind? He hadn't done anything carnal with Addy yet. At this point he would be free from any guilt if Marla wanted to make a new start. But how long could he last? Just thinking about Addy, those curves, that rose-tinged ivory skin, that enrapturing scent drove him crazy. He took a deep breath and closed his eyes, trying to fade out the two women.

His mind drifted to the murder case. When he had stopped by Achak's neighbor's house yesterday, the neighbor had told him he had tossed Achak's note into the trash. The waste company had collected the garbage earlier that morning. Dugan couldn't tell if the guy was lying or not. He checked the receptacles, and they were empty. Agent Goodwin wasn't too happy when he heard the news—no search warrant would be issued without the note. The murder weapon, the bone knife with the miniscule broken tip, might be lying on Achak's kitchen table, but there was nothing they could do about it.

Dugan's cell phone erupted from his front pocket, a strident, old-fashioned ringtone. He slid the phone out and cupped it to his ear. "Sheriff Walton speaking."

"Dugan, it's Addy. I'm being followed."

"Where are you?"

"Just south of Buxton. I was heading to the Twiford Funeral Home in Manteo to make final arrangements for Rowland."

"Are you sure you're being followed, or is it just someone tailgating you?"

"It's a black SUV. It's been right behind me since I left Hatteras."

Dugan suspected Addy's imagination may be in overdrive. "Turn off on a side street and see if they stick with you."

"Okay. I'll make a right at this next road. "

"What street is it?"

"I'm turning onto Billy Mitchell Road."

Billy Mitchell Road, Dugan thought, that's a mistake. That's a lonely road that heads out past the Billy Mitchell airstrip. Very few people hang out there this time of year. "Is the SUV still following you?"

"Yes! What do I do?"

"Don't panic. I'm five minutes away. I'm coming."

"Dugan! I think they are going to ram me."

Dugan heard the rev of an engine—*Addy must have hit the gas to prevent a collision*. He whirled and bolted across the gallery deck to the door. The steps spiraled downward like an unending corkscrew. He descended as quickly as possible, his feet a blur as they pinged on the metal stairs, his hand sliding down the rail. The descent was broken by an occasional checkerboard landing. The black and white squares followed by the twirl of more steps spun his vision, making it difficult to keep his balance. Finally, he reached the bottom.

He sprinted out the entrance, past the attendant, and toward the Ford Interceptor. As he reached into his pocket for his keys, he clasped the phone to his ear. "Addy, are you there?" He heard the roar of the engine and hysterical cries. He unlocked the door, jumped in the vehicle, started the engine, and engaged the siren. Adrenaline surged through his body as he peeled out of the parking lot. He flew down Lighthouse Road, cutting the turns and hoping not to encounter any oncoming traffic. A maintenance truck sped around the approaching curve, blasting its horn. Dugan hit his breaks and veered to the right, just missing the truck.

As he neared Route 12, he slowed to check for traffic. Seeing an opening, he stomped on the gas, turned left, and spun out onto the highway. Billy Mitchell Road was still three miles away. He held the phone to his ear and heard a scream and the rumbling of a vehicle out of control. *Then silence. Please God, no. If someone got to Addy . . . if someone murders her, it's my fault. I'm responsible for her.*

He moved into the center turning lane to pass a line of cars as he flew toward Cape Hatteras Secondary School. *Careful.* The siren should have given ample warning, but people didn't always heed sirens. The last thing he wanted to do was crash into a teenage driver exiting the school parking lot.

The Cape Hatteras Baptist Church blurred by on the right. Traffic thinned, and he picked up speed as he passed the Frisco Mini Golf and Go Cart Park. He checked his speedometer— almost ninety mph. Not far now. He knew Billy Mitchell Road was near the Frisco Native American Museum where Achak Rowtag worked as a volunteer. He spotted the museum coming up on the right and hit his breaks. *There it is on the left.*

He gripped the wheel tightly, his arm muscles tensing, and turned. The Interceptor squealed and slid through the turn, but Dugan spun the wheel to readjust its momentum back toward Billy Mitchell Road. There were no houses on either side, just a barren landscape of green shrubbery and brown dune grasses. To the right Dugan saw the Billy Mitchell airstrip, a landing runway for small planes. The unattended public airport was empty, but that didn't surprise him. He picked up speed, keeping an eye out for any vehicle that might be trying to flee from the scene. It had been several minutes since the sounds of wreckage blared from his phone.

He hit the brakes as he came to a "Y" in the road. Turning right would lead to the seashore. Four-wheel-drive vehicles were permitted to cruise along the beach for various recreational purposes like fishing or surfing. Dugan veered left onto the road which headed to the Frisco campground. This time of year the park was empty. The camp road circled the grounds and returned to the entrance. Where was Addy's car—that silver

Cadillac Escalade?

Up ahead the road turned sharply left to circle back to the entrance. *There!* Dugan spotted the undercarriage of a vehicle that had rolled over onto its side. It had careened into a dune, flipped, and landed under an old live oak. Dugan slammed on the brakes and slid to a stop a few feet from the Escalade. He sprung out of the car and darted to the other side. A spider web of cracks sprawled across the windshield. Through the fractured glass he could see Addy suspended by her seat belt. The Escalade had landed on its passenger side.

Dugan mounted the vehicle and tried to pull open the driver's side door, but it was locked. Addy's eyes were closed, and blood dripped down her face from a gash on her forehead.

Dugan pounded on the driver's side window. "Addy! Addy!"

Chapter 14

Addy turned her head and opened her eyes, blinking from the blood that trickled across her eyelid. She wore a yellow sun dress, and several drips of blood dotted the halter strap.

"Can you unlock the door?"

She nodded and reached for the unlock button. The lock popped up, and Dugan slung open the door and blocked it from shutting with his backside.

"Are you in pain?"

"I think I'm okay. Just a few nicks from the glass."

Dugan reached and touched her forehead where the line of blood flowed down. "You may need a stitch or two. Can you climb out?"

"I think so."

"Put your arm around my neck and release the seatbelt with your other hand. I'll hang on to you."

Addy released the belt and clung tightly to Dugan, the side of her face warm against his as he lifted her through the door.

Slowly he rolled onto his back pulling her with him, trying to keep the car door open with his extended leg. She worked with him, intertwined but still making her way across his body until she came to rest on top of the rear door. Dugan whipped his leg away, and the front door slammed shut.

Dugan sat up and slid to the edge of the car, his legs hanging over. "Stay there until I get down." He scooted as far forward as he could and jumped. Then he reached up. "Can you jump? I'll catch you."

Addy slid forward and dangled her legs over. She leaned and extended her hands toward him. A drop of her blood fell and struck him on the cheek.

"I've got you. Go ahead and jump."

She nodded and dropped from the car. Dugan caught her and managed to keep them both from falling to the ground.

Dugan pulled his phone from his shirt pocket. "I'm calling a rescue squad and tow truck."

"I don't want to go to the hospital." There was desperation in Addy's voice. "It's just a small cut."

Dugan made the calls and then pulled a handkerchief from his back pocket. He carefully wiped the blood from her face and inspected the wound. "You'll at least need a butterfly bandage on this cut. Did you bump your head?"

"I got smacked by the airbag, but I'm fine. Hold still." With her index finger she wiped the splotch of blood on Dugan's cheek. "There. My blood looked like a red spider on your cheek."

"Tell me what happened."

She laid her palm on her forehead. "It seems like such a blur now. When I turned onto Billy Mitchell Road, the black SUV followed me. I glanced in my rearview mirror and thought the driver was about to ram me, so I hit the gas. I went faster and faster."

"Did he stay with you?"

"I don't know. I didn't look back again. He may have stopped for all I know. I was trying to keep control of the car. I panicked. It felt like we were heading down one of those deserted country roads where victims disappear for good. Then I made a left toward the campgrounds, hoping people would be there. Nobody in sight. I didn't realize the road made a U-turn at the end of the campground. I hit my brakes, ran up against the dune and flipped onto the car's side."

"Did you see the SUV?"

"No. I didn't have a good angle. When I looked out the driver's side window, all I could see were branches of that tree." She waved toward the live oak.

"Did you hear another car?"

"I don't remember. I don't think so. I kept thinking I'm trapped, I'm a goner. If someone wanted to kill me, wouldn't that have been the perfect opportunity?"

Dugan nodded. "But maybe they had second thoughts when you took off toward the campground. They knew they would have to come out the same way they went in. If the law came down that road, they'd be rats in a trap."

"And you would have caught them."

"Maybe. Either go after them or check on you."

"Which would it be?"

Dugan smiled. "I would have checked on you first. They probably would have gotten away."

Addy threw her arms around him and hugged him tightly. "You're my Captain America."

Dugan hugged her back feeling her softness and warmth rush through him. "Just doing my duty, Ma'am."

It didn't take long for the ambulance and tow truck to arrive. The EMTs wanted to transport Addy to the Outer Banks Hospital in Nags Head to go through a few x-rays and make sure there were no internal injuries, but she insisted she was fine. They warned her that tomorrow she'd be sore and may need a pain prescription, but she stood her ground. After one of them patched up her forehead, they got tired of coaxing her and took off. By then the tow guys had the Escalade turned over and hooked up. Dugan suggested they haul the vehicle to Auto Banks Car Repair a mile or so north on Route 12.

On the way back down to Hatteras, Addy reached and clasped Dugan's hand as it rested on the police radio compartment between the seats. "Would you please come into my house and check all the rooms again?"

"No problem. I planned on doing that anyway." He squeezed her hand.

"I'm really looking forward to the séance tonight."

"Yeah, I almost forgot about that."

"Are you still picking me up at 11:30?"

"Of course, I wouldn't miss it. My boat will get us there by midnight."

"If Darrin Brownstown is as good as I think he is, we may solve this murder tonight."

Dugan chuckled to himself. "That would be not only impressive but a good break for U.S. taxpayers considering the cost of a drawn out federal investigation."

Addy smiled. "Well, I guess I shouldn't get carried away."

"You never know. We'll see who Mr. Brownstone conjures and listen to what the spirits have to say."

"I hope he can bring Rowland back."

"Do you miss Rowland?"

"Yes, of course. Not so much as a lover but as a good friend. I know he felt bad that he couldn't give me physical satisfaction these last several years, but I never complained. We still dreamed together, wheeled and dealed together."

"Sounds like you were devoted to one another."

"We were. The relationship wasn't complete, but sex isn't the only thing that makes a relationship complete. I know a lot of couples who make love like college kids and brag about it but don't share their minds. We were closer than most couples. How about you and Marla? Were you good in and *out* of the bedroom?"

Dugan felt his face flush. "Uhhh . . . well, I thought we had a great connection mentally. We shared our thoughts and ideas almost daily. When you work with someone, you can get pretty close. We agreed sex was something that should be saved for marriage."

"Really. That's old fashioned but admirable."

"I didn't say that we always succeeded in keeping our high ideals."

Addy snickered. "Sometimes that's hard to do."

"Yeah, we slipped a few times but then always felt guilty. I guess it was our Sunday school upbringing. Anyway, it is what it is—over."

"Well . . . I can see we have something in common."

"What's that?" Dugan took a sideways glance at her.

Addy's playful smile grew. "We both haven't got much lovin' lately."

Dugan chuckled and refocused on the road. "You've got that right."

* * *

At Addy's beach house they quickly covered the three floors and found nothing out of the ordinary. With a high-end security system and video cameras stationed around every turn, the house was well monitored. Dugan figured only a fool would try to make a move on her there. But then again the prisons were filled with fools.

Addy rode the elevator back down to the first floor with him and walked him to the door. She placed her hands on his shoulders. "Well, my wonderful Captain America, thanks again for coming to my rescue."

"I'm sorry I didn't get there sooner."

"You don't realize how much safer I feel knowing you aren't far away."

"Listen. Because of this incident today, I'm going to need more help protecting you. When I get back to the office, I'm going to assign two more deputies to the task. They'll make rounds every hour."

She tugged him a little closer, her eyes tensing. "I hate being this much trouble."

"No trouble. It's our duty to keep you safe. I want you to do me a favor, though."

"Anything."

"Whenever you leave the house, call me and let me know where you're going. I'll make sure someone stays close."

She pulled him closer and took a deep breath, the space between them disappearing as her body pressed against his. "I like that word."

Dugan could feel heat rising. "What word?"

She grasped the sides of his head with her hands, pulled his face toward her, and kissed him softly and then leaned back. "Close."

Dugan's rational center swayed and plummeted. He wrapped his arms around her and clamped her body against him. He pressed his lips on hers, sensing their fullness and wetness. She responded by sighing and opening her mouth.

The strident ring of his cell phone snapped him back to rational thought. He broke the kiss and straightened. She released him, her blue eyes wide.

Dugan slipped the phone out of his front pocket, stuck it to his ear, and cleared his throat. "Sheriff Dugan Walton speaking."

"Dugan, this is Marla." Marla's voice strained with the edge of anxiety.

"Hi uh . . . uh . . . Marla. Is everything all right?"

"I just needed to talk to you."

"Okay. What about?"

"Well . . . not now, but when I get back we need to sit down somewhere alone and talk."

"Okay. Uh . . . that would be fine. Well . . . I guess . . . I guess we'll set up a time to meet when you get back."

"Dugan, why do you sound so uncomfortable? Where are you?"

Chapter 15

Marla knew something was up with Dugan. Okay, so he was at Adelaide Brackenbury's house checking the premises for her safety. That's fine. But why did he act so strange?

"You're quieter than a cold rattlesnake," Mee Mee said as she drove east on State Route 250 in east central Ohio, a hilly road with excessive curves.

"I've got a lot on my mind." The sun had set, colors fading from the landscape, but they didn't have far to go. The twists and turns and ups and downs of the state highway exacerbated Marla's already unsettled emotional state. Too many catastrophes had happened in the last couple days. Marla's stress level rose with every curve of the road.

They passed the Dairy Jean on the right, a popular soft ice cream stand out in the middle of nowhere. During her high school years, she worked there in the summer. Those were some of the most wonderful days of her life, days of innocence, serendipity, and young love. She missed the way life felt back then, and she missed her son, Gabriel, and ached for her late husband, Gabe.

"Please don't blame yourself for that man's death. My gracious, girl, everyone at the rally was so thankful you were there. You saved lives."

"I know, but still, a man is dead and I'm responsible. That's the reality, and I've got to deal with it. Something bad happens wherever that bird shows up, but why did I have to be a part of it?"

"You're looking at this all wrong. Without you this could have been a much worse tragedy. Who knows how many people that guy would have shot? The Youngstown Chief of Police had nothing but praise for your quick response."

Marla waved her hand. "I guess you're right, but I didn't come here to be a hero. Anyway, that's not the only thing that's on my mind."

"The phone call?"

Marla sighed. "Yes. There's something going on between Dugan and Adelaide Brackenbury."

"You don't know that for sure."

"I know Dugan better than anyone. His voice wavers, and he stutters when he gets in a tight spot, and I definitely cornered him."

Mee Mee shook her head. "But Russell asked him to keep his eye on Addy."

"He's got more than his eye on her. Let's change the subject."

Mee Mee gripped the wheel with both hands and straightened her arms, trying to stretch. "Okay. How far are we from Negus Road? These turns and valleys are starting to get to me."

"I thought you grew up with valleys and hills back in West Virginia. Doesn't everybody from your hometown have one leg shorter than the other from walking on the sides of mountains?"

"Watch it, girl." Mee Mee raised a finger. "I may have grown up in West Virginia, but my last thirty-five years have been spent on the Outer Banks where everything is flat and fairly straight."

"Right now I'm missing my little beach house on the Outer Banks and my son. But I guess we gotta keep chasing this

Thunderbird—North Carolina, West Virginia, Pennsylvania, and now Ohio."

"Bet you didn't expect it to appear in your old hometown, did you?"

Marla clasped her hands behind her head. "Not really, but come to think of it, Belmont County has become the big fracking hotspot in Ohio. So it shouldn't surprise us that the bird showed up here."

"Russell said about eight people spotted it. The local TV station in Steubenville reported on the sightings. Word got back to Russell very quickly. We're lucky you knew one of the eyewitnesses."

Marla arched her back and stretched her arms. "Pastor Byron didn't officially see the bird, but two farmers who belong to his congregation did. When I talked to him earlier today, he was all pumped up about this Thunderbird hunting expedition."

"It could get exciting if the bird shows up again tonight."

Ahead, Marla spotted the Colerain Presbyterian Church where the 4-H Club held their regular meetings when she was a kid. She loved raising lambs and showing them off at the Belmont County Fair. She wondered where all her friends from back in the day were now. She fought off a strong urge to order Mee Mee to pull around back into the church parking lot just to see if there was a 4-H meeting going on. One of her old buddies would probably be the adult leader. She shook her head, trying to escape this overwhelming flood of nostalgia. "Quick." She pointed to the left. "Turn down that road—County Road 4."

Mee Mee spun the wheel, and the Jeep Cherokee lurched off the main road, jolted over the crown, and plunged down a narrower side road. "Hey! How about a heads up before the next turn."

"Sorry. My mind is jumbled. Everything's coming back to me from the good old days. It's hard to think straight."

They drove about a half mile downhill and around a few turns. Modest homes, mostly ranch-style built in the sixties, perched on the slopes on both sides of the valley. Directly in front of them, the half-moon hung above the rim of the Allegheny foothills to the east, and stars began to appear, twinkling against the darkening sky.

"Make a left after this next curve and go up the hill. The Quaker Cemetery is near the top next to the old meeting house. Pastor Byron said he'd meet us there."

"Wonderful," Mee Mee groaned. "An old spooky building and a cemetery—the ideal place to go hunting for a phantom eagle at night."

They drove about a half mile up the hill, and the headlights brightened Pastor Byron Butler's blue Chevy Equinox parked along the gravel road next to the Quaker Meeting House. The old brick building looked like a one-room school house with its closed-shuttered windows and wide wooden door. Mee Mee parked behind the pastor's vehicle.

Marla jumped out of the car and rushed toward Byron Butler who had just stepped out of his car. He clicked on a flashlight and directed the ray toward them.

"Pastor Byron!" She opened her arms, and he greeted her with a big hug. He was a tall, thin man, slightly over six feet with receding brown hair edged with gray around the ears. He wore sporty wire-rimmed glasses and dressed in baggy jeans and a dark blue long-sleeved T-shirt.

The pastor leaned back to get a look at her. "Marla, it's so good to see you. It's been a while."

Marla released her embrace and stepped back. "Bet you didn't expect we'd meet again under these circumstances."

Pastor Byron shook his head. "No way. What a weird turn of events. Your phone call startled me, especially when you mentioned the bird."

Mee Mee stepped up to them. "Hi, Pastor Byron. Remember me?"

"Sure." He extended his hand. "Mee Mee Roberts, right?"

"That's right." Mee Mee shook his hand.

"Do you still own the bookstore in Buxton?"

"Yes sir. Been selling books down there for more than thirty years."

"On the phone this morning, Marla mentioned that you are writing your own stories now."

"That's why we're here. I'm writing a feature for the *Island*

Free Press about the Thunderbird that's been spotted along this road. "

"That's very cool," Pastor Byron said. "Marla mentioned you've seen the creature."

Mee Mee let out a low whistle. "Oh yeah. On Ocracoke Island. Believe me, if you see it tonight, you will be impressed. It's definitely an unearthly creature."

Pastor Byron rubbed his hands together. "I'm excited. The bird was spotted about a quarter mile from here." He turned and pointed up the hill. "At the top the new pipeline crosses the road. They've been digging a huge trench across the county for miles. The farmer that owns this land, Alvin Mitchell, came to church Sunday morning all worked up. He was driving home from the VFW on Saturday night when the creature flew over top of his pickup truck and stayed about thirty yards ahead of him. Then it peeled off to the right and flew along the big pipeline ditch the backhoes had dug that day."

"Did anyone else see it?" Marla asked.

"Yeah, his wife Luella. Old Alvin drove back to the farmhouse and told her all about it. She thought he was crazy, so he dragged her out into the field to look for it. It came right at them, and they ran back to the house for cover."

"The creature chased me, too," Mee Mee said. "It's very aggressive. Has anything bad happened since the energy companies moved in? This Thunderbird has been linked to tragedies and other negative incidents wherever it shows up."

"Plenty. All the rents have gone up around here because of the influx of out-of-town workers. Local families who struggle financially can't afford the monthly housing payments. Then there's the increase in violence and crime. Last month an oil and gas worker beat a college student to death over an argument at a sports bar. He knocked the poor kid down and then just kept kicking him in the head until he died. Last week one of the workers who moved up here from down South lured a teenage girl into his apartment in Martins Ferry and then raped her. It's sad. We thought this would be a big financial blessing for the county, but the energy companies rarely hire local people. There has been a rise in construction, which is a good thing. A bunch of new hotels have been built to accommodate these transient workers, but these guys really don't care about the local community. In a few years they'll move out, and the hotels will be empty. What a waste."

Mee Mee pointed across the valley to where the dying glimmer of day contrasted against the dark ridge. "There it is! The Thunderbird!"

Marla turned and focused. "That thing's huge! Look at the wingspan."

"I told you so."

Pastor Byron directed his flashlight up the road. "It's heading towards Vickers Hill Road. Quick, up to the top! We can see better from there." The pastor broke into a fast trot up the gravel lane.

By the time they covered the quarter mile to the top of the hill, Marla's leg muscles burned. Far off she could see the glow of the bird fading into the darkness.

"Should we chase it on foot?" Mee Mee asked.

Pastor Byron spread his hands. "This is where Alvin Mitchell spotted the bird. Let's wait and see if it comes back."

"That makes sense to me," Mee Mee said. "We'd waste time and energy by running a mile in that direction if the bird doubles back on us."

Pastor Byron directed the swath of light at the hayfield before them. "See the trench and the backhoes?"

Marla gazed at the big ditch gouged through the field and noticed several large earth-moving machines looming on each side of the trench. The backhoes resembled the silhouettes of dinosaurs with their long necks and shovels. A sudden chill went through her as if she had been transported through a portal back in time. She turned away from the backhoes and gazed across the other side of the road to the western hills. "What's that light?"

They crossed the road and stared at the odd glow atop the farthest ridge.

"I'm almost sure that's a natural gas well," Pastor Byron said. "They've drilled quite a few in the county and keep them lit all night. I'd say it's about a mile from here."

Marla squinted. She detected a sliver of black crossing the glow. She blinked. The sliver grew, moving slightly up and down. "Do you see what I see?"

"Where?" Mee Mee asked.

"Look at the glow."

"I see it," Pastor Byron said. "Do you think it's the bird?"

Marla eyed the dark shape." It has to be. It's huge." As it neared, it reminded her of the large model of a pterodactyl hanging in her son's bedroom.

Mee Mee reached and grasped Marla's elbow. "It's coming our way."

Pastor Byron cast the light in the direction of the creature, but the ray lacked the power to illuminate it. "Do you think it knows we're here?"

Marla glanced at the flashlight. "I'm sure it can see your light."

"I'll wave it to see if we can attract it." Pastor Byron circled the flashlight in front of him.

"I wouldn't do that if I were you," Mee Mee cautioned.

The bird looked to be about a quarter mile away. Its phosphorescent glow against the violet sky sharpened its form.

Pastor Byron stopped circling the light. "Uh oh."

"Kill the light. It's going to attack. Run!" Mee Mee whirled and sprinted down the hill.

Marla met Pastor Byron's surprised eyes. They turned to refocus on the Thunderbird. It was only about a hundred yards away.

"Eeeeeeeaaaaaaaaaarrrrrrraaaaach!" The bird's screech ripped through the chilly night air.

Pastor Byron dropped the light, and it tumbled on the gravel at their feet.

Marla's heart jolted in her chest. She turned and bolted down the hill towards the car. Mee Mee had a good lead, but Marla could see she was catching her.

"Eeeeeeeaaaaaaaaaarrrrrrraaaaach!"

The cry pierced through her. Marla glanced over her shoulder and saw the huge glowing wings and sharp talons. She felt a blast of air from the wings. Her toe caught on a rock, and she tumbled onto the gravel road. The Thunderbird passed over and then rose, peeling off to the right. Pain shot through her knees and palms. Gravel had embedded into her skin. *I've gotta get up. I've gotta run.* She tried struggling to her feet but stumbled again and fell.

"Eeeeeeeaaaaaaaaaaarrrrrraaaaach!"

She looked over her shoulder. The bird had circled back. It was descending.

A hand grabbed her arm. "Get up and run!" Mee Mee shouted. She pulled Marla to her feet.

"Eeeeeeeaaaaaaaaaaarrrrrraaaaach!"

The bird plunged toward them, and they collapsed to the road, screaming, and covering their heads with their arms and hands.

The blast of air from its wings rushed against them. Marla peeked through her fingers and saw large talons clawing toward them.

"Be gone you damned demon!" Pastor Byron yelled. He swung a large branch at the creature, barely missing it. The bird screamed. He swung again and caught the bottom of its tail feathers. Immediately the creature shot skyward and turned in the direction of the oil well.

He tossed the branch to the side of the road. "Are you ladies all right?"

Mee Mee put her hand on her chest. "My heart's beating like a jackhammer."

"Hurry, let's get back to the cars," Marla said.

Pastor Byron extended his hands and helped pull the women to their feet. "I'll catch up in a minute. I'm going back for my flashlight."

Marla and Mee Mee walked quickly down the road. Every few steps Marla kept glancing over her shoulder to see if the Thunderbird had circled back. She took a deep breath once they reached the Jeep Cherokee and quickly climbed into the passenger's side.

Mee Mee closed the driver's side door, and the interior light slowly faded. "I'm shaking like a lonely leaf in a windstorm."

Marla picked gravel out of her palm but couldn't stop her

hand from trembling. "I'm right there with you. That was terrifying."

"No kidding. That's the second time for me. I told him not to swing that light."

"I could use a big glass of wine right now to take the edge off of these nerves."

"Looks like you need a Band-Aid too."

A sudden knock on the driver's side window startled them.

"It's only me," Pastor Byron pressed his face to the window.

Mee Mee started the engine and powered down the window. "How many heart attacks do you want to give me tonight?"

Pastor Byron clicked on his flashlight and held some long brown feathers in its glow. "Look here. We've got proof that the bird exists."

"Let me see." Mee Mee reached and took a couple of the feathers. "I'd say these are golden eagle feathers because of the white markings. I'll have to check with Lou Browning, our bird rehab guy." She shook her head. "But a golden eagle's wingspan is only seven or eight feet. I don't know."

Marla grunted. "Maybe it was a freak of nature, somehow biologically altered. You never know nowadays."

"I'm glad you found these," Mee Mee said. "This could be key evidence in the investigation."

"Great." Pastor Byron thumbed toward his car. "Follow me back to my house. I want to hear more about this investigation. "

"Do you have room to put us up for the night?" Marla asked.

"Plenty of room. I'll even cook you breakfast in the morning."

Mee Mee pointed to the top of the hill. "Watch yourself. Here comes a vehicle down the road."

Pastor Byron squinted into the glare of the headlights. "Must be more Thunderbird hunters."

An old white Chevy cargo van whizzed past. Pastor Byron shifted the flashlight, illuminating the back of the vehicle. "That's odd."

"What's odd?" Marla asked.

Pastor Byron pointed towards the vanishing van. "I'm almost sure that license plate said North Carolina."

"It did," Mee Mee said. "That was Achak Rowtag's van."

Chapter 16

Late Monday night Dugan pulled into Addy's driveway. He wondered what kind of weirdness awaited them at the Ocracoke Lighthouse. He kept telling himself to be a calm observer. There was no need to play the skeptic or expose the fraud—just listen, observe, and take detailed mental notes. Let the paranormal researchers believe him to be a naive participant.

When it came to spiritualism, Addy was exceptionally vulnerable—a true believer. It was his job to protect her from the suspected environmental extremist who murdered her husband. Did that job extend to preventing con men from dipping their hands into her bank account? Not really. But he cared about her. Maybe it was her vulnerability that attracted him. They say opposites attract.

Marla used to be vulnerable. Not anymore. The cold world had hardened her, made her scrutinize life much more suspiciously. A con man had murdered her husband. That was a major contributing factor to her lack of trust in people. Of course, police work will harden anyone. She'd been his deputy now for three years, a damn good one. Perhaps it was her acquired distrust that led to their breakup. She couldn't trust him to be the man she needed to complete her.

But why did she call? Was she having second thoughts? Did she come to her senses? If she did, he might have blown it. He probably sounded like a stammering fool on the phone, like a kid caught with his hand in the cookie jar. Could she tell by the sound of his voice and how he fumbled for words that he was trying to conceal his attraction to Addy? Yeah, they were alone together at her house, but he was just doing his job. Why did he get so flustered? Obviously, because Addy's appeal had penetrated beyond fleeting lustful thoughts. Guilt! Women could pick up on that immediately. That phone call didn't reinforce any hope that Marla wanted to renew their relationship. Oh well. Not much he could do about it now. Dugan stepped out of the car and headed to the rear entrance.

Addy swung open the door and waved. "I've been waiting for you. I'm so nervous." She reached for his hand.

He clasped her hand, and they turned toward the dock. "Why so nervous?"

"This could be a very important night. Darrin Brownstone is a world class clairvoyant. Who knows what we'll discover." She squeezed his hand. "Besides, I get to spend the evening with you."

"I hope I don't make you nervous."

"No. You make me feel excited." She winked at him.

Dugan took a deep breath and let it out slowly. *Oh boy.* As they passed under a street light, he admired her low-cut pink sweater and tight jeans. *Settle down now. Let' not get too excited. The night has just begun.*

On the boat ride over Addy talked a mile a minute. She went on about the mysteries of the netherworld and how it could be considered one of the last frontiers. She wanted to open herself up and discover the possibilities like a pioneer or an explorer venturing into the wilderness. Dugan didn't need to say much to keep her talking. That was fine with him. He sat back, relaxed, and enjoyed the ride across Pamlico Sound. The night was warm and clear. His Scout Dorado skimmed over the unusually smooth water with nary a bump. In twenty minutes they arrived at Ocracoke Harbor. Dugan cut the engine down to a crawl and crossed Silver Lake to the docks nearest the lighthouse.

After he secured the boat, they found their way to Creek Road and then made a right on Lighthouse Road. A strong breeze met them, and Addy let go of his hand.

She secured her arm around his waist. "Warm me up, would you please?"

Dugan put his arm around her shoulder and pulled her close. "How's that?"

"Much better."

They passed a small parking area and made a right onto a wooden walkway. Dugan spotted the lighthouse about fifty yards away. It wasn't a huge lighthouse like the one on Cape Hatteras or even as tall as the Currituck Lighthouse in Corolla. He estimated it to be about seventy-five feet high. It had been painted white and seemed to glow against the blue-violet of the cloudless September sky. Dugan chuckled to himself. Maybe it glowed because it was haunted by so many ghosts. That's what the locals claimed anyway.

They reached the entrance, a white wooden door with louvers on the bottom half. Dugan turned the knob and swung the door open. The redbrick interior was aglow with candlelight. Several candles had been placed on the metal spiral staircase that ascended to the top. A small round table had been set up at the base of the staircase, and two women, Sienna Bryce and Luna Holiday, sat at the table facing him. He didn't see Brownstown. Luna waved. He stepped aside to let Addy enter first.

Addy waved back. "Hi, ladies."

They proceeded through a short entryway and entered the round room. Immediately, Dugan caught sight of a figure leaning against the wall to the left of the entrance. He wore a black turtleneck and dress slacks. His ponytailed dark hair, goatee, thick eyebrows, and narrow eyes reminded Dugan of a character right out of a Vincent Price movie.

Sienna, the middle-aged blonde he had met at Springer's Point, stood up. Her dark sweat shirt and sweat pants blended her figure into the shadows. "Addy, it's so good to see you again." Sienna circled the table and hugged her.

Luna, wearing the same black ball cap she had worn the other night, rose to her feet and embraced Addy also. She had long, black curly hair and wore a black long-sleeve T-shirt and dark blue jeans. "I'm so sorry for your loss. That was a terrible night."

Dugan's red flannel shirt made him wonder if he had missed the memo about appropriate dress for a séance.

Addy stepped back from the two paranormal researchers. "It was a terrible night, but I'm so thankful you were able to arrange this session. I hope we can communicate with Rowland's spirit and get some answers."

"Addy and Sheriff Walton," Sienna motioned toward Brownstown, "this is Darrin Brownstone. He is one of the leading spiritualists of our time."

The man in black stepped from the shadows and extended his hand toward Dugan. "It's a pleasure to meet you, Sheriff. I have great respect for those who uphold the law."

Dugan shook his hand, wondering how many people the guy had defrauded in his career. "I've heard a lot about you."

"All good, I hope."

Brownstone turned to Addy and extended his hand. "Mrs. Brackenbury, it's so good to meet you, and I also offer my sympathies."

Addy's eyes widened as she gazed at him. "Thank you, Mr. Brownstone. I'm a big fan of yours. I've seen many of your séances on television and on the internet. It's amazing how you can channel deceased loved ones."

"It's a gift." Brownstone placed his hand gently on his chest. "I don't take credit for it."

"You truly are gifted," Addy said. "I'm so excited about being a part of this gathering tonight. I believe I have strong spiritualist tendencies myself. There's no doubt in my heart that we can contact the departed."

"I'm sure we will," Sienna said. "The Ocracoke Lighthouse is one of the most supernaturally energized locations on the island. So many people have encountered spirits here."

Dugan cleared his throat. "Any particular ghosts?"

"Yes indeed," Luna piped. "Everyone knows about Blackbeard. Springer's Point was his favorite harborage. It's no wonder he's been spotted around here by so many credible witnesses. But he's just the tip of the iceberg. There's the old lighthouse keeper. He appears to be a solid person with long hair and a beard, wearing striped pants and white shirt. He will walk toward you and then pass right through you. His appearance has been documented over and over again. Then there's Theodosia Burr Alston, the daughter of Aaron Burr, the famous vice president. She lost her life in a shipwreck just off shore. People see her walking in the vicinity of the lighthouse wearing a long, flowing white dress."

Dugan raised his eyebrows. "Very impressive. This is quite the confluence of paranormal activity."

Sienna nodded. "Two of the strangest ghosts were twin sisters, young girls whose remains were found buried near the wall of the lighthouse. They are thought to be the daughters of one of the early lighthouse keepers. Forensic scientists believe they died of typhoid back in the mid-1800s. People often see them strolling along the Pamlico Sound and even playing around the base of the lighthouse. Ghost sightings of Indians, other shipwreck victims, pirates, and settlers are common occurrences around here. It's no wonder that Ocracoke is one of the most haunted islands on earth."

"That's quite a diverse collection of the dead," Dugan said. "They might have to take a number if they want to get an opportunity to address tonight's assembly."

"Very funny," Brownstone said. "You sound like a skeptic, Sheriff Taylor."

"Not really. I'm neither a believer nor unbeliever. Consider me an open-minded observer."

Brownstone rubbed his goatee. "I hope you are open-minded. If that's the case, don't be surprised if your horizons are widened tonight."

"My horizons could use some widening. Why don't we get started?"

Brownstone circled the spiral staircase, blowing out the

candles. One candle was left burning, the one in the middle of the table. Dugan sat on a wooden chair next to Addy. Brownstone took the seat on the other side of Addy, and the two women sat in the remaining seats. The old oak table had numbers and letters spaced evenly around the rim. In the middle next to the candle sat an upside-down wine glass between the words "YES" and "NO." When the candle's flame wavered, their shadows on the curved brick walls shuddered.

Brownstone spread his arms. "Shall we join hands?"

Dugan clasped Addy's and Luna's hand and rested them on the edge of the table.

Brownstone leaned forward slightly. "I want all of you to stare into the flame of the candle. Please blank your minds and open your spirits to the realm beyond this world."

Dugan stared at the candle but didn't empty his mind. He tried to be supersensitive to all that was happening around him.

"Very good. Very good. Stare at the flame and let the thoughts and concerns of the day drift away. In the solitude and tranquility of these moments, open yourself to the transcendent and eternal realm."

Dugan noticed Brownstone's voice was low, rhythmic, and soothing. Addy's hand began to tremble slightly.

Brownstone's voice became lower. "We are united in our efforts this evening. We are open to the spiritual world. Is there a spirit here among us who would like to communicate with us?"

Nothing.

"I will ask again. Is there a spirit among us who would like to communicate with us?"

The upside-down wineglass near the candle began to vibrate. Dugan blinked and shifted his focus to the glass. Addy squeezed his hand tighter.

The glass slowly edged to the left. It moved a couple of inches and stopped. Dugan's mind raced trying to figure how the object moved but could not detect any kind of clandestine impetus.

Luna gasped, "The glass moved over the word 'YES'."

Brownstone nodded. "There is a spirit with us." He released Addy's and Sienna's hands and raised his hands. "Oh spirit, I invite you to enter me and speak to us."

Dugan could feel his heart thudding. *Calm down and pay attention. This is a show. Don't get caught up in the theatrics.*

Brownstone sighed deeply, his face contorting. He made a guttural noise and shifted in his seat as if involuntarily adjusted by an unseen force. He closed his eyes, and his head swiveled slightly back and forth. His voice became that of an old man, gravely and unsteady. "IIII...IIII...am...here. I am the keeper of the light. Why do you want to cross over into my world?"

Sienna leaned forward. "We need to communicate with departed spirits who still roam the island."

A strange smile altered Brownstone's face. "To whom do you wish to speak? Blackbeard?" He half coughed and half chuckled. "He's the popular one. Do you want me to summon Blackbeard?"

"N-no, n-not B-Blackbeard," Luna said, nerves edging her voice.

"Good!" Brownstown slammed his fist on the table, and everybody flinched. "You do not want to cross paths with Blackbeard. He is not a contented spirit. There are many others who would be willing to talk to you—Indians, those who died on the shoals and washed ashore, fishermen, children who met an unfortunate fate. Whom shall I summon?"

Addy squeezed Dugan's hand even harder. "Do you know Rowland Brackenbury? He recently died. Someone murdered him here on Ocracoke."

Brownstone sat back, his head slowly nodding. "Yes, I have met the Englishman. He is a good fellow. I will summon him." His head tilted back. "Rowland Brackenbury, I call you to join us. You are walking this island with much sorrow and confusion. Come and speak to these people. Unburden your restless heart."

Dugan noticed the candle flame wavering wildly. The shadows on the brick walls gyrated like spectral dancers. The flame went out, and the women let out brief gasps.

"Shhhhhhhhhh."

Dugan couldn't see a thing but assumed the shooshing came from Blackstone.

In the utter darkness an odd light appeared a few feet above them where the smoke of the extinguished candles had collected. Dugan examined the glow and noticed the rippling of facial features.

"I- I-It's Rowland," Addy quavered.

"I am here, my love."

The voice reminded Dugan of Winston Churchill. Brownstone had to be talking, but the words seemed to emanate from above.

"Is it really you?" Addy asked.

"It is, and I have come to warn you. The man who murdered me is also a threat to you."

"Who was it? Why did he do it?"

"He has powers of concealment and conjury but do not let his menace dissuade you. Be brave. Carry out our plans for Ocracoke. The spirits that roam the island want a voice. You can bring their story to the world through our project. But beware, my dear Addy. Beware."

Dugan couldn't hold his tongue any longer. "Can you tell us anything else about the murderer?"

"Yes. He also crosses over into lands where spirits roam. He is a destroyer of lives. He is . . . aruuugghh. I can't . . . I can't . . . argggguuuhh. . ." The glow above them faded and strange noises came from the direction of Brownstone like someone struggling to keep his head above water. Then a loud thud shook the table.

Next to Dugan a spark flashed into a flame on a matchstick, and Luna leaned over and lit the candle. Brownstone had slumped onto the table, the candle's light fluttered over him.

Sienna shook his shoulder. "Mr. Brownstone? Are you okay? Mr. Brownstone?"

He stirred and pressed his hands on the table, pushing himself erect and blinking. "I'm sorry. I couldn't maintain my connection with Rowland Brackenbury. Something, some kind of entity pulled him away from me."

"I sensed its presence also," Luna said.

Sienna leaned toward the candle and whispered, "I did too, and it is still with us."

Addy drew in a deep breath and closed her eyes. A stream of odd words flowed from her mouth. To Dugan it sounded like some kind of Native American dialect, but the words jumbled together and became more like glossolalia. Her head wobbled as if she'd lost control of her neck muscles.

Dugan grabbed her arm and shook her. "Addy! What's the matter with you?"

She tried to pull away and screamed. She began to shake like someone suffering from an epileptic seizure. Dugan lowered her to the floor and tried to steady her by grasping her shoulders.

She screamed several times and continued to jabber in the odd Native American dialect. Finally, she went limp.

Dugan pulled out his cell phone and activated the flashlight app. "Does anybody have some water?"

"Yes," Luna said. "I have a bottle in my carryall bag." She hurried to the other side of the spiral staircase and knelt in the shadows. A few seconds later she returned with a bottle of water.

Dugan uncapped it and sprinkled some onto Addy's face.

Addy blinked, her facial muscles tensing and eyes squinting into Dugan's light. "Where am I?"

"You're with me," Dugan said, "at the Ocracoke Lighthouse."

She reached and caressed Dugan's cheek. "I want to go home."

"Me too," Dugan said.

Brownstone had lit several of the candles on the spiral staircase generating a soft glow against the red bricks. "Will she be all right?"

"I think so," Dugan said as he slid his cell phone back into his pocket.

Sienna stepped closer. "This happened the other night on Springer's Point. Addy became possessed by the spirit of an Indian maiden."

Brownstone knelt and reached toward Addy. She grasped his hand, and with Dugan's help, they raised her to her feet. Brownstone held her face between his hands. "Tell me about the spirit who possessed you. What happened?" He lowered his hands.

Addy took a deep breath and let it out. "It's the same spirit that always possesses me—a Native American girl. I relive a terrifying scene in her life over and over again. She seems to be a part of my past. I'm near Springer's Point when a dark figure chases me. I run through the woods, but I can't get away. I

132

stumble and fall, and he pounces on me. I know he wants to violate me and kill me."

Brownstone reached and touched Addy's shoulder. "The Native American girl is trying to reveal something to you. She wants to empower you so that you are not overwhelmed by your opposition. Your husband mentioned that you have a particular enemy, the same person who murdered him. I can help you discover who that enemy is and what to do if you are attacked. Let me help you, Addy."

Addy shook her head. "I don't know. I'm dizzy and tired. Give me some time to think about all that's happened."

"Of course, but we can't wait too long. I sense a great desperation in your circumstances."

Addy stepped closer to Dugan and leaned her head on his shoulder. "I'm ready to go."

Dugan put his arm around her shoulders and nodded toward Luna and Sienna. "It's been interesting, but we've had enough paranormal activity for one night." He glanced at Brownstone. "Addy will be in touch if she needs your services."

Brownstone handed Addy a business card. "Please call me."

Dugan ushered her through the short entryway and out the door. They made a left and headed down the wooden walkway.

Dugan pulled her closer. "To say the least, that was very weird."

She slipped her arm around his waist. "I'm glad you were there with me. I can't get that dark figure out of my mind."

"Do you see his face at all during the struggle?"

"Not clearly. He's dressed in black and has long hair and a beard."

Hmmmmm, Dugan thought that sounds a lot like Brownstone.

Chapter 17

The boat ride home was much quieter. Withdrawn and tense, Addy sat with her arms crossed and stared at the dark waters in front of them. She seemed lost in her thoughts. Dugan tried to lift her spirits by talking about the beauty of the night sky, the myriad stars that flickered above them, and how when he was a kid he would make a wish whenever he saw a shooting star. Addy smiled weakly but didn't add much to the conversation.

When they drew near Hatteras Harbor, Addy said, "Dugan, I'm afraid."

"You don't have to be afraid. I'm with you."

"But you can't be with me all the time. Someone wants to kill me. He almost succeeded when I wrecked my car earlier today. Tonight Rowland's spirit warned me, and Darrin Brownstone said my circumstances were desperate."

"I wouldn't put much stock in Brownstone's opinion."

"Why not? You saw what he could do. His abilities are

amazing."

Dugan turned into the harbor, slowed the engine, and steered the boat toward the dock. "I'm not as impressed as you are with his talents. I think he's a fraud."

She sat up and faced him. "A fraud? Then how did he do it? How did the wineglass move? How did my husband's spirit appear above us?"

"I don't know. I can't explain what happened tonight. It's just a gut feeling. I could be wrong."

"Do you think I was putting on some kind of histrionics?"

Dugan cut the engine and drifted toward the dock. "No. I believe you do have some kind of connection to the spirit realm. I just don't know enough about those matters to help you sort things out."

"But Brownstone does. He said he could discover the identity of Rowland's murderer. He said he could help protect me from harm."

Dugan reached for the edge of the dock and steadied the boat, then quickly secured it to a cleat. "Like I said, I might be wrong, but if you ask him for help, I can guarantee you one thing."

"What's that?"

Dugan stepped up onto the dock, turned, and offered Addy his hand. She grasped it, and he pulled her onto the deck. "That help will come at a price. He'll ask for a substantial amount of money."

"But he didn't charge me a penny tonight."

"I know." He took her hand, and they walked toward the back entrance, stopped under the porch light, and faced each other. "That's part of the plan," Dugan said. "The first time is free to hook you, but after that you pay dearly."

She stared at the ground and shook her head. "I hope you're wrong, but I'm afraid you might be right."

"Do you want me to check the house and make sure it's safe?"

Addy shook her head. "I haven't been this frightened for a long time. What I really want is for you to stay with me tonight."

In the glow of the porch light Addy's beauty stirred him, her dreamy blue eyes, soft features, and that enticing body. But then

Marla's face appeared in the back of his mind, and a pang of guilt jabbed him. "I'm not sure if that's a good idea."

She patted his cheek. "Listen, Sheriff Walton. I don't want you to sleep in the same bed with me, just in the same house. This has been a horrendous day. I need you near me. There's several bedrooms on the second floor. Mine is on the third floor."

Dugan shrugged. He knew he had to be at the office early in the morning, but that shouldn't be a problem. Acknowledging the threats that had recently arisen and his responsibility to protect her, he reasoned it might be a good idea for him to stay. "Considering all that has happened, I guess I could bunk here tonight and make sure you're safe."

"Thank you." Addy turned and entered the code into the door lock.

Dugan executed his usual search of the premises floor by floor and found nothing out of the ordinary. Once he completed his check of the third floor he looked around for Addy and noticed the bedroom door slightly ajar. He drifted over in that direction. "Addy, I'm heading down to one of the guest bedrooms. I'm dead tired, and I have to be at the office early in the morning."

"Wait. I'll be out in a few seconds."

Dugan tapped his foot, wanting to peek through the opening and perhaps get a glimpse of her changing clothes. He took a deep breath and stepped back to counter the temptation. She exited the bedroom wearing a long white terrycloth robe. He felt relieved it wasn't a slinky nightgown. That temptation would have been difficult to resist.

She gazed up at him. "Help yourself to whatever you need. Every bedroom has its own bathroom. I'm sure you'll make yourself comfortable."

"I'll figure it out."

She stepped closer. "Thank you so much for staying tonight. I couldn't have made it through these last few days without you." She embraced him.

Slowly, he wrapped his arms around her. Her warmth charged through him. He breathed in the fragrance of her hair, the smell of cherry blossoms. They stood holding each other for what seemed like minutes. He wanted to kiss her but knew that would be a bad idea. Finally, he broke the embrace and stepped back.

"I'll see you tomorrow morning," he said, and then turned and headed down the stairs.

* * *

The bedroom Dugan chose was large and comfortable. A king-size bed sat in the middle of the opposite wall with tall ebony posts and a blue-and-white checkered bedspread. Centered above the bed, an Impressionist painting of colorful sailboats brightened the wall. To the left he noticed a sliding glass door that led out to a balcony facing the Pamlico Sound. An ornate fan hung from the ceiling slowly turning. He figured the door on the right must lead to the bathroom.

He entered the bathroom and inspected his face in the large mirror above the granite counter-topped sink. Dark bags rimmed his eyes. His brick-red hair was disheveled and in need of a good styling. He wiped his hand across a freckled cheek and wondered how a girl like Addy could be attracted to him. Then he thought about her late husband and reasoned that physical appearance wasn't that important to her. The notion seemed a little insulting but made him smile. *C'mon you son of a monkey, cheer up. You're not that bad looking.*

He stripped off his clothes and swung open the large glass door to the shower. He edged to the side and turned on the water. From a large rain shower head, the water spouted down. He checked the temperature with his palm and adjusted the handle. Just right. Lowering his head, he entered the downpour. It felt like heaven. He stood there several minutes not thinking, allowing the stream to warm and massage his backside.

Eventually, thoughts of Addy infiltrated the inactive mental zone created by the steady pelting. He had known very few women who possessed her allure. Whenever she hugged him his testosterone levels skyrocketed. Their one kiss nearly slayed him. If it weren't for Marla's phone call, that kiss would have led to something much more intimate. He knew if he stepped out of the shower and marched up to her bedroom, she would welcome him. They definitely wanted each other, physically anyway.

But Dugan knew that yielding to passion may lead to disaster. He'd seen it in a hundred faces of impulsive men he had arrested. They had sacrificed their future for a few minutes of pleasure or revenge or material gain. He didn't want that to happen to him. Giving in to that desire would put his reputation, his occupation, and his destination in jeopardy. During moments of weakness, he was definitely vulnerable to fleshly delights. He needed to stay strong and guard against those natural cravings, but boy, she was desirable.

He stepped out of the shower, quickly dried off, and slipped into his boxer shorts. He collected the rest of his clothes and hung them on the back of a chair next to a mahogany desk. Glancing around the room, he noticed the door to the balcony and decided to step out for some fresh air before hitting the sack.

After tripping the lock, he slid the glass door open and greeted the brisk night breeze. The wooden deck chilled the bottom of his bare feet. He peered skyward and noticed the stars appeared even brighter than earlier that evening. A silvery flash caught his eye as a shooting star streaked overhead. He chuckled to himself, thinking, if I were still a kid, I'd make a wish. *What would I wish for now?* He knew the answer, although he had tried to bury it in the soil of resentment and bitterness. More than anything he wanted Marla to love him and commit to him for a lifetime. He wanted to be the stepfather to her son, Gabriel, and he hoped she would conceive his child, maybe two or three kids. If that shooting star could grant a wish, he'd wish for a happy family and wedded bliss with a woman he loved more than anyone on this earth.

Could that shooting star be a sign? He truly doubted it. Marla had made it clear that he didn't meet all of her standards of romantic love and fulfillment. If she changed her mind and they ever married, the relationship would be unbalanced. He'd always love her more than she loved him. He guessed most relationships were that way.

What would happen if he and Addy did the wild thing? Would she want a commitment or just a fling? She seemed quite enthralled with him. That was nice—a beautiful women desired him. What a rarity. Could he love someone like her? She was a little kooky but very rich and sexy. More than likely he would lose his job as sheriff for crossing that forbidden line of maintaining professional distance. Making love to someone he was assigned to protect was a major no-no. If they stayed together, he would probably become dependent on her financially. That didn't sit right with him.

Dugan yawned and shook his head. He needed sleep, and wrestling with these thoughts would only keep him up most of the night. He headed back into the bedroom, closed the door, and crawled onto the king-size bed. Tomorrow was another day. If he could get a good night's sleep, things may be more manageable in the morning. The silky comforter felt wonderful as he settled into his favorite sleeping position on his right side. It didn't take long for his mind to empty and blessed sleep to descend.

Somewhere deep in the night, Dugan heard a woman call his name. In that state of half sleep he struggled to open his eyes and enter full consciousness.

"Dugan."

He managed to break through the thin film of slumber and force his eyes open. He saw a figure standing in the half-open doorway backlit by the glow of hallway light.

"Are you awake?"

He recognized Addy's voice. "I am now. Are you okay?"

"I had a bad dream." She pushed the door all the way open.

Dugan squinted as more light flooded into the room. "Do you want to talk about it?"

Wearing a sheer pink negligee that tied in the front, she drifted toward him and sat on the edge of the bed. "Yes. I couldn't fall back to sleep. I'm so stressed."

Dugan propped a pillow against the headboard and sat up. "What happened in your dream?"

"The usual." She placed a pillow against the headboard, lifted her legs, and scooted back against it. "But there were some differences this time."

"How so?"

"A different man chased me."

"Not the same guy dressed in black with long hair and a beard?"

"No. He was an Indian. His hair was braided, and he wore these beads around his neck. All he had on was some kind of loin cloth."

"Did he catch you?"

"Yes. He tackled me. Then he pulled an odd looking knife out of his belt. I thought he would stab me, but he didn't. He held the knife flat in his hand and said, "It is your choice." I knocked the knife away, broke from his grasp, and managed to roll out from under him. That's when I tumbled out of bed. Didn't you hear the thud?"

"No. I must have been sound asleep."

"Do you think it means something?"

"Maybe." Dugan recalled the results of the autopsy and how Brackenbury had been stabbed three times with an unusual knife. "Do you think the man in your dream was Achak?"

"This man was young and strong, but his voice was similar to Achak's. Why?"

"He's the obvious suspect in your husband's murder."

She leaned toward Dugan and rested her head on his shoulder. "I don't know. Maybe he was a younger version of Achak. Maybe it was just my imagination running wild." She took a deep breath. "I'm so tired."

"Dreams can't convict murderers. Only evidence can do that. But it certainly is interesting."

Addy sat up, scooted farther down the bed, and rested her head on the pillow. "I just want to sleep."

Dugan gazed at her as she lay beside him. Only a few feet separated them. He wished she would have put the terrycloth robe back on. Her eyes were closed, and her breasts beneath the sheer fabric rose and fell with each slow breath. Now what? Did she fall asleep already? "Addy."

She groaned softly.

"Addy."

She groaned again and turned onto her side facing away from him. She definitely didn't want to snuggle. Good. He lifted the comforter and gently covered her. Then he eased himself onto his back and stared at the ceiling. He did the best he could to fight off lustful thoughts. After a few minutes weariness weighed on him again. He decided to turn onto his right side and move closer to the edge of the bed to be as far as possible from her. There. Now if he could only get a couple hours sleep before his phone alarm went off.

* * *

Something wet tickled the side of Dugan's neck and he opened his eyes. The fragrance of cherry blossoms filtered through his nostrils, and he knew Addy had drawn near. He focused on the wall and tried to remain calm, but could not quell the fire charging through him. She nibbled his ear and murmured indistinguishable words. He turned onto his back, and her lips greeted his, wet and soft.

She placed her hand on his chest and rose up. Her eyes were closed and her lips moved, but he could not decipher the strange language coming from her mouth. She lowered herself again and kissed him passionately. The rapture of her flesh overwhelmed his senses. He felt himself slipping into the bliss of her warmth and touch, as if he was sinking into a pool of pleasure.

She shifted her legs to move on top of him. He sensed the pressure of her body against him from head to foot. He ran his hand down her backside as far as he could reach, and she moaned. She placed her hands on the pillow at each side of his head, raised herself slightly, and kissed his cheek, chin, ears, and neck. Then she sat up slowly, still straddling him, rocking gently back and forth. She tilted her head toward the ceiling and spoke unintelligible words, the same sounding ones she had uttered at the séance. Was she dreaming, possessed by some spirit, or was this some kind of role play?

Dugan had lost his grasp on self-control. He stared at the tie on the front of her negligee. Her breasts heaved as she inhaled and exhaled. He wanted to undress her and see the full beauty of her body. He wanted to make love to her. He reached for the tie and began to pull one of the strings.

From the dresser his cellphone erupted with the blaring sound of a trumpet playing reveille—his alarm had gone off.

Addy's eyes sprung open. She glanced down at his hands. "Dugan! What are you doing?"

Dugan pulled his hands away, and she clasped the top of her negligee.

He snatched his phone off the dresser and killed the alarm. "What do you mean? You're the one who climbed on top of me."

"Oh. I'm sorry." She rolled off of him, scooted to the edge of the bed, and stood with her arms crossed over her breasts. "I was dreaming again."

"Yeah. That was some dream." Dugan swung his legs over the edge, sat up, and planted his feet on the floor. "I've got to get dressed and be on my way."

"We were in the middle of making love, weren't we?"

Dugan stood. "I'd say we at least made it to second base, maybe halfway to third."

Addy giggled. "I hope you're not mad at me."

"For what? Starting the fire or putting it out?"

She raised her eyebrows. "For putting it out."

Dugan slipped into his flannel shirt and began buttoning it. "Believe me, it's not the first time I've had my fire put out."

"Are you in a big hurry?"

"Why?"

"I think I could fan those flames again."

Chapter 18

On the drive back to Manteo, Dugan thanked God he didn't go all the way with Addy. The timing of his cell phone alarm must have been divine intervention. He berated himself for his fleshly weakness. But what man could have withstood that kind of enticement? He wondered if she intentionally orchestrated the circumstances. If so, should he take it as a compliment that a beautiful woman wanted to make love to him? Her offer to reconvene sexual congress startled him. By then, though, he had come to his senses. He apologized and insisted he had to get to the office. He had already put his reputation at risk by staying the night and wondered if any deputy had spotted his Ford Interceptor parked in her driveway.

He arrived at the Dare County Sheriff's office in Manteo at 8:15, only fifteen minutes late. The redheaded receptionist, Doris Bonner, gave him an odd look, but he smiled, waved, and said, "I know. I'm a little late today. I was uh . . . conferring with uh . . . a concerned citizen."

Doris shrugged and pushed her horned-rimmed glasses up on her nose. "You're the boss. I'm not gonna yell if you're late. It's just unusual, that's all."

"I know. I'm usually here fifteen minutes early." Dugan hurried down the hall to his office, his face heating up. He wondered if the staff was talking about Addy and him. Now he wished he would have parked the cruiser somewhere less noticeable. Surely, someone spotted it when making rounds.

With all the paper work he had to catch up on, he pushed thoughts of Addy and possible rumors to the back of his mind. He plopped down in his swivel chair and began sorting through the stack. He'd meet with his day-shift deputies about nine o'clock. That gave him a half hour to make some progress. He hated paperwork. Had to be done, though.

At nine o'clock he headed down to the squad room. About ten deputies had gathered, drinking coffee, chatting, and laughing. He informed them of Mrs. Brackenbury's accident and instructed them to keep an eye out for a black SUV in the Hatteras neighborhoods and especially near her beach house. He carefully observed his deputies' expressions as he described the circumstances of the accident, but nothing seemed to hint at any kind of insider's knowledge of his previous night's whereabouts. No winks. No nudges with elbows. No sly smiles.

Several deputies updated him on arrests and other recent incidents, but nothing demanded change in their routines or a refocus of priorities. After a discussion about the increased use of heroin in the county and a review of procedures with addicts and overdoses, he wished them a good day and sent them on their way.

Back in his office he worked for another hour and a half on all the reports that had been submitted. Taking a break, he checked with the dispatcher to see what kind of calls had come in: nothing too alarming—a stray dog knocking over garbage cans in Buxton, a shoplifting incident in Avon, and a domestic dispute in Rodanthe. If things remained this quiet, he'd be caught up in an hour or two.

Back in his office the phone rang at about 11:15. He picked up. "Sheriff Taylor here."

"Sheriff, this is Russell Goodwin. How're things going?"

"Not bad."

"Anything new concerning the Brackenbury investigation?"

Dugan remembered Goodwin's warning about keeping things on the professional level with Addy. He tried to sound levelheaded and relaxed. "We did have an incident yesterday and an interesting paranormal encounter. Mrs. Brackenbury was followed by a black SUV just south of Buxton. She panicked and ended up wrecking her vehicle in the Frisco Campground. Then at the séance last night her husband showed up."

"Whoa, that was an eventful day. I'm assuming she's okay since she attended the séance."

"Yeah, she's fine. Just a slight cut on the head."

"Have you been keeping a close eye on her?"

Dugan coughed and swallowed. "Uh . . . yeah, I've been watching out for her, and I've assigned a couple of deputies to swing by her beach house once an hour to make sure she's all right."

"Good. Well, I want to hear all the details about the wreck and the séance. I'm about ten minutes north of Manteo heading in your direction. Could we meet somewhere for lunch?"

"Sure thing. How about Poor Richard's Sandwich Shop near Festival Island?"

"Sounds great. I'll tell my GPS to look it up and lead the way. See you there in about fifteen minutes."

* * *

Poor Richard's Sandwich Shop was located on Queen Elizabeth Street near the waterfront. One of Dugan's favorite lunch spots, it was housed in an historic building with a combination of white wooden siding and cedar shingles. A balcony hung out over three large front windows, and the sign painted on the side of the building featured a skull and crossbones. Dugan entered and waved at Ed Durbin, the owner, who was standing behind the oak bar to the right. Good ol' Ed, tall, bald, and bearded, had been running the place for decades. A few locals and four or five vacationers occupied the stools along the bar. A dozen or so oak tables and booths were evenly spaced throughout the restaurant. The walls were covered with original paintings, old photographs, and mounted fish. Dugan's favorite, a blacktip shark, hung above the entrance.

Dugan weaved through the tables of chatty customers to an empty booth in the back corner. He glanced at the big screen TV to the right of the liquor cabinet behind the bar. An ESPN reporter announced yesterday's baseball scores. Dugan could care less about professional sports. To Dugan, America's infatuation with athletes and movie stars proved how far the nation had strayed from sound principles and priorities. A cop protects local citizens, and a fireman lays down his life for his neighbors, and both get paid about $35,000 a year. A movie star hams it up on film, and a pro athlete plays a game, and both make about $35 million a year. Yeah, that makes sense. Considering the examples America idolizes, Dugan wasn't surprised that so many people try any shortcut they can to make a fast buck.

Glancing up, Dugan caught sight of Russell Goodwin entering the restaurant. He waved to get his attention, and Goodwin waved back. Dugan stood and greeted him with a firm handshake.

Goodwin slid into the booth. "I'm starved. What's the best sandwich here at Poor Richard's?"

Dugan eased back onto the seat. "I like the hot roast beef with provolone cheese. The clam chowder's great too."

"Sounds good." He patted his stomach. "I've got room for both."

The waitress, a pudgy brunette in her late forties, sauntered over with pen and pad in hand. "Usual, Sheriff?"

"Yeah, and give me a large coffee with two creams."

She turned and gazed at Goodwin.

"I'm assuming Sheriff Walton's usual is the roast beef sandwich with provolone cheese. Put me down for that too and throw in a bowl of clam chowder. Let's see, to drink I'll take a tall glass of iced tea."

The brunette jotted their orders. "Be right back with your drinks."

Goodwin sat back in his chair and linked his hands behind his head. "Tell me about the accident."

"I was at the Cape Hatteras Lighthouse when Mrs. Brackenbury called. Said she was being followed by a black SUV. I told her to make a turn onto a side street to see if the vehicle was just tailgating her or actually following her. Unfortunately, she turned onto Billy Mitchell Road."

"The one by the airstrip?"

Dugan nodded. "That's an isolated stretch of highway until you get to the campground, and there aren't many campers this time of year. She panicked and hit the gas."

"That doesn't surprise me. She gets agitated. I've seen her upset a few times when I was assigned to accompany them for protective services."

"I'm not sure if the SUV followed her into the campground or not. She was flying down the camp road and didn't realize it made a 180-degree turn at the end. That's when she lost control and flipped the car."

"Where were you?"

"I eventually turned onto Billy Mitchell Road. I didn't see any SUV coming the other way. It's possible the aggressor exited the campground and made a left onto the beach. That's one way to get out of there unnoticed."

Goodwin put his hands on the table and leaned forward. "That would have been a lucky break if you got a glimpse of the driver."

Dugan shrugged. "That's true, but I didn't. When I got to the scene of the accident, I pulled Mrs. Brackenbury out of the Escalade and called the rescue squad. She had a cut on her forehead but refused to go to the hospital."

"That doesn't surprise me either. She's a strange one, a little crazy. When I was on assignment with them, she always wanted to talk about the supernatural realm—spirits, ghosts, past lives. I indulged her, but only out of a sense of duty. I wanted to tell her to get off at the next stop—the *Twilight Zone*."

After the waitress delivered their drinks, Goodwin updated Dugan on the complications of the investigation on his end. His research team felt confident the murderer had no terrorist ties to the Middle East or other known terror organizations. They were convinced the killer had more regional motives. The agency's public relations coordinator did her best to keep the news media from wild speculation, promising more information in the near future. Goodwin reasoned the killer had two intentions: Number 1 -Stop Brackenbury from proceeding with his development plans on Ocracoke; Number 2 - Discourage his wife, other politicians, and investors from taking up Brackenbury's objective. Currently, his team focused on researching possible persons of interest including all members of the Ocracoke Preservation Society.

Dugan rubbed his chin. "When you think about it, we *are* dealing with a terrorist."

"You're right, but not the conventional kind. This person is so obsessed with Ocracoke Island that he is willing to kill to preserve it."

"The killer must have known the kind of power Brackenbury could wield."

Goodwin took a big gulp of his iced tea. "No doubt about it. Clearly, there's a lot of money to be made if this theme park concept is realized. Adelaide Brackenbury, the politicians who can pull the legal strings, and the investors could still strike gold on Ocracoke."

Dugan sat back in his chair. "That makes me wonder about the séance last night."

"Yeah. I'm anxious to hear about the séance. What happened?"

"Talk about getting off in the *Twilight Zone*. The two paranormal researchers, Sienna Bryce and Luna Holiday, were there along with some world famous medium by the name of Darrin Brownstone. The guy was definitely good. We all sat around this table that reminded me of an Ouija board. Brownstone opened up by asking if there were any spirits present willing to speak to us. Now this is crazy, but I saw it with my own eyes—a wine glass in the middle of the table moved by itself and stopped at the word 'YES'."

"Did the glass vibrate?"

"Yes."

"There had to have been some kind of mechanism. Remember playing the vibrating football game when you were a kid?"

"Sure."

"With the right gizmo, a glass can be directed by vibrations. It was probably located directly under the table. What happened next?"

"Brownstone channeled the old lighthouse keeper. It was quite a production. The lighthouse keeper claimed he knew all the ghosts on the island. Then Addy . . . I mean Mrs. Brackenbury asked if we could speak to her dead husband." Oh no, Dugan thought, I slipped.

Goodwin eyed Dugan and nodded slowly. "Go on."

"Well . . . this is the spooky part. Something blew out the candle in the middle of the table. Now it was pitch black. Above us this odd glow appeared, like a wavering face. Then a voice started talking in a British accent. The voice sounded like it was coming from above."

Goodwin chuckled. "That Brownstone is good. What did the ghost of Brackenbury have to say?"

"He told Mrs. Brackenbury to beware because the same person that murdered him was out to get her. Then he insisted that she proceed with the development plans. He said the spirits of the island wanted to be heard. That's when I cut in and asked him who the murderer was."

"I'm guessing he didn't name names."

"No. There was a loud thump and the glow vanished. One of the paranormal researchers lit the candle. Brownstone had thudded onto the table. He came to and claimed he couldn't maintain contact with Brackenbury. Then Mrs. Brackenbury went into some kind of trance and started screaming. When she came out of it, she said she was being chased by a man dressed in black."

"Geeesh. Bet you felt like you landed in a cuckoo's nest."

"For sure. I still can't figure out how Brownstone made Brackenbury's ghost appear."

"Had to be some kind of projection triggered by remote control. After the candle was blown out, the smoke hovered above you. The wavering face reflected off of the smoke. All Brownstone had to do was hit the remote and throw his voice."

"That makes sense. If that's the case, then Sienna and Luna had to be in on it. They are the ones who invited Brownstone to come and were with him at the lighthouse before we got there. Certainly they saw him set up the devices to pull off the ghost tricks."

"No doubt about it. The question is why did they want to do this?"

"Because . . ." Dugan linked his hands together on the table, ". . . they're invested."

"I agree. They have something to gain if Adelaide Brackenbury moves forward on the development of Ocracoke."

The waitress brought their food, and they spent the next fifteen minutes scarfing down their sandwiches and clam chowder. In between bites they volleyed ideas back and forth concerning the motives of various suspects.

Dugan wiped his mouth with a napkin, sat back, and stretched. "So we've eliminated Brownstone and the paranormal researchers as potential killers."

"More or less. I'm guessing Rowland Brackenbury hired them to convince Adelaide to move forward on the project. They're partners in the development business, and she can be stubborn. He knew her weakness was spiritualism. Perhaps he offered the paranormal researchers and Brownstone stock options and promised their investment would soar once the theme park opened. They would have nothing to gain by Brackenbury's death. Once he was murdered, they conspired to sway Adelaide to proceed with the plans by means of the séance. That would insure their investment."

"That leaves Achak Rowtag as the prime suspect."

Goodwin tilted his head and closed one eye slightly. "My money is on Rowtag, but we've discovered that several members of the Ocracoke Preservation Society could also be categorized as extreme environmentalists. They may be working behind the scenes in concert with Rowtag."

"No kidding. I figured most of those people were harmless tree-huggers."

"You'd be surprised by the level of their commitment. Here's something else to consider. This morning Mee Mee called. They spotted the strange bird last night in the Ohio Valley. The creature attacked just like it did at Springer's Point."

"Did she say it was the exact same bird?"

Goodwin nodded. "That's not all. After the bird flew off, a white Chevy cargo van with North Carolina plates passed them. Mee Mee swears it's the same van that drives past her bookstore every day, one that belongs to Achak Rowtag."

"Interesting. That means that Achak is the Birdman of Frisco."

A Beach Boys' song, "Good Vibrations," resounded from Goodwin's shirt pocket. He pulled out his cellphone and pressed it to his ear. "Agent Goodwin speaking. . . .Judge Hawkings, it's good to hear back from you. . . Okay . . . Sounds good . . . I really appreciate this . . . Would it be possible for you to fax it to the Sheriff's office in Manteo? . . . That would be great. Thanks again." He sat up and slid the phone back into his pocket. "Excellent."

"What's up?"

"Judge Hawkins just approved a search warrant for Achak Rowtag's premises. I called him this morning after talking with Mee Mee. Her identification of Rowtag's van was just enough to convince him to approve the search warrant."

Dugan threw a twenty dollar bill onto the table. "What are we waiting for? Let's go find the murder weapon."

Chapter 19

Pastor Byron lived by himself in a small subdivision known as Floral Valley at the north end of Martins Ferry, Ohio along Route 7. His wife had lost her battle against cancer several years before, and Mee Mee noticed the house needed dusted and freshened up. The spare bedrooms were comfortable, though, and Mee Mee had slept like a tired toddler despite having to deal with the frenzy of another Thunderbird attack the night before. Was she getting used to it, or had the last few days worn her out? She was sure it was the latter. The morning had passed quickly, eating a good breakfast, catching up on all the news, and relaxing. Mee Mee and Marla planned on heading back to North Carolina later that afternoon.

About noon Mee Mee climbed into the passenger seat of Pastor Byron's Chevy Equinox to head to Martins Ferry City Park. When Pastor Byron discovered Mee Mee had recently taken up running, he wanted to take her on his favorite run—the Four-Bridge Five Miler. The out-and-back route crossed the Ohio

River four times. Mee Mee agreed to go on the condition that they run at her pace—ten minutes per mile. Pastor Byron had no problem with that, claiming his competitive days were over. Now he ran to clear his mind and burn calories. Marla had no interest in joining them. She planned on stopping by her aunt's house to check on her son, Gabriel. She looked forward to catching up with her relatives.

Pastor Byron parked in the city pool parking lot behind the recreation center. They walked past the deserted pool and entered the shade of the park's towering elm trees. An old sandstone fountain, ten feet high and somewhat shaped like an hour glass, spouted water which splashed into a circular moat surrounded by a wrought iron fence. The temperature had risen into the 70's, and the sun filtered through the boughs above, spattering a nearby copper-colored statue of a World War I soldier with golden splotches.

As they went through basic stretches, Pastor Byron said, "The old bones are creaking this morning."

Mee Mee smiled. "I didn't realize my creaks were that loud."

"Not you. I'm talking about me."

"I'm just glad I can still run five miles."

"Me, too. Most of my old running buddies can't do it any more—bad knees, bad hips, heart problems, plantar fasciitis, you name it."

"Knock on wood." Mee Mee reached and tapped on the trunk of the nearest elm tree. "Let's hope nothing serious happens to us."

"Yeah, I want to keep running on into my seventies and even eighties."

They finished their stretches and headed out at an easy pace. Running along the streets of Martins Ferry, Mee Mee noticed the town resembled her old home town of Star City seventy miles southeast of here in West Virginia. Most of the old houses with their peeling paint and tired porches needed updating. The cracked and uneven sidewalks posed a challenge when it came to sure footing, but the town had a nostalgic feel with friendly people waving and kids playing in the yards. The foothills of the Alleghenies rose up on both sides of the river reminding her of the hilly terrain back home.

As they jogged along, Pastor Byron asked, "So what have you learned about this Thunderbird on your travels up in these parts?"

"The creature is definitely the same one I saw on the Outer Banks. Clearly, someone has trained it and transported it up here to terrorize people who live in fracking zones."

"But who and why?"

"We believe the person to be a Native American by the name of Achak Rowtag. He's an extreme environmentalist. An influential British diplomat with political ties in the U.S. threatened to develop Ocracoke Island. Now he's dead. It seems like something bad happens wherever the bird shows up."

"Did anything happen up in Pennsylvania when you were there?"

"Yeah, there was an explosion in a house where methane gas built up in the kitchen from a contaminated well. An old guy died in the explosion when he lit his morning cigarette."

"Good golly, that's a terrible thing to happen to someone. I guess the shooting in Youngstown adds to the curse of this bird."

"Right. I feel bad for Marla, but if she hadn't been there, who knows how many of those oil and gas workers would have been shot."

"Poor Marla. Things haven't been easy for her these last few years." Pastor Byron pointed to an old rusty blue bridge on the left that spanned the Ohio River. "That's the Aetnaville Bridge, the first of four that we'll be crossing. It was built back in the late 1800's."

"Is it safe?"

"Oh yeah. I've been running across it for forty years. About twenty-seven years ago inspectors declared it unsafe for vehicular traffic, but pedestrians can still use it. Lots of people on the south end of Wheeling Island appreciate that they can walk across to get to their jobs on this side."

Steel mesh comprised the flooring of the bridge. Mee Mee focused through the grating to the brownish-green water forty feet below. The flow of the current unsettled her, so she looked up and kept her eyes on the roadway at the end of the bridge.

"Looking at the river made me a little dizzy."

"You get used to it."

After crossing the bridge they made a right on the street that ran along the river on the east side of Wheeling Island. Mee Mee could see the city on the banks of the other side. A row of Victorian houses followed by red-brick and beige-brick buildings ten to twelve stories high lined the shore. "I'm guessing we'll be crossing over to Wheeling on another bridge."

"Yep. The Wheeling Suspension Bridge is about a half mile from here. It's older than the Aetnaville Bridge."

"Wonderful. Can you see the river through the walkway?"

"Yep. Like I said, though, you get used to it."

No problem, Mee Mee thought. I used to wind surf on the ocean. I'm not afraid of river water, but then again, there wasn't a forty foot drop into the ocean.

"So why do you think this Achak Rowtag wants to terrorize people with his eagle?" Pastor Byron asked.

"Good question. If it is Achak, I'm guessing he wants to create fear in people living in areas where the environment is threatened. The Thunderbird becomes a symbol of nature's protest against man's mismanagement of the earth."

"That makes sense, but why do bad things happen wherever the bird shows up?"

"That's even a better question. Rowland Brackenbury's murder was intentional, but everything else appears to be coincidental. The explosion and water contaminations in Pennsylvania, the earthquakes and shootings in Youngstown, the murder of the college student and rape of the high school girl here in the Ohio Valley wasn't caused by a particular person or organization with specific goals."

"Maybe so, but with the fracking industry you don't need to make bad things happen. They just do. Everything you named could be attributed to the fracking industry."

"Good point," Mee Mee said.

"Of course, there's no hydraulic fracturing on Ocracoke Island. Maybe the murderer killed Brackenbury to maintain the mystique of the Thunderbird."

"The murder may have accomplished that, but I don't believe

the goal was to build the bird's legend."

"What was the goal?" Pastor Byron asked.

"To stop the development of Ocracoke before it started. Murdering one man wouldn't stop the fracking industry, but it did stop Rowland Brackenbury in his tracks. "

"What about his wife? Has she given up on the project?"

"Not yet. She's still weighing the decision, but that possibility puts her life in jeopardy."

"Sounds like they need to arrest this Achak Rowtag."

"They're working on it. But he might not be a lone wolf. There may be a group of radicalized people in cahoots with him. The Secret Service agent working on the case informed me that Adelaide Brackenbury was followed by a suspicious vehicle yesterday. It couldn't have been Achak because he was here."

"I wouldn't want to be in her shoes." Pastor Byron pointed to the left toward the river. "There's the Wheeling Suspension Bridge. At one time it was the longest suspension bridge in the country."

The tall sandstone towers, nearly one hundred feet high, rose majestically from the base of the masonry. The impressive span arched over the river suspended by hundreds of thick cables. Red railings along the walkway and the blue and white cables combined to foster a sense of patriotism within Mee Mee. A topless lime green Jeep passed them on the steel mesh roadbed, the driver waving and smiling. The wind had picked up by the time they reached the middle of the span, increasing that uplifting sensation. Mee Mee spotted several pleasure boats cruising on the water and noticed a large amphitheater to the right near the water's edge. Farther down she noticed some kind of civic arena. Wheeling appeared to be a happening place.

A sudden jolt almost tumbled Mee Mee to the walkway. "What was that?"

Pastor Byron had kept from falling by catching the railing.

The jolts continued even harder. The bridge began to rock and waver.

Pastor Byron shouted, "It's an earthquake!"

Mee Mee glanced at the far tower. The large sandstone blocks cracked and crumbled with each shudder of the bridge. Cables snapped with loud zings. As the bridge swayed back and forth, the lime green Jeep tumbled off and made a humungous splash in the river. Mee Mee held on to the nearest cable for dear life as other vehicles and people fell through the rupturing metal and dropped forty feet into the water. A few hundred yards downriver, she glimpsed the interstate bridge snapping in half mid-way. Cars slammed on their brakes and slid off the edge, spiraling downward.

A tremendous groan erupted from only a few feet away. Mee Mee watched with terror as the metal roadway split in half. The swaying stopped for a second, but then came the downward descent as the bridge plummeted toward the water. Mee Mee let go of the cable and tried to gain control of her body position as she fell. The slow-motion descent felt like a nightmare filled with the shrieks of tearing metal and falling debris. She managed to rotate toward the brownish-green abyss just before she hit the surface.

Chapter 20

Mee Mee slammed into the surface of the water. Coldness and blackness swallowed her. She sank into the depths, her body growing numb. Struggling to overcome the shock, she forced her eyes open. Brownish-green murkiness clouded her vision. Lifting her head, she saw a glimmer of light above her. Odd muffled noises reverberated around her. She needed air, needed to get to the surface, but her stunned arms and legs wouldn't cooperate. Her feet touched the bottom. One foot sunk into mud, but the other came to rest on a hard, smooth surface. A flat stone? She plucked her foot out of the mud and managed to slide it onto the stone next to the other. Now she could surge upward.

Her lungs ached for oxygen. Gathering all her strength, she sprung off the rock towards the surface. She had to breathe but not yet, not yet, not yet. She couldn't hold off any longer and sucked water into her nostrils and mouth. Darkness enveloped her.

Slowly, the light appeared again. She reached for the surface. Was she rising? The light became brighter. Was she breathing? Her head broke the surface. She kept rising. What was lifting her? Now she was above the river. She glanced down. Debris and bodies were scattered across the surface. One man lugged a body towards shore, one arm wrapped around the victim and the other stroking the water. Was that Pastor Byron? The back end of a red car jutted up out of the water, bobbed, and slowly sank. Tangled and ruptured cables sagged into the water, some extending back towards shore. Several people struggled to keep their heads above the surface. She wanted to help, but the chaotic scene drifted away.

Everything blurred, as if she had entered a cloud. An overwhelming sense of peace pervaded her being, lifting her higher. She moved through a tunnel of clouds towards a small blue opening. *Did I die? Where am I?* It didn't matter. She felt free, no longer imprisoned by her body. She stared at the blue opening and noticed a soft glow of light. *Was that God?* Warmth flowed over her. She felt connected to this glow and assured that nothing could harm her.

The scene of the bridge collapse flashed before her but did not upset her. *Will I be sent back to help?* She was willing to go back but didn't want to lose this connection, this sense of wholeness and unconditional love. In the distance she heard an odd chanting. Another path opened before her. Do I go that way? The chanting became louder, a male voice with steady rhythm but indistinguishable words. She felt compelled to move in the direction of the voice. She drifted towards the chanting as the sense of tranquility faded and anxiety increased.

The Thunderbird appeared, and fear surged through her. It spread its wings and hovered on an updraft. Its fierce eyes and huge talons menaced her. She wanted to turn back and escape the creature's presence, but she felt obligated to seek out the voice. Far below, she could see the man. He stood bare chested with hands raised. His long black hair spilled from his receding hairline and dangled to the middle of his back. He was chanting some kind of Native American prayer or anthem. She recognized him—Achak Rowtag.

The Thunderbird descended and hovered just above Achak. He appeared to be worshiping the creature. She floated downward, suspended above the bird and Achak. *Does he know I'm here?*. Although she could not understand the language, she sensed the meaning of the words. Achak was praising the Animikii for bringing its wrath upon the earth because of the greed of men. He asked the creature to protect Ocracoke Island and destroy anyone who threatened its shores.

Mee Mee cried out, "Achak! Achak Rowtag! Can you hear me!"

Achak's words slurred and stopped. He opened his eyes and focused on Mee Mee.

The Thunderbird rose as if lifted by an updraft and faded into the clouds above.

Achak's eyebrows knotted. "Who are you?"

"Mee Mee Roberts."

"Why have you entered the spiritual realm?"

"I don't know why I'm here. I don't even know if I'm still alive."

"From where have you come?"

"From a place where the earth shook violently. I fell off a bridge into a river and sank to the bottom, but then something lifted me up. I went through a tunnel of clouds, but then I heard your voice. I felt led to come to you."

Achak smiled, closed his eyes and lifted his hands, his mouth moving, chanting quietly.

"Why am I here?"

Achak opened his eyes. "You are a messenger."

"I am?" Mee Mee scoured her mind but could not think of any kind of message to share with him. "But I don't have anything to say."

"You have already told me what I need to know."

"Do you mean about the earthquake?"

"Yes. The Animikii has answered my prayers and brought great destruction upon the earth. It is only the beginning if man does not change his ways."

The fire of indignity burned within her. "Why are you praising this creature for such destruction? Many innocent people fell to their deaths."

The creases in Achak's brow and cheeks deepened. "Do not be angry with the Animikii. He is only the agent of consequence. Be angry with the ones whose actions bring forth the consequences."

"If the Thunderbird brings death and destruction, I could never applaud its mission."

"Often men will not listen unless death and destruction assail them."

"Is that why Rowland Brackenbury had to die? So that people would fear to cross the line you have drawn in the sand?"

Achak laughed. "Yes, but the line I have drawn is not mine. I am only an emissary of our Mother, the Earth. Wherever my people have roamed, lived, and died is sacred. The soil is sacred. The animals, trees, wind, and water are all sacred. I have been called to protect the land."

The threat against Adelaide Brackenbury's life entered Mee Mee's thoughts. "But how many more people must die to protect your sacred land?"

"I do not determine who or how many must die. They determine their own fate by their choices. I enter the spiritual realm to call upon the Animikii to seek out those who have doomed themselves because of their foolish decisions. Their deaths demand a decision from those who have the means to pollute or preserve our Great Mother."

Mee Mee felt exasperated. "But I didn't pollute Mother Earth, yet I'm here. What did I do to deserve this?"

Achak's dark eyes intensified. "The question is what will you do? You must make a decision."

"What kind of decision?"

"To live or die."

Mee Mee tried to grasp the essence of his words. Did she have the power to return to her body? As she stared down at him, she noticed his form diminishing as if she were floating upwards again. The anxiety and frustration faded as she ascended through the tunnel of clouds. A peace, one that she could not describe or understand, flooded through her being again. She sensed the warmth, love, and unity of an all-powerful being. Then she suddenly knew she could not stay in that paradise. Her responsibilities on earth had not been completed. She agreed to let go and felt herself slipping back like a skydiver parachuting down through the clouds. The warmth and unfathomable peace faded as she descended.

Looking down, she saw the twisted metal of the bridge sagging from the shores into the river. As she neared the surface she moved horizontally, gliding just above the choppy water. She passed over bodies and debris. A child struggled to hang onto a floating log. Mee Mee tried to reach out but did not have the physical capability to grasp the child's hand. She glanced up as she neared the shore. She recognized Pastor Byron. He knelt over a drowning victim, leaned over the body, and administered mouth to mouth resuscitation. Then he straightened up, placed both hands on the person's chest, and applied heart compressions. If only she could help.

She hovered above him, observing his desperate efforts. Finally, he straightened again, arched his back, lifted his hands to the sky and prayed, "Help me, God! Save this woman!" Now she could see the victim. She stared in horror as she recognized the pale, lifeless face—her face.

Chapter 21

Dugan turned on to Timber Trail at the north end of Frisco. Pine trees and live oaks lined the narrow asphalt road. Every few hundred feet modest homes could be spotted along its route, most serving as residences for the locals. Achak lived near the end of the road. As soon as Dugan pulled into Achak's driveway, barking erupted from the back of the house. He spotted an old white Chevy cargo van parked in the shadows under the residence, which was elevated by eight-foot pilings.

"Looks like our boy made it back safe and sound," Russell Goodwin said.

"Yeah." Dugan put the car in park and turned off the engine. "He must have driven all night."

"At least we won't have to break down the door."

They exited the Ford Interceptor and walked to the steps on the side of the house.

Goodwin stopped at the bottom and held up his hand. "Do you hear that?"

Dugan tilted his head and listened. A muffled chanting came from inside the house. He glanced at Goodwin. "We might be interrupting some sacred meditation. Achak claims to be a shaman."

"I'm surprised the dog's barking didn't snap him out of it. He must be totally entranced."

They mounted the wooden stairs as quietly as possible. Everything had been stained a drab brown—the steps, the railings, the siding, and the deck, which extended across the full length of the side of the house. At the top, Dugan eased toward the window and leaned to look. Achak faced the opposite wall wearing only a loincloth. His black hair dangled to the middle of his back. With his hands raised, he bobbed his head as he chanted some Native American prayer. An abstract painting of the Thunderbird hung above the fireplace. Wisps of smoke rose from bowls placed on each side of the mantel.

Achak stretched his arms upward, hands open, then clenched his fists and drew them down toward his chest. He kept repeating the motion and words. After several intervals Achak's body shook as if a cop had just tasered him. Once he regained composure, he went back to the hand motions. The intense gestures and incantations sent an odd sensation up the middle of Dugan's spine. Was the shaman beseeching the Thunderbird to do his bidding, to bring down its wrath upon the earth? That was Dugan's interpretation of the ritual.

Goodwin stood behind Dugan, peering over his shoulder. He grasped Dugan's elbow and pulled him away from the window. Goodwin raised his eyebrows. "Enough of this. Let's knock." He rapped loudly on the door, and the chanting stopped.

About thirty seconds later the door opened. Achak stood there half naked, his tanned, middle-aged body sagging around his belly and chest. The strong smell of incense, possibly cedarwood, assaulted Dugan's nostrils. "Good afternoon, Sheriff Walton. Please excuse my appearance. Seeking the spirit realm is part of my daily routine."

"We apologize for interrupting," Dugan said. "This is Agent Russell Goodwin from the Secret Service."

Achak extended his hand. "Nice to make your acquaintance."

Goodwin shook his hand. "We have some important questions to ask you."

"Certainly." Achak swung the door wide open. "Please come in."

They entered, and Achak motioned to a threadbare brown couch with a geometrically designed blanket draped over the back. The blanket with its red, white, and black zigzagging pattern added zest to the dull room. "Please, have a seat." Dugan and Goodwin settled onto the couch, and Achak sat on a wooden rocking chair next to the fireplace.

Dugan noticed the painting of the Thunderbird and the blanket had similar colors and patterns. He pointed above the fireplace. "Nice painting."

Achak nodded, rocking gently in the chair. "Thank you. It's the image of the Animikii."

Goodwin scooted forward on the couch. "Is that similar to the Thunderbird?"

"Yes. The Animikii is the Thunderbird, the great bird who brings the storm."

Goodwin rubbed his chin. "Interesting. Do you believe the Animikii made its appearance at Springer's Point a few nights ago when you were there with Rowland Brackenbury?"

Achak crossed his arms and stopped rocking. "Yes. I believe so."

"Do you own or train a large eagle?" Goodwin asked.

Achak smiled. "Eagles and ospreys are my friends. An osprey nests in my back yard. But no one owns these birds. They are free."

Goodwin persisted, "But have you ever trained an eagle or an osprey?"

"No."

"Why did you leave town shortly after Brackenbury was murdered?" Goodwin asked.

Achak shrugged. "I did not know Brackenbury was murdered. I did not know he died until I read it in the papers."

Dugan cleared his throat. "Where did you go?"

"I do a lot of traveling up along the east coast and as far west as Ohio. Most of my trips are prompted by environmental concerns."

Goodwin said, "Our records show that you have been arrested several times at environmental protests."

Achak nodded. "I'm willing to sacrifice my freedom for my beliefs. These threatened lands where we protest are sacred."

Goodwin's eyes narrowed. "How far are you willing to go to protect these sacred lands?"

"As far as I need to go."

"So you would be willing to kill another human being, if necessary, to protect the land?"

Achak placed his arms on the armrests, rocked slowly forward and stopped. "That would be an option. Are you accusing me of murder?"

Goodwin shook his head. "Not yet, but if you're willing to confess, we'll certainly take your statement."

The creases in Achak's face deepened. "I'm no murderer."

"In that case . . .," Goodwin reached into his shirt pocket and pulled out the search warrant, unfolded it, and held it up, ". . . we have a warrant to search your premises and your vehicle for evidence in the murder of Rowland Brackenbury."

Achak began rocking slowly again. "Search to your heart's content. I have nothing to hide."

Goodwin glanced at Dugan and shrugged. "Okay." He stood. "We'll start in this room and work our way to the back of the house. We prefer that you stay with us as we go through the premises."

Achak slowly bobbed his head. "You want to keep your eye on me."

Goodwin held out his hands and jutted his chin. "Obviously, we don't want you wandering to another part of the house and removing items that may have a connection to this case."

"Fine. I will stay with you. I guarantee you won't find anything that can be used as evidence against me in the murder of Rowland Brackenbury."

"We'll see," Goodwin said.

Dugan thought Achak sounded overconfident, as if he knew this probe was coming and prepared by tucking away anything that could incriminate him. Perhaps he recognized Mee Mee's

Jeep Cherokee when he passed them last night on that country road and accurately calculated the possibility of being linked to the Thunderbird. Investigators, of course, would consider the Thunderbird tie a possible thread leading to the murder.

They quickly searched the front room as Achak rocked and watched them. The room was furnished simply with a couch, recliner, the rocking chair, and a couple of lamps. One lamp stand had a drawer, but Dugan discovered it contained only a few nature magazines and a small flashlight.

A hallway led to the back of the house. They entered the first door on the right, Achak sandwiched between them. It was a bedroom, sparely furnished and probably the guest bedroom. An old black and white photograph of a famous Native American hung above the queen size bed. Dugan had seen the image before in history books. The Native American sat facing the camera and holding a peace pipe. He wore a buckskin shirt, and one large feather stood straight up from the back of his head.

Dugan pointed to the portrait. "Is that Geronimo?"

Achak grunted. "Geronimo wouldn't pose so peacefully. That is Sitting Bull, the Lakota holy man."

"Was he a shaman like you?" Dugan asked.

Achak smiled, a smile that struck Dugan as eerie. "Yes. He was a shaman and a medicine man. You may find this interesting: Sitting Bull had a vision of many government soldiers falling down as thick as grasshoppers in the Lakota camp."

Goodwin closed a drawer of a pine dresser he was inspecting. "Is that right? Was there anything significant about the vision?"

Achak's smile grew wider. "He received this vision right before the Battle of Little Big Horn."

"Hmmph." Goodwin's eyes met Dugan's. "He prophesied Custer's Last Stand. Old Sitting Bull must have been consuming some high octane mushrooms that day."

It didn't take long to inspect the rest of the room. The dresser drawers contained some clothing but nothing significant. In the bottom of the only closet Dugan found a variety of shoes including Nike cross trainers, moccasins, and hiking boots. A few light weight jackets hung on the rod above the shoes, and books were stacked on the shelf above the jackets.

They walked down the hall and made a left into the second bedroom. Immediately, Dugan noticed the knife display hanging above the king size bed. Six bone knives were mounted in columns of three against a burlap backing presented in a plain oak frame.

Goodwin walked to the foot of the bed and motioned toward the knives. "Are those Native American relics?"

Achak nodded. "Yes. All six were found on the Outer Banks. Two of them are estimated to be over three hundred years old."

"Very impressive," Goodwin said. "Do you mind if I take a closer look?"

"You've got a warrant that says you can do what you want."

Goodwin smiled. "Good point." He climbed onto the bed, reached above the headboard, and took down the display. After scooting back off the bed, he motioned Dugan to check out the knives.

They ranged in length from about six inches to fifteen inches. Their handles were wrapped in worn leather, and several had patterns of varied colored bands of fiber wrapped around the leather. The bone blades varied from a dull white to a yellowish shade. Dugan leaned closer and examined the tips of the knives. Three were sharp and undamaged, but Dugan could see where the other three lacked a sharp point. A small fragment had been broken off each of them.

Dugan pointed to the tip of the top right knife, the one with the smallest bit of tip missing. "What do you think? A possible match?"

"We may have found the missing piece to the puzzle." Goodwin glanced over his shoulder at Achak. "We'll be taking this knife display with us as possible evidence."

"Just so I get it back."

Goodwin chuckled. "Well . . . if these prove to be immaterial to the case, we'll certainly return them. But if they serve to convict you, I'm guessing the state prison system won't approve of knife displays in your cell."

Achak shrugged. "So that's how Brackenbury died—a knife in the back."

Goodwin eyed Achak. "How did you know he was stabbed *in the back*?"

"Just a logical guess." Achak smiled, that eerie smile.

Dugan wondered what was going through the shaman's mind. His expression seemed to reveal hidden knowledge, as if he had just made a mental connection to something very significant. Oddly, he didn't seem worried at all that a Secret Service agent had just confiscated a possible murder weapon.

They headed to the back of the house to inspect the kitchen. Again, the room was simply furnished with basic oak cabinets and a pine table with four wooden chairs, scuffed and worn. It didn't take long to go through the cabinets and food pantry. They found nothing out of the ordinary.

Goodwin gazed out the window above the sink. "Is that your pet osprey in the nest on top of the totem pole?"

Achak edged closer to the window and tilted his head to see over Goodwin's shoulder. "That's my friend, not my pet. It looks like feeding time for the young."

Goodwin faced Achak. "Yeah, the bird caught a snake for lunch. Nice catch."

Achak nodded. "Snakes are good eating."

Dugan smiled. "I've caught a few snakes myself."

Achak continued to stare out the window. "That's a moccasin. Be careful if you try to pick up a moccasin. They are . . . shrewd . . . and sometimes deadly."

"The ones I've captured are now in cages, and I'm still alive and well."

Achak nodded, the odd smile furrowing his cheeks. "Count yourself lucky to this point in life."

"Not lucky, just well trained."

Goodwin said, "We're about done here, but we'd like to take a look at your van before we leave."

"Not a problem. Give me a minute to get dressed." Achak sauntered down the hallway and into his bedroom.

Dugan motioned toward the hallway. "He doesn't seem overly concerned about a possible murder charge."

Goodwin nodded. "He lives on a different level."

"What do you mean?"

"He has his own spiritual perspective. What we call murder, he would consider a righteous judgment. In his mind he's not a murderer."

A few minutes later Achak emerged wearing jeans, flip flops, and a denim shirt with frayed short sleeves. "Follow me." At a leisurely pace he led them to the front of the house, out the door, and down the steps.

"Wait here a second." Goodwin took the knife display and placed it in the back seat of the Interceptor. Then he returned and said, "Okay, go ahead and open up the van."

Achak walked between the pilings into the shadows under the house and used his key to unlock the front door of the van. He pulled open the door and stood back. "Search to your heart's content."

"Open the back doors too," Goodwin said. "Sheriff Walton, could you check out the back and I'll inspect the front?"

"Sure thing."

Dugan and Achak walked to the back of the van, and Achak unlocked the doors and opened them. Dugan noticed a few random items scattered in the back—a black, collapsible umbrella, jumper cables, a tire pump, a box of wrenches, and a couple of soiled rags. Dugan could see Goodwin in the front of the vehicle sitting in the passenger's seat, probably rummaging through the glove compartment. Dugan climbed into the back on his hands and knees. He spotted a brown feather, about four inches long next to the umbrella. He picked it up and took a closer look. Gently, he tucked it into his front pocket. Farther up into the bed of the van he found two more, one smaller and one slightly larger. All three matched in color and texture. He slid them into his front pocket. Other than the feathers, he found nothing unusual.

As Goodwin and Dugan finished their search, Achak waited patiently with his arms crossed, that eerie smile pasted on his face. Dugan glanced at him occasionally, wondering what in the world he knew that created such an odd expression. Finally, Dugan backed out of the van and walked toward Achak. Goodwin joined him.

Dugan reached into his shirt pocket, extracted a feather, and eyed Achak. "I found three of these in the back of your van. They appear to be eagle feathers."

Achak leaned toward Dugan and examined the feather. "Could be."

Goodwin asked, "Have you transported a large bird in the back of your van recently?"

"No. Perhaps the feathers were stuck to the bottom of my shoes and fell off when I was loading the back of the van for one of my trips."

"That seems unlikely," Dugan said.

"Unlikely, maybe, but possible," Achak said.

Goodwin cleared his throat. "Listen, Achak. It shouldn't take us long to examine and evaluate these confiscated items to see if they establish conclusive evidence in this case. Until we do, you are not to leave town. Postpone any trips you may have scheduled until we give you the all clear. Do you understand?"

Achak nodded. "I have no plans of traveling in the near future."

"I'm curious," Dugan said. "When we arrived, we saw you performing some kind of ritual in front of the painting of the Thunderbird. It looked to me like you were calling upon the bird to bring down some kind of wrath upon the earth. Is that anywhere close to being an accurate interpretation?"

"You are very observant, Sheriff Walton. That was exactly the intent of the ritual."

Goodwin straightened and placed his hands on his hips. "What kind of disaster were you trying to conjure up?"

Achak smiled that eerie smile. "An earthquake."

Chapter 22

Dugan drove north on Route 12 through the town of Buxton on the way back to the Sheriff's office in Manteo. With the knife display in their possession, he felt confident they would wrap up the investigation soon. Achak's eerie smile kept infiltrating his thoughts. "What do you think? Is Achak the snake that bit the diplomat?"

"I'm sure he is." Goodwin glanced at the knife display in the back seat. Now we just have to match up one of those bone blades with the missing tip."

"He's a weird one, isn't he?"

Goodwin wobbled his hand in front of him. "He's out there. I've seen it again and again: If a person embraces extreme beliefs about a cause or religion, he is willing to cross society's boundaries. To me, these kinds of people are more dangerous than common criminals. They're motivated by what they consider to be a higher truth. Humanity takes a back seat to their fanatical views. Rowland Brackenbury was the unfortunate victim of Achak's fanaticism."

"Yeah, he's definitely off the charts. Watching him go through that ritual in front of the Thunderbird convinced me he's psycho. He actually thinks he can bring down a natural disaster upon the earth. I wonder where he keeps the eagle."

"Hard to say. He may have a storage barn on some secluded part of the island. He's smart enough to keep the bird out of sight. We'll find it. If the knife evidence pans out, and we arrest him on murder charges, I'm sure he'll fess up about the eagle's whereabouts."

"Right. If he cares for the bird, he won't let the poor thing starve in some cage while he awaits trial in jail."

Dugan's cell phone rang, a strident old fashioned ringtone. He hit the Bluetooth button on the steering wheel to engage hands-free calling. "Sheriff Walton here."

"Dugan, this is Marla." Her voice sounded tense.

"What's up?"

"There's been a terrible disaster."

Dugan's heart ramped up. "What happened?"

"An earthquake. Mee Mee's in a coma. She almost drowned."

"Almost drowned?" Dugan's mind reeled: *Earthquake? Drowning? How can you drown during an earthquake?*

"Where are you?" Goodwin asked.

"We're at the Ohio Valley Medical Center in Wheeling, West Virginia. Pastor Byron is with me."

Goodwin thumbed over his shoulder. "Turn the car around. Head back to Frisco. My plane's at the Billy Mitchell Airstrip."

Dugan checked for traffic, hit the brakes, and spun the wheel. The Interceptor screeched and whirled sideways. He hit the gas, completing a 180, rumbled off the road a few feet and back on again heading south. Needling chills charged up his back. *An earthquake!* The vision of Achak worshiping before the image of the Thunderbird replayed in his mind.

"We'll be there in about three hours," Goodwin said.

"Mee Mee's on life support. Please hurry and please pray."

"We will." Duggan ended the call and hit the siren, punching the gas pedal to the floor.

From Buxton it took about five minutes to get to Park Road, the same road Adelaide Brackenbury had turned onto as she tried to elude the black SUV. The airstrip was only a few hundred yards down the road. Dugan let off the gas and peeled to the right toward the airstrip parking lot. He crossed the lot, hit the brakes, and skidded into a parking space.

"Let's go!" Goodwin shoved open the door, leapt out, slammed it shut, and trotted toward a small white plane with red and blue stripes.

Dugan hurried to catch up. He wasn't a fan of flying, especially small aircraft. Mee Mee's condition trumped his fears. He didn't want to get airsick in front of Goodwin. That would be a sign of weakness. He hoped his relationship with Goodwin would open a few career doors for him on the federal level. Oh well, he thought. He'd deal with his stomach if it went south on him. He opened the door and climbed into the passenger seat.

"How long have you been flying?" Dugan asked.

"About thirty years." Goodwin started the engine, the propellers on each wing whirring to life. "Bought this back in the late nineties. It's a Beechcraft Baron, a great plane. Cruises at about 200 miles per hour. Won't take us long to get there."

One other plane sat on the asphalt lot a few empty spaces to their right. Goodwin taxied his plane to the left toward the beach where the airstrip ran almost parallel to the ocean. Once they reached the airstrip, he turned the plane hard left to angle onto the two-lane runway. Dugan could feel the strong breeze from the ocean shimmying the plane. Goodwin pulled back on the throttle lever, and the plane picked up speed. About halfway down the runway it lifted, and Dugan's stomach dropped. There it goes, Dugan thought. Hang in there lunch. He took a deep breath and tried to relax.

The aircraft climbed steadily. Dugan gazed at the Buxton woods below, the tops of trees passing under in a furious blur. He knew this was the widest section of the Outer Banks, but the bird's eye view exposed its impressive breadth. To the right he caught a glimpse of the Cape Hatteras Lighthouse. The tall spire diminished with every second.

"Are you a religious man?" Goodwin asked.

"Well . . . I'm a Christian but definitely not a great example. I've slipped a bit since my high school days."

"Do you pray much?"

"Yeah. Usually, every morning I'll say a prayer. You know, I'll ask God to watch over my deputies and give me wisdom in my decision making. Why do you ask?"

"I haven't been to church for years. Haven't prayed for months." Goodwin took a deep breath and blew it out. "I'm worried about Mee Mee. Her condition is serious. Could you say a prayer for her?"

"Sure." Dugan swallowed. Public prayer was not one of his natural gifts, but he bowed his head and cleared his throat. "Dear Lord, we humbly ask you to watch over Mee Mee. We pray for her recovery. Please don't let her . . . slip away from us. Get us to her side safely and quickly. Amen."

"Amen."

Dugan glanced at Goodwin. "How well do you know Mee Mee?"

"We spent a week together long ago. Most people would say that's not enough time to know someone. I'd disagree. There are a few people in life with whom you make an instant connection. Mee Mee and I had that kind of relationship."

"If it was so great, why only a week?"

Goodwin shrugged. "Back in the early eighties before I headed off to the Federal Training Center in Georgia, I decided to vacation a week on the Outer Banks. I've always been fascinated with Blackbeard and the history of his escapades on Ocracoke and Hatteras Islands. Mee Mee was a young entrepreneur back then. She had just opened her bookstore in Buxton. I walked in to pick up some books on Blackbeard and the general history of the area."

"So you two hit if off right from the start?"

"Yeah. She had read all the books on the subject. We talked for several hours. Of course, there was a physical attraction too. She's a good looking woman."

"No doubt. So you spent a lot of time together that week?"

"As much as we could. I took her out to dinner that night at a local seafood restaurant, a place called the Captain's Table. I remember every detail. The dining room was simply furnished with wooden chairs and tables, pine paneling on the walls. There was an old wine bottle in the middle of our table with a candle on top."

"Sounds romantic."

"Very. It was a great time. Later that week we took a ferry over to Ocracoke late one afternoon to check out Springer's Point. We were both convinced Blackbeard had buried his legendary treasure there. It was exciting. We walked around the point and through the woods several times, speculating about possible treasure locations. In one of the books there was a map with an X-marks-the-spot illustration, but, of course, we knew that was someone's educated guess."

"So you didn't find the treasure?"

Goodwin chuckled. "No, but I'm sure it's there somewhere."

"Maybe you two will have a second chance at romance."

"I hope so."

Dugan thought about Marla and wondered if she'd ever give their relationship another chance. His mind drifted to the good times they had after they first became engaged. The memories felt more like a dream, as if their intimacy only happened in his imagination. Perhaps he tried to hold on too tightly to someone who seemed out of his league. All the while that small voice in the back of his mind kept telling him she'd slip away. When she did, he sensed that dread of realizing his worst fear. He hated that feeling of being swallowed up by his self-doubt. Maybe that's why Addy appealed so much to him. He could sense the heat of her desire for him whenever they were together.

"What about you?" Goodwin asked.

"Huh?" Goodwin's question caught Dugan off guard.

"Is there someone special in your life?"

"There was—Marla Easton. We were engaged until recently."

"Hmmm. I'm assuming she broke it off with you."

"Yeah. Story of my life."

"Any chance of getting back together?"

"I guess there's always hope. I just don't think she wants me as much as I want her."

Goodwin nodded. "I see. How about Adelaide Brackenbury? Do you think she wants you?"

"What?"

"You heard me."

"Well . . . I uh . . . uh . . . " Dugan wondered if Goodwin was testing him.

"I'm guessing she does," Goodwin said.

"Why's that?"

"She was with Brackenbury all those years. He wasn't the most desirable of men. Don't get me wrong now. I don't believe she cheated on him. At least, I didn't pick up on that kind of illicit undercurrent whenever I was around them. But I could certainly see her needs weren't being met."

"So you think she wants me to meet those needs?"

"You're a young, handsome, single guy that has come to her rescue. I'm sure she felt a sense of release when her husband died. Suddenly she was free after years of marriage to an older man. You were there to fill the vacancy in her life."

Dugan wanted to be selective with his words. "You might be right. She does seem to be attracted to me."

"How do you feel about her?"

"Probably the way most men would feel if a Marilyn Monroe look-a-like entered their lives—somewhat stirred up."

Goodwin chuckled. "She definitely has some impressive physical attributes."

"That's one way of putting it."

"Be careful. Don't let your libido direct your brain."

Dugan nodded. "I'll try to keep a reign on my urges."

"Getting tied up in a relationship with her could mean trouble. She's not a stable woman."

"She definitely has some odd ideas." Dugan inhaled and blew out a long breath. "I'll try to keep my wits about me. I realize I'm flesh and blood. It's hard not to think about . . . uh . . . uh"

"Being literally tied up by her?"

Dugan chuckled. "That's one possibility, but I'm a professional. I don't intend to cross that line."

"If you did, you'd probably lose your job."

Goodwin's words hit Dugan like a bucket of cold water. "Right."

"Who knows? Maybe Marla Easton wants you more than you suppose."

Dugan shrugged. "I doubt that. She did say she wanted to talk when she got back to the Outer Banks."

"There you go. That should give you some hope."

"She probably wants to make sure we can still work together professionally after going through a break up."

Goodwin stretched and linked his hands behind his head. The plane seemed to be flying itself. "You must be a glass-half-empty guy."

"When it comes to Marla, I am. She was the 'it' girl in high school, the kind guys like me never dared to date."

"The only thing I can tell you is don't give up hope yet. I stayed single most of my life. In my early forties I met a girl a lot like Adelaide, a real beauty. Had a body that made men trip over their tongues. She was about fifteen years younger than me. We got married, and it was fun for a few months. But soon I realized you can't base a long-term relationship on physical attraction. The mental and spiritual connection just wasn't there, not like it is with Mee Mee. We stayed together for about a year, but it got to the point where we couldn't stand each other. We divorced and went our separate ways. If you and Adelaide do cross that line, you'll regret it."

Dugan glanced at Goodwin and smiled. "But it would be fun for a month or two."

Goodwin shook his head. "Listen, if you and Marla have that deeper connection, she'll come around. She'll realize that love is more than some emotional high you feel when you're a teenager. She'll come to her senses. "

Dugan stretched and linked his hands behind his head. "I don't plan on making any foolish mistakes with Adelaide, but I have my doubts about Marla."

* * *

Throughout the flight Dugan noticed mostly woodlands and

small towns whenever he glanced downward. After about an hour they flew over the outskirts of Richmond, and then an hour later they passed over another sizable city, Morgantown, West Virginia. In between those metropolises were lots of trees, hills, valleys, and a few rivers. The flight was fairly smooth, and Dugan managed to keep his stomach under control by keeping his mind occupied. He questioned Goodwin about the life of a secret service agent and the process of qualifying for the program. Goodwin didn't paint a rosy picture but gave him a clear idea of the ups and downs of the profession. Overall, Goodwin's account appealed to Dugan and stirred the pot of future possibilities.

The Wheeling Ohio County Airport was located on top of one of the foothills of the Alleghenies that rose up from the banks of the Ohio River. It had two runways that crossed forming an "X" on top of a flattened ridge. As Dugan gazed downward, he saw four helicopters parked on a large rectangular slab in front of what appeared to be the flight building. They looked to be military choppers. He reasoned that the buildings on the west side of the hill were some kind of military headquarters.

Goodwin had contacted the Secret Service field office in Pittsburgh to arrange transportation from the airport to the hospital. Pittsburgh was about an hour north of Wheeling. As the plane landed, Dugan caught sight of a black Chevy Suburban in the parking lot next to the flight building. Goodwin brought the plane to a crawl, taxied to a parking place just off the end of the runway, and shut down the engine.

"Our ride is here. No time to waste." Goodwin released his seatbelt, popped open his door and climbed limberly out of the plane. Dugan fumbled with his seatbelt for several seconds and finally unfastened it. By the time he managed to get the door open, Goodwin had a thirty yard lead. Dugan leapt from the plane and sprinted toward the Suburban.

* * *

The Ohio Valley Medical Center was located about six blocks east of the Ohio River on a steep hillside just south of downtown Wheeling. Special Agent Harry Hoffman, Goodwin's associate from the Pittsburgh field office, dropped them off at the main entrance. Marla met them in the lobby. Dugan noticed her red-rimmed eyes and assumed she'd been crying. He wanted to comfort her but waited to see if she offered to embrace first. She didn't. Her appearance worried him. Marla didn't cry often. *How bad was Mee Mee's condition?*

"How's Mee Mee doing?" Goodwin asked.

Marla blinked and shook her head. "Not good."

Dugan reached and touched her shoulder. "Are you okay?"

She stared at the floor and nodded. "I'll be fine." Marla pointed towards a hallway on the other side of a spacious reception area. "The elevators are that way. ICU is on the third floor. Follow me."

She walked quickly past the information desk and angled towards the hallway. They stopped in front of three elevators to the right. Marla poked the up button, and the center elevator doors separated.

"Is Mee Mee still in a coma?" Goodwin asked as they entered the elevator.

"Yes. They administered an EEG. We're still waiting for results." Marla took a deep, trembling breath. "Pastor Byron's daughter, Dr. Christine Taylor, showed up to help with the casualties. She said that drowning victims who are comatose rarely regain consciousness but not to give up hope. A few come out of it."

The elevator doors parted, and Marla led the way to the ICU unit. At the end of the corridor she pressed a large, square button that activated double doors. They entered the large room sectioned off by patient cubicles. The room buzzed with activity. Medical personnel scurried back and forth as machines beeped and whirred. The tragedy precipitated a full house of patients and visitors, but the overflow of people spoke with hushed and serious tones.

Marla pointed to the last glassed-in cubicle on the left. "Mee Mee is in number twelve."

Goodwin strode in that direction where two people were standing just outside the doorway. Marla followed him.

Dugan's heart lifted when he recognized the familiar faces of the two people—Pastor Byron Butler and his daughter, Christine. Pastor Byron, his thinning hair disheveled, sported a black and red running outfit; and Christine, a tall, good-looking blonde, was clad in a white physician's lab coat with a stethoscope dangling from her neck. They had known each other for a long time. Dugan's uncle, Elijah Mulligan, had brought him along on a vacation to the Outer Banks with the Butler family when he was ten years old. He and Christine had managed to navigate a two-man kayak through the waves and past the breakers several hundred yards out into the Atlantic Ocean. Unfortunately, a bull shark showed up and about tipped the kayak. He had never paddled so hard in his life to get back to shore.

A smile cracked their somber faces as Dugan spread his arms for a group hug. The preacher and his daughter embraced him. For the first time in a long time he felt a deep connection to the past. For the last fifteen years he had been pursuing his career in law enforcement on the Outer Banks. His youthful days spent in the Ohio Valley had drifted into a fog bank in his mind. He didn't look back on those years of childhood with fondness. His broken home and father's rejection combined with the social awkwardness of never quite fitting in to the various cliques at school tarnished his hometown memories. Pastor Byron and his family had provided a welcoming haven along an unstable path. In their company he had always felt loved and accepted.

They broke their embrace and stood back from one another.

Christine's smile flashed a bright set of perfect teeth. "Sheriff Dugan Walton, you sure have grown up since the day we battled that bull shark."

"Twenty-five years will do that to a kid. Look at you—a successful physician practicing back in your old stomping grounds. I thought you were going to make the world your oyster."

"I tried." Christine winked at her father. "But there's no place like home."

"I'm glad she came back home," Pastor Byron said. "We've got plenty of sick and hurting people right here in the Ohio Valley, especially on a day like today."

"What happened today?" Dugan asked.

"A massive earthquake. We think it was triggered by all of the fracking in this region. Let me start with what happened last night." Pastor Byron told about the encounter with the Thunderbird along the ridge near the drilling site. Then he related how Mee Mee decided to join him on a jog over to Wheeling and back that morning. He tried to describe the scene on the middle of the Wheeling Suspension Bridge when the earthquake struck, but his voice faltered and his eyes seemed to stare into another world. He took a deep breath and blinked back tears.

"Dad has been through a difficult day," Christine said.

"I tried to save her. . . She floated to the top in the middle of the river . . . Somehow . . . somehow I toted her back to shore. She was unconscious and all gray. I gave her CPR . . . I tried to . . . I tried to bring her back to life. She wouldn't . . . wouldn't respond."

Christine rubbed her father's back. "You did all you could possibly do."

Pastor Byron lowered his head and stared at the tiled floor.

"Listen, Dugan, I need to take Dad down to the cafeteria and get him a cup of coffee. We're still waiting for the EEG results on Mee Mee. All I can say is she's in God's hands now."

Dugan nodded. "I understand. Thank you, both of you, for all you've done."

Pastor Byron raised his head, eyes widening. "The Thunderbird." He shook his head. "They say something terrible happens wherever that bird shows up."

"Come on, Dad, let's get some coffee."

Christine directed her father to the ICU exit. She turned and waved goodbye before the double doors closed behind them.

Dugan took a deep breath and pivoted toward Mee Mee's cubicle. The sign cautioned only two visitors at a time. Through the glass he saw Goodwin and Marla standing on either side of Mee Mee's bed, a tangle of beeping and blinking monitors and machines surrounding them. He wondered if he should enter. Then Dugan heard a man's baritone singing softly a very familiar tune—"Take Me Home, Country Roads."

That's odd, Dugan thought. Goodwin was singing to Mee Mee. He walked into the cubicle. The Secret Service agent held Mee Mee's hand as he sang, his voice smooth and melodic. Dugan neared the bed and observed the tender scene. A heart monitor beeped steadily above her, a red light flashing with every beat. Marla stood on the other side, her hand on Mee Mee's shoulder. Mee Mee's face was pale and motionless. But then Dugan noticed her lips quivering slightly. He stepped nearer. Her mouth moved as if she were trying to speak. Then Dugan realized she wasn't trying to speak. Her mouth movements matched the lyrics of the song. She was trying to sing.

Mee Mee's eyes popped open, and she immediately sat up. She glanced from face to face. "Where am I?"

Marla leaned and grasped her hand. "Wheeling, West Virginia."

Mee Mee tilted her head. "Almost heaven."

Chapter 23

Mee Mee tugged on the heart monitor wires and anxiously eyed the intravenous tubing and needle inserted into her wrist. Then she glanced from face to face. "Listen. We need to get back to the Outer Banks right now."

"Calm down," Goodwin said. "You just came out of a coma."

Her eyes widened. "You don't understand. Someone's life may be in danger."

"Whose life?" Dugan asked.

"Adelaide Brackenbury's. He said one more person may have to die to stop the development of Ocracoke. She's the most logical choice."

Marla leaned closer. "Who said that?"

"Achak Rowtag."

"When did you talk to Achak?" Dugan asked.

"I . . . I . . . Just a few minutes ago."

Dugan met Marla's gaze and then eyed Goodwin.

Goodwin shrugged. "You were dreaming."

Mee Mee shook her head. "It was *not* a dream. It was a . . . an out-of-body experience. I died and crossed over into the spirit realm."

Dugan remembered Achak's chanting in front of the image of the Thunderbird, calling down disaster upon the earth. Could the timing of his ritual and Mee Mee's experience have coincided?

Marla asked, "How could Achak have met you in the spirit realm? He isn't dead."

Mee Mee held out her hands, fingers spread. "He's a shaman. That's what he does. He can see into a world we never venture into unless . . . unless we die."

"Take a deep breath and relax," Goodwin said. "We'll sort this out."

"There's no time. We need to go now."

Dugan raised his hand and bobbed it gently as if patting the air. "Marla and I will take your car and head back to check on Addy. Once the doctors give their approval, you can fly back with Agent Goodwin."

Mee Mee slowly nodded and lay back on the bed. "Where's Pastor Byron?"

Dugan thumbed over his shoulder. "He's down in the cafeteria with his daughter."

"I wanted to thank him for lugging me to shore and giving me CPR."

"How did you know he was the one who tried to save you?" Marla asked. "You were unconscious."

Mee Mee wrung her hands and shook her head. "Like I said, I was no longer imprisoned in my body. I could see everything that was happening below me. I was free."

Marla and Goodwin stood frozen by Mee Mee's words, skepticism hardening their expressions. Dugan, however, couldn't help wondering about the possibility. He had heard about out-of-body experiences many times. During his career as a law enforcement officer, people who had revived from serious accidents made similar claims to him when he had questioned them at the hospital. Adelaide's face formed in his mind. Something inside, perhaps instinct, pressed him to head back home. Hopefully, they'd get back before anything happened.

* * *

Speeding along Interstate 70 in Mee Mee's Jeep Cherokee, Dugan wondered if a state trooper would cut him slack for going 90 in a 65 mph zone. His explanation may sound a little crazy—*I'm trying to prevent a murder, sir. A lady had an out-of-body experience and informed us that someone is in danger.* Dugan shook his head. Nope. He'd get the ticket.

"Slow down." Marla put her hand on the dashboard. "You're going to get us killed."

Dugan took a deep breath and blew it out. "Right." He took his foot off the gas and dropped down to eighty. "With all the evidence we have on Achak, it's just a possibility, that's all."

"I agree, but you're not going to save anybody if you lose control of this vehicle."

"You think that Mee Mee could be right?"

"Yes, but not because she went floating around in the netherworld. If Achak is the murderer, Adelaide Brackenbury could be next. I'm guessing she makes the decisions now concerning the development plans of Ocracoke."

"Good guess. She's meeting with investors and politicians in a few days to make a final decision. If she dies, that stops the whole works."

"What all do you have on Achak?"

"We've matched his handwriting up with an anonymous letter threatening the Brackenbury's lives. When we executed a search warrant on his house, we found several bone knives that could possibly match up with the tip of the murder weapon. Then when I searched his van, I found large feathers, very possibly from the eagle that's been terrorizing these environmentally threatened locations."

Marla crossed her arms. "Maybe you better give Adelaide Brackenbury a call."

"I should have thought of that earlier." Dugan reached in his shirt pocket and pulled out his cell phone. "Crap! It's dead."

"You can use my phone."

"I don't remember her number."

"Mee Mee has a charger." Marla took Dugan's phone, connected it to the charger and inserted the charger prong into the port. "Give it a minute or two."

Dugan glanced at his watch. "It's 4:30 in the afternoon. I don't think Achak would do anything in broad daylight unless ..."

"Unless What?"

"Unless she left the house, and he followed her to some isolated place."

"Considering the circumstances, she should know better."

Dugan shrugged. "She's an unusual girl."

"Do you like her?"

"What?"

"You heard me. You've been spending a lot of time with her."

"She's okay."

"Most men would say she's beautiful."

Dugan kept silent.

"Have you slept with her?"

"Marla!" Dugan felt his face flush.

"You have, haven't you?"

Dugan took a calming breath. Time to come clean. "One night she was having a bad experience, the night of the séance. She felt threatened and asked me to stay at her house to make sure she was safe."

"Of course, you obliged."

"Yes, I stayed but in a different bedroom."

"Don't you think that's crossing professional lines?"

"Possibly ... Okay, it was a poor decision. ... but ... I want to tell you exactly what happened. In the middle of the night she came down and got into bed with me."

Marla straightened in her seat, the muscles in her arms tensing. "Did you make love to her?"

"No! I swear we didn't have sex."

"But you wanted to."

"Marla, why are you doing this? You tossed our relationship out like yesterday's garbage. Why would you care about what I do with Adelaide Brackenbury?"

Marla's head dipped and her arms relaxed. "Because I think I'm still in love with you. That's why I said we needed to talk when I got back to the Outer Banks. I am still considering the possibility of marriage."

Marla's words turned Dugan upside-down like a whirling rocket ride at a small-town carnival. "Give me a few seconds. I wasn't expecting this."

"I know. My mind and emotions have been all over the place these last few days, but I keep coming back to you and me and our future together."

"Okay. Does that mean you do want to get married, or do you need more time to think about it?"

This time Marla took a deep breath and blew it out slowly." I need more time, but marrying you seems to be the right decision."

"Hmmmph. Seems to be? What needs to happen to convince you? Does an angel need to ring a bell?"

Just then Dugan's cell phone dinged.

Marla stared at the phone. "You just got a text message."

"Check it for me would you please."

Marla picked up the phone. "I've been trying to reach you. Achak wants to meet with me this afternoon at Springer's Point. He says it's important and could impact my decision about the development. He claims the spirits have spoken to him. I wanted you to go with me. You know I don't trust him. Please call me back as soon as you can. I love you." Marla sat back and gave Dugan a sideways glare.

"What do you want me to do? I can't help it if she's fallen in love with me."

"I want you to call her back."

Chapter 24

With Dugan unavailable, Addy had to take the ferry over to Ocracoke Island. The ride was peaceful. The hot sun blazed from a clear blue September sky. She stood on the deck and let the breeze cool her. The hum of the engines and the rhythm of the ferry's passage through the gentle waves of the Pamlico Sound calmed her spirit. No one bothered her. That was fine as far as she was concerned. Usually men would hit on her when she traveled alone.

She wondered if Dugan was falling in love with her. It had been so long since she had made love to a man. Her husband had been impotent for five years. Five long years. Now he was literally dead. She tried to block his roly-poly image from her mind. What did she have to do to get Dugan to loosen up? She smiled and glanced down at her low-cut yellow blouse and tight-fitting jeans. I'll figure something out, she thought.

The walk from Silver Lake, the small harbor where the ferries docked, to Springer's Point wasn't far, maybe a half mile. She needed the exercise to firm up her thighs. She had skipped her daily workout routine several times over the past week, but that was understandable considering the circumstances. She enjoyed having a body men noticed and wanted to maintain that advantage as long as she could. Now that she was a widow, she could play the field again. Being a rich widow meant she had to be careful. No man was going to worm his way into her financial estate. She had worked too hard to be made a fool by some Romeo with dollar signs for eyes. Maybe that's why she liked Dugan. He didn't seem to be interested in her money or try to make out with her at the first opportunity. She admired his ideals but enjoyed the challenge he presented. If they became lovers, would he be happy to stay out of her financial affairs? She hoped so. With Rowland gone, she didn't want any help.

As she neared Springer's Point she wondered what Achak would say to her. On the phone he had promised that his revelations would open her eyes to things unseen. He wanted to give her an ancient Indian necklace with spiritual powers. That intrigued her. She did not like the man but felt a strange connection to him.

Certainly, he hoped to influence her decision about the development of Ocracoke. She'd listen to what he had to say and accept his gift. He was a shaman. They did have the spiritual realm in common. Who knows? His secret knowledge may help her achieve new spiritual levels. However, she realized he would try to use his powers to sway her over to his environmentalist ideology. What if she resisted? Would he become angry? Threatening? She'd play it cool and let him have his say. But the decision was hers alone.

This would certainly be a test. She was cautious but not anxious. He wasn't the only one with inner spiritual power. She knew she had the gift to commune with entities beyond this earth. Were her abilities equal to his? Maybe. He definitely had developed his abilities to the highest levels. That's what she lacked—spiritual refinement and control. Whenever the Indian maiden possessed her, she lost control. The frightful dreams of being chased, raped, and murdered made her shudder. Perhaps the spirit of the maiden wanted to empower her and help protect her from abusive and controlling men.

She knew Dugan would never approve of her meeting with Achak, but he never replied to her text message. He was probably behind on all of his sheriff's duties. She'd manage this encounter by herself.

She stopped and peered down the sound side of the beach. Achak stood near the point, a lone figure staring across the water to the North Carolina mainland. The wind ruffled his long black hair. He turned and waved, the fringe from his suede jacket swishing. She waved back. Fortunately, they were meeting in broad daylight at a location frequented by tourists. She wasn't too worried.

As she neared, she noticed his demeanor had changed. The stern, hard-edged expression from the night of the paranormal gathering had been replaced by a warm smile.

"Thank you for coming, Mrs. Brackenbury." His voice was gentle and welcoming.

"You said this meeting was incredibly important."

"It is. I hope you are open to what I have to say."

"I'm assuming you are referring to my decision about developing Ocracoke."

Achak nodded. "The first thing I want to do is offer my condolences concerning the death of your husband."

"Really? His murder benefited your cause."

Achak held up his hand as if to offer a pledge. "I swear I do not subscribe to murder as a means to achieve a righteous end. The appearance of the Animikii was a warning for your husband."

"Some warning. I spoke to my husband's spirit last night at a séance. He warned me to watch out for people like you. Then he told me to move forward with our development plans."

"You have nothing to fear from me, and developing Ocracoke would be a grave mistake. Do not be deceived by people motivated by greed who are trying to influence your decisions. Your husband died because he was not willing to heed the Animikii's warning."

She examined Achak's eyes and the solemnity of his expression. "I'm not sure what you're trying to say to me.

Rowland was the major force behind all these plans. Now he's dead. Are you saying this Animikii somehow orchestrated his death?"

"When the Animikii appeared, spiritual forces were mobilized. Death resulted."

"So the Animikii motivated someone to murder my husband. Sheriff Dugan Walton believes you did it."

Achak shook his head. "I do not murder. But the Animikii did not have to look far to find someone who does."

"That scares me. If it wasn't you, then one of your obsessed preservation society friends must have done it. Will I die if I don't heed the Animikii's warning?"

"We will all die sooner or later. The question is: How will you live until that day? You are not like your husband. You know there are powers beyond this world that keep the universe in balance."

"I know there's much more to existence than what's on the surface."

Achak nodded, his eyes fixing upon hers. "You can see beyond the surface. You have a rare gift."

"Do you think so?"

"I know." He turned and motioned toward the woods and then pivoted toward the Pamlico Sound. "I know you know how sacred this island is." He laid his hand on his chest. "Deep inside you know."

She could not deny his assumption. "I . . . I agree. This is a special place."

"It's more than a special place to you. Tell me about your past life here."

"Well . . . " Adelaide wasn't expecting an invitation to talk about her spiritual journey but sensed a sincerity in Achak's tone. She loved to converse about past lives and the possibility of channeling spirits, especially the girl who often possessed her. "I lived on this island as a young Native American girl. She was sixteen or seventeen years old."

Achak nodded and closed his eyes. "Yes. She is near right now. She feels like she is one with you."

Adelaide straightened, pinpricks scrambling up her back. "I

sense her presence too."

"Her name is Kimi."

"Kimi?"

"Yes. The name means 'secret.'"

Deep inside she felt a strange affirmation. "Yes, her name *is* Kimi. She has secrets."

"Kimi wants you to make the right decision."

A cold wave flowed over Adelaide. Was Achak taking advantage of her spiritual inclinations? "I'm willing to listen to what Kimi has to say."

Achak reached into his pocket and pulled out a beaded necklace, the beads old and faded. Adelaide could tell the strand was once brightly colored. He held up the necklace, a half-moon carved from bone dangled from the middle of the drooping string of beads.

"This is what I wanted to give to you." He extended the necklace to her.

Adelaide held out her hand. "It's old . . . but very beautiful."

He dropped the necklace into her palm.

She examined it closely. What was the odd, rust-colored stain on some of the beads? Blood?

"Listen carefully. I found this artifact in a cedar box not far from here after a bad storm. The wind had uncovered a corner of the box. I knew immediately it held something significant. Along with the necklace was a note written by the son of the island's constable. The young man wanted to marry Kimi. Unfortunately, he found her body at the edge of the woods with her throat slashed." Achak turned and pointed to a stand of live oaks near the edge of the field. "That's where I found the box, and that's where he found Kimi's body." Achak took the necklace from Addy's hand and carefully looped it over her head and around her neck. "Do you feel the necklace's power?"

Addy nodded as she sensed a tingling around her neck.

"Do you know who killed her?" Achak asked.

Addy blinked and sucked in a quick breath. "Yes. I know. The man dressed in black with a beard. I thought he was a pirate, but . . . but . . . he was the constable."

Achak clasped Addy's shoulders. "That's right. That was

Kimi's secret. She'd been raped by the boy's father. When the constable found out his son was in love with her, he murdered her before she could tell the boy."

Addy placed her hands on top of her head and closed her eyes. Her breathing accelerated. Her vision of being brutalized by the constable flashed on the screen of her mind like scenes from a late-night horror flick. She became dizzy.

Achak shook her by the shoulders. "Listen to me. Tomorrow at midnight I want you to come here to Springer's Point. Make sure you wear the necklace and stand at the edge of the woods where I found the box."

Addy caught her breath and steadied herself. "Why?"

"Kimi will possess you, and the Animikii will appear."

Addy shook her head. "No! I'm afraid of the Animikii."

Achak's hands slid from her shoulders to the collar of her blouse, firmly gripping the back of her neck. His eyes widened. "Do not be afraid. You must become one with the Animikii. Kimi's spirit will embolden you. The answer you are seeking will be made clear."

"Let her go, Rowtag!"

Addy jerked away from Achak's grasp, whirled, and caught sight of a tall deputy standing at the edge of the woods. He pointed a pistol directly at Achak's chest.

Chapter 25

The Wright Memorial Bridge spans the Currituck Sound from Point Harbor on the North Carolina mainland to Kitty Hawk on the Outer Banks. The three-mile span is actually two bridges—a two-lane bridge traveling east toward the ocean and the other heading west back to the States. In the mid-sixties the concrete structure replaced a wooden bridge. That marked the beginning of the incredible growth of the tourist industry on the barrier islands. Whenever Dugan crossed the bridge he felt vulnerable. Traveling for several miles suspended twenty feet above the choppy sound waters made him edgy—that sense of having very few options if catastrophe would strike. He knew his fears were unfounded. Not much could happen crossing that bridge unless he tried to cross it in the middle of a hurricane.

This evening, however, he and Marla were happy to be so close to home. They had made the trip from Wheeling in record time, less than nine hours. He could hardly keep his eyes open. Marla had offered to drive several times, but he remained stubborn. Did his refusal give him some kind of psychological advantage, proving he could manage to maintain control of himself and the vehicle without her help? Marla probably thought he was being insecure or immature or both. But she hadn't complained much and had drifted off to sleep a few times.

Marla stretched her arms, pressing her hands against the ceiling of the Jeep Cherokee. "I don't understand your new friend Addy."

"Yeah. Doesn't make sense, does it?"

"Not at all. If Achak had his hands around her neck, why would she defend him?"

"Good question. Deputy Dufresne said she swore up and down that he meant her no harm. With her being so adamant, Dufresne had no grounds to arrest him."

"She's an odd one. I'd be careful around her if I were you."

Dugan nodded, wondering if Marla believed his plea of innocence in regards to her accusations of sexual intimacy with Addy. "I'm just wondering if Achak exercised some kind of power over her."

"Now you're starting to sound like Mee Mee."

Dugan lifted his right hand from the steering wheel and held it out pleadingly. "Not so fast. You have to agree that there are people with the ability to exercise control over others. Haven't you seen those hypnotists who can make a grown man act like a chicken?"

Marla chuckled. "Yes, but come on, Dugan. A guy strutting around, pecking at the ground, and cackling like a hen must have putty for a brain."

"Right. But my point is there are people who are highly skilled at controlling others."

"Point taken."

On the drive down to Rodanthe to drop Marla off at home, things became quiet. Dugan's mind drifted to Addy. Could Achak somehow have brainwashed her? He wanted to call her but knew he had to wait until he was alone. Marla had a way of making him feel guilty whenever he mentioned Addy's name. Now that Marla had reintroduced the possibility of their future together, he wanted to be careful about everything he said. He definitely needed to cool his relationship with Addy, but that didn't mean he no longer cared about her. He took seriously the responsibility to keep her safe. He couldn't quell an odd feeling that she was drifting in the wrong direction because of Achak.

"I want to cook dinner for you."

Marla's words snapped Dugan out of his reverie. "Dinner? Do you mean tonight?"

"No. Not tonight. It's late, and I'm dead tired. Besides, I'm on duty tomorrow morning."

"When? This weekend?"

"No. My cousins are bringing Gabriel back home this weekend. Next week some time. Hopefully, this murder mess will be cleared up, and Achak, Addy, and the ghosts of Ocracoke will be out of our lives. We'll have a nice dinner and talk about the future."

"Sounds good to me. I'll bring dessert. Chocolate cream pie."

Marla smiled. "You know my weakness." She reached and rubbed Dugan's knee.

He took a deep breath and felt his face flush. Wow, he thought. Something happened to Marla on that trip up north. Maybe there's hope for us after all.

When he pulled into Marla's driveway, she leaned and kissed him on the cheek. "You be good now," she said. "I'll see you sometime tomorrow."

As she climbed out of the Jeep Cherokee, Dugan wanted to call out, "I love you," but thought better of it. He didn't want to seem too easily won back. Better wait to see what happens after that dinner.

At the end of Marla's lane, Dugan turned south onto Route 12 and headed toward Buxton. The long stretches of protected shoreline became monotonous at night, especially when he was dead tired. The dunes to his left resembled dark, misshapen walls, and the land that stretched out toward the sound was fairly flat and swampy with thick brush and the silhouettes of trees that vacillated in the steady breeze against leaden gray water. Now was the time to call Addy. He preferred hands-free calling, but his phone wasn't paired to Mee Mee's Jeep. Oh well, he thought, perhaps phoning Addy would make him more alert.

He picked up his phone, scrolled to Addy's number, and initiated the call while doing his best to keep his eyes on the road.

The phone rang three times. "Dugan?"

"It's me."

"I was hoping you'd call. Where have you been?"

"It's a long story. There was an earthquake near Wheeling, West Virginia. Mee Mee Roberts fell from a bridge and ended up in the hospital. Agent Goodwin and I flew up to see her."

"How terrible. Is she okay?"

"By the time we left she was doing much better. Lucky to be alive, I guess. Quite a few weren't so lucky."

"Didn't she go up there to investigate the Animikii sightings for the local paper?"

"Yeah, and she spotted the Thunderbird the night before the earthquake. Strange, isn't it?"

"Very strange."

"Kinda like your encounter with Achak."

"You've heard about it?"

"Of course. After I listened to your message, I called Deputy Dufresne and ordered him to head to Ocracoke just in case Achak tried to kill you. He told me all about it."

After a long pause, Addy said, "There was no need to do that."

"Believe me, with the evidence we have against him, your life was in danger."

"What kind of evidence?"

"The murder weapon. We confiscated several knives that belong to him. We believe he used one of them to kill your husband."

"You . . . you have the murder weapon?"

"We're pretty sure. We haven't had time to match it up with the evidence yet."

"Hmmm . . . you might be right about him, but I still don't think he wants to kill me."

"No. He could have killed you easily out there in that field and tossed your body into the Pamlico Sound, but he didn't. Do you know why?"

"Yes. He wants to control me."

"I'm glad you realize that."

"I'm not stupid, Dugan. I gave him the impression that I'm open to his way of thinking. He gave me an old Indian necklace. He said it belonged to Kimi, the girl that possesses me."

"Do you believe him?"

"Yes. I think the necklace is authentic. I can feel the power of her presence when I wear it. He wants me to wear it tomorrow night."

"Why?"

"He said the Animikii will appear at Springer's point and give me the answer that I've been seeking."

Dugan shook his head. "In other words his trained eagle will show up and somehow convince you not to proceed with your development plans."

"Should I not go?"

"Of course not . . . unless . . . " Dugan considered the opportunity to gain more evidence against Achak. ". . . unless I go with you."

"You can't. He insisted I come alone."

"Don't worry. I'll keep my distance. He won't know I'm there."

"Well . . . I'd definitely feel better if you were there. That Animikii scares me."

"Believe me. I won't let it harm a hair on your pretty blonde head. "

"Would you shoot it if it attacked me?"

"If it attacks, we'll be eating Thunderbird for Thanksgiving."

* * *

Mee Mee gazed out of the passenger window at the West Virginia forest below. Flying in a small private plane wasn't her travel preference, but it definitely beat a ten-hour drive. Sitting next to Russell Goodwin made up for the bumpy ride. It felt good to be heading home. It felt good to be alive. "How did you know to sing 'Country Roads Take Me Home' when I was in a coma?"

"The oldie goldies." Russell glanced at her and smiled. "They have special powers."

"Really?"

"I'm not kidding. Medical researchers have been studying the impact of old familiar songs on Alzheimer's patients. For example, patients will sit unresponsive for hours, not communicating, just staring. Then headphones would be placed on them and popular songs from their youth would be played."

"What happens?"

"The patients come to life, start singing the songs, and then they communicate with the researchers. They talk and talk as if the disease had been temporarily lifted. Their personalities reemerge. Music reaches a part of their brain nothing else could reach."

"That's amazing." Mee Mee sat back in her seat and stared through the windshield at a bank of clouds. "I was drifting in this odd state of existence wondering how to get back. Then I heard the song. As I started to sing, I could feel myself moving toward you. I recognized your voice."

"Do you remember when we sang that song together?"

"Yes, when we were on Ocracoke Island looking for Blackbeard's treasure nearly forty years ago."

A wide smile broke across Russell's face. "I remember like it was yesterday."

Mee Mee shook her head. "Believe me, that memory is much better than my ones from yesterday. I keep hearing the loud whine of metal tearing and cables snapping. Then I see cars falling forty feet into the river and people struggling to keep their heads above the surface."

Russell reached and grasped her hand. "Try not to think about it."

"I can't help it. My out-of-body experience was the strangest thing. I know you think I'm crazy, but I really did communicate with Achak. Then I drifted back to the river. I keep telling myself I've been given a second chance at life for a reason." She squeezed Russell's hand.

Russell let go of the control wheel and tapped his chest. "Maybe I'm the reason."

Mee Mee chuckled. "Maybe, or perhaps I'm supposed to dedicate myself to some worthy cause like feeding the hungry or housing the homeless."

"Well . . ." He gripped the wheel again. "I can't compete with those callings. However, I would like to propose a possibility that would require you and me to join forces in a common quest."

"That sounds interesting."

"It would definitely be an adventure."

"Well . . . what's on your mind?"

"I would like you to help me find Blackbeard's treasure."

A burst of laughter spurted out. "Very funny."

"I'm not kidding."

"I know you were obsessed with that treasure when we met, but we were very young and wide-eyed back then."

Russell blinked several times at her. "Do I look narrow-eyed now?"

"No. I'm just saying . . ."

"Listen. My eyes are wider now than they were when we were in our twenties."

Mee Mee tilted her head. "What do you mean?"

"In my position as a Secret Service agent I have access to resources few treasure hunters can claim. There are special government archive rooms and documentation centers which require a level of authorization for entry."

Mee Mee turned in her seat and examined his expression. His eyes beamed with passion, or was it fanaticism? "So you've been on a quest researching Blackbeard's treasure all these years?"

Russell nodded.

"I'll bite. Where is it?"

"Very near where we were looking so long ago—the southern end of Ocracoke Island."

"How do you know?"

"You've read most of the biographies of his life. Do you remember what one of Blackbeard's crew members asked him the night before he died in that battle against the British naval force near Ocracoke?"

"No."

"The crew member asked him if his wife knew where he had buried the treasure. He responded, 'Nobody but me and the devil knows where it is, and the longer liver shall take it all.'"

"Okay, so what does that mean?"

"It's a clue to the location, of course."

Mee Mee scratched her head. "And you have deciphered the clue?"

"I think I'm on the right track. The Queen Anne's Revenge, Blackbeard's flagship, was discovered in 1996 about one mile off the North Carolina coast sixty miles south of Ocracoke. The research company that discovered the wreck found no treasure. Blackbeard was sailing north from Charleston, South Carolina when the ship ran aground near the Beaufort Inlet. Obviously, his crew had time to remove the treasure and find a hiding place. Blackbeard's favorite anchorage was the south end of Ocracoke Island. Back then it was the perfect place for pirates to keep a lookout for enemy ships. Logically, it would also be the perfect place to bury the treasure."

"Makes sense. A lot of people have come to that conclusion, but tell me more about the clue. Blackbeard said that only he and the devil knew where it was. So where the hell is it?"

"Exactly! Hell is the key."

"What are you talking about?"

"Like I said, I have access to archives of historical documents which require a high level security clearance. These files should have been declassified and handed over to the National Archives years ago, but very few people know they exist. I guess you could say these documents have been illegally hoarded. I'm sure one of these days they will be made public, but for now I am one of the few who have had access to them."

"What kind of documents are they?

"Mostly historical documents. Some date back to the late 1500's. I've focused all my research energies on any documents dealing with Edward Teach and his men. Did you know that Blackbeard intentionally ran the Queen Anne's Revenge aground?"

"I think I read that somewhere, but refresh my memory."

"Teach and his fleet reaped quite a harvest by blockading Charleston. They sailed north with their loot to Beaufort Inlet. There he ran the Queen's Anne Revenge onto a sandbar with the intension of downsizing his crew to increase his share of the take. He ordered his favorite crewmen to load the spoils onto the remaining sloop. They marooned the rest of the crew on the grounded ship. Then they headed to Ocracoke to bury the treasure."

Mee Mee nodded. "Yes. Now I remember. Some historians believe he did it intentionally. Others disagree."

"The local authorities sailed out to the wreck of the Queen's Anne Revenge and arrested the abandoned pirates. Of course, they questioned them thoroughly about Blackbeard and recorded their answers. In the documents I researched, several of the marooned crewmen claimed Teach grounded the boat intentionally to cut them out of the profits. I kept reading these documents to find any references to the devil or hell to help with the clue."

"Did you find anything?"

"Yes. One of the crewman claimed Teach was Satan himself. He told the judge that one day he went hunting in the woods at the south end of Ocracoke. Whenever he stood quietly, he could hear scraping like someone sharpening a large knife. Following the sound, he came upon Blackbeard right in the middle of the woods. The pirate was on his hands and knees, his eyes wild as he dug the tip of knife into a large flat stone. The crewman said it was a sight to behold –Teach's bedeviled expression and beard and hair all in tangles. He asked Teach what he was doing there. That seemed to snap the pirate out of his fixation on the stone. Teach glared at him and said, 'I'm about to open the gates of Hell. Now get out of here!' The crewman was so frightened by Blackbeard's demonic voice that he turned and ran clear back to the beach."

Mee Mee rubbed her chin. "That is an unusual story. What do you think he was carving on the stone?"

"I don't know, but I want to find out. If that stone is the gateway to Hell, then Blackbeard's treasure is buried beneath it."

Chapter 26

Dugan had insisted Addy take the 10:45 ferry from Hatteras to Ocracoke and hang out at the Ocracoke Bar and Grille until it was time to head over to Springer's Point. He didn't want Achak to catch sight of them together. He checked his watch as he drifted up to an empty dock at Silver Lake Harbor. Right on time—fifteen minutes before midnight. He quickly secured the boat and hurried across the wooden walkway to shore. Wearing a black hooded sweat outfit, he blended easily into the darkness as he covered the few blocks from Silver Lake Harbor to the restaurant on Irvin Garrish Highway. He leapt over a wooden fence on the left side of the property and slipped into the shadow of a large tree near the front porch of the cedar-shingled building. The twang of country music filtered from the windows and doors, a Willie Nelson tune, "Angel Flying Too Close to the Ground." There he waited for Addy to exit the establishment.

About 11:55 he heard the door swing open and footfalls on the porch. A nearby floodlight lit up her form as she descended the steps. Her platinum blonde hair and white, sheer maxi dress made her appear ghostlike. Dugan noticed the beaded necklace that hung across her cleavage. He gave a low whistle and whispered, "Addy, it's me, Dugan. Don't look this way. Just listen."

She stopped at the bottom of the steps and stared at the starlit sky.

"I'll follow behind at a safe distance. Don't worry. I've got you covered."

She nodded, took a deep breath, and headed for Lighthouse Road.

He kept about 100 yards between them. He figured Achak was hiding out somewhere on the edge of the woods with his trained eagle. How would Achak broadcast his *Save Ocracoke* directive to her? Maybe with a remote transmitter and some kind of small amplifier device attached to the eagle. Possibly, he would command the eagle to fly to her and hover above while transmitting the message. Dugan wanted to catch him in the act to help fortify the case against him. He reasoned Achak used the eagle to chase the ghost party into the woods the night he stabbed Rowland Brackenbury.

The fastest approach to Springer's Point was located at the end of Lighthouse Road where it turned and narrowed into Loop Road. It wasn't the official path, which was located on up Loop Road a ways. However, cutting between two residential properties offered a shortcut. On a late mid-September night, most people had gone to bed or were getting their late-night snacks. Dugan wondered what the residents would think if they peered out their windows at the shimmering figure in the long white dress gliding in the direction of Blackbeard's favorite hangout: *There goes another Ocracoke ghost.*

The three-quarter moon hanging high in the blue-violet sky helped to keep her in view, but Dugan lost sight of her when the path turned slightly. He stepped up his pace but kept to the shadows. The sandy trail led along the edge of the sound for about two hundred yards and then opened into a clearing at Springer's Point. Addy had informed him that Achak instructed her to walk along the beach about seventy yards past the spot where the point jutted into the water. There she would wait by the edge of the woods. Dugan cut up toward the woods much sooner, staying low, and making his way through the scrub brush and sea grass which covered the triangular clearing.

He stepped between two live oaks, their long branches winding and bending like giant octopus tentacles. Staying low, moving from tree to tree along the edge of the woods, he kept his eyes on Addy as she angled around the point and headed to the prearranged spot. She had told him that the son of the constable had discovered the Indian maiden's body there. He wondered if Achak had fabricated the tale to take advantage of Addy's metaphysical persuasions. Then he capped it off with the story about the necklace he dug up nearby. Clearly, the man was a master manipulator. She stopped at the edge of the woods and peered upwards.

Dugan froze, leaning on the rough bark of a live oak, and gazed at her. She began to chant odd words that sounded like some kind of Native American dialect. He remembered the night of the séance when she channeled the Indian maiden's spirit. Pin prickles charged up his back. He listened for other sounds. A mosquito buzzed around his ear, but then he heard rhythmic flapping. The Thunderbird was about to make its appearance. Addy stopped chanting and raised her hands skyward. Dugan crouched and moved slightly forward beyond the edge of the trees to get a better look. The large eagle glowed in the sky, circling about fifty feet above her.

He knew Achak had to be close by. He edged back into the woods, stood, and carefully weaved his way through the trees. He stopped and listened. The eagle screeched, but from his position below the trees, he could not see it. Peering between the trunks, he spotted Addy. Her face and hair glowed white in the moon's light as she gazed skyward. Then he heard a ghostly voice between the eagle's screeches: *Honor your ancestors. Protect the land. Honor your ancestors. Protect the land.*

Looking to his left he noticed the silhouette of someone crouching behind a bush and speaking into some kind of transmitter. The figure had to be Achak. He glanced back at Addy. He could now see the eagle through the branches. The flapping and screeching became louder as the eagle descended. The oddly distorted voice kept repeating *Protect the land. Honor your ancestors.*

Dugan knew he had to move fast. He pulled his Smith and Wesson revolver from his shoulder holster and aimed it at the dark form. "Hold it right there, Achak. You're under arrest."

The man turned and sprang into the woods. Dugan rushed towards where he had bolted, but his foot caught on a root. When he hit the ground, his gun discharged.

Addy screamed, and the eagle screeched.

He crawled between the trees toward her and peered up. Ten feet above, the eagle went berserk, swirling erratically and shrieking like a cat afire. The huge bird plunged and rose with the sweep of its expansive wings. Each dip drove its large talons closer to Addy's upraised arms as she tried to protect her face.

Dugan sprang like a panther and tackled her with one arm as the eagle's talons swiped and missed.

He rolled over, raised his pistol, and fired. Sparks shot from the beast's chest. Its wings convulsed, and more sparks spurted, igniting feathers. *What the hell?*

Addy screamed and clutched his arm.

The eagle's wings kept flapping but lost their rhythm. Flames clambered up its body and quickly spread across its wings. The bird turned over like a wing-clipped airplane and tumbled into a heap on the ground.

Dugan pulled Addy closer and shielded her from the flying sparks. "Are you okay?"

Addy squeezed him tightly and buried her head into his chest. "Get me out of here."

Dugan managed to slowly rise with Addy hanging on to him. They turned and stared at the smoking eagle.

Addy put her hand to her mouth and gasped. "It's . . . it's some kind of machine."

"Yeah." Dugan stepped closer and leaned to inspect the wreckage. "It's a drone."

Chapter 27

Dugan touched the contact number on his cell phone. It rang three times.

"Agent Goodwin speaking."

"Russell, this is Dugan. Where are you?"

"Well . . . I'm at Mee Mee Roberts's house in Buxton. We flew in about an hour ago. Where are you?"

"Ocracoke Island. You won't believe what crash landed in front of me."

"Crash landed? I have no idea what you're talking about."

"The eagle has landed . . . in a smoking heap."

"The Thunderbird? What . . . what happened? Is it alive?"

Dugan chuckled. "No. It's not alive and never was. You need to come see for yourself. I wish I could tell you I arrested the guy at the controls, but he got away."

"Okay. I see. It was some kind of sophisticated drone?"

"You guessed it."

"And Achak was operating it?"

"That would be my guess, but it was dark. I couldn't tell for sure. He took off through the woods."

"My plane is down the road at the Billy Mitchell Airport. There's a landing strip near Springer's Point. I'll be there in less than twenty minutes."

"We'll be waiting."

Dugan ended the call and eyed Addy.

She shook her head. "I can't believe I fell for a mechanical eagle."

"Don't question your judgment on that." Dugan pointed at the smoking rubble of feathers and gears. "Before it went wacko, it was pretty convincing."

She embraced Dugan and nuzzled her face against his neck. "You're my knight in shining armor. That thing would have torn me up if you hadn't have acted so quickly."

"I can't claim hero status. When I tried to arrest Achak, I tripped and fell. That's when my gun went off. He got away, and the Thunderbird went crazy."

"I thought you were shooting at Achak."

"No. I couldn't pursue him because you were in danger. Luckily, I tackled you before the drone could do its damage. "

"I should have dived out of the way. I was too hysterical to think clearly."

"Once we were clear, I fired, and down it went, right where you were standing."

"You saved me from a horrible thrashing. The thing could have killed me."

"I doubt it would have killed you, but it certainly could have severely disfigured you. Those talons were sharp."

She clasped his face in her hands. "You are an amazing man."

"Not really."

"I feel so charged up." She hugged him tightly. "I wish we could make love right now on this bed of sea grass."

"What?"

She planted a wet kiss on his lips. "I want to show you how much I appreciate all you've done for me. Make love to me. Right here. Right now."

"Addy, Agent Goodwin is on his way. He'll be here soon. We

can't do anything like that right now."

She released him, crossed her arms over her breasts, and took a deep breath. "I know. I know. You're right. I'm just so on edge. My emotions are out of control, but I do love you, and I want to prove it."

Dugan tried to calm himself but couldn't help imagining the pleasurable possibilities. Memories of his last conversation with Marla kept intruding upon his visions of Addy—*I want to make dinner for you. I think I'm still in love with you. I am still considering the possibility of marriage.*

Addy stepped closer. "Please hold me."

Dugan hesitated but then put his arms around her. "Addy, we need to talk."

She took a deep breath, and he could feel her soft warmth against him.

"We'll talk later. I just need you to hold me now."

After a few minutes Dugan broke the embrace and convinced her to sit down on a nearby sand mound. The breeze had picked up, and a few clouds had drifted over, smudging the starlit sky.

She reached and clasped his hand. "You were right."

"About what?"

"This isn't the time or place, but soon I'm going to show you what heaven is like. Once we make love, you'll know exactly how I feel about you."

Dugan felt dizzy with conflicting thoughts. "Listen, Addy, I've got to make things clear. On the drive home yesterday, Marla and I had a long talk."

Addy let go of his hand. "Really? And what did you talk about?"

"About the possibilities of getting back together."

"Possibilities? So it's possible that you might get back together, and it's possible that you might not?"

"Yes. It could go either way."

"Which way do you want it to go?"

Dugan shrugged. "I want to marry Marla, but I'm afraid she might grow cold towards me again."

Addy rested her arm on his back and leaned her head against his shoulder. "With me you'd never have to worry about that."

Dugan breathed in the wonderful citrusy fragrance of her hair. "Believe me, I can imagine what it would be like to love you and be loved by you."

She lifted her head and winked at him. "Believe me. You have no idea what it would be like. I can make a man feel like a Greek god. All I'm asking is that you give me a chance."

Dugan shook his head. "It sounds amazing, but I want to wait and see what happens with Marla. I'm sorry."

She rubbed his back. "Don't be sorry. I'm going to pray to Eros, the Greek god of love. I think I'll get my chance."

* * *

Dugan noticed a light hovering just above the sea grass a hundred yards to the east along the sound shore. He stood and reached for his gun just in case Achak had decided to return for his drone.

"What is it?" Addy asked. She reached up to him. "Give me a hand."

"Stay down until we know who it is."

"Sheriff Walton! Is that you?" Goodwin yelled.

"Yeah, it's me." Dugan waved. "It's Agent Goodwin." Dugan clutched Addy's hand and pulled her to her feet.

Goodwin jogged the last fifty yards. "Sorry it took me a little longer than I expected. That trek from the landing strip to here was farther than I figured. I had to work my way around some marshy spots."

"We knew you'd get here sooner or later," Dugan said.

Addy grasped Dugan's arm. "Sheriff Walton kept me safe and sound."

Goodwin eyed Addy and nodded.

Dugan felt a flush of embarrassment, wishing Addy would let him go. "The drone's over this way." He broke away from her grasp and led Goodwin closer to the woods where the drone lay.

Goodwin shone his powerful flashlight on the wreckage. "Paint me silver and call me the Hindenburg."

"Yeah," Dugan said. "It went down in flames."

"Exactly what happened here?"

Addy stepped forward. "Achak asked me to come here tonight. He gave me this necklace." She lifted the strand of beads from her chest, holding it by the end of the half-moon carved from bone. "He told me it belonged to the Indian maiden who possesses me." She shook her head. "I wanted to believe him. Everything he said made sense. When he told me I had great spiritual powers and a deep connection with the past, I felt tremendous pride." She let go of the necklace and raked her fingers through her hair. "He said the Thunderbird would come to me and guide me in my decision about developing Ocracoke."

Dugan cleared his throat. "I wouldn't let her go unless I could follow her and make sure she was safe. I knew Achak would be in the woods somewhere with his trained eagle. My plan was to cut through the woods, find him, and arrest him before anything happened. I reasoned that tying him to the eagle would help our case against him. I figured he used the bird to chase the ghost party into the woods last week so that he could isolate Rowland Brackenbury and murder him. Now that we know the Thunderbird was a drone, I'm guessing he pre-programmed its flight."

Goodwin's eyes narrowed, and his jaw tightened. "Coming here tonight was a mistake."

Dugan hung his head. "I realize that now."

"It was too risky. He may have intended to kill Mrs. Brackenbury. We don't know for sure. Maybe he only wanted to use the drone to sway her decision. Either way her life was in jeopardy."

Dugan glanced up. "I apologize to both of you. I made a bad decision."

Addy placed her hand on Dugan's shoulder. "Maybe it was risky, but I was willing to take the risk. I know that if Dugan wasn't here . . .," she pointed at the drone, "that thing would have attacked me."

"Okay." Goodwin waved his hands in front of him. "What's done is done. Let's focus on Achak. He took off through the woods, correct?"

"Yes. I tried to go after him but tripped on a root. By the time I got to my feet, Addy, I mean Mrs. Brackenbury, was in trouble.

Something had gone haywire with the drone."

"That's when Dugan sprang out of the woods and tackled me," Addy said. "If he would have hesitated a second more, those talons would have ripped me up."

"With the bird going crazy, I had to shoot it. To our surprise it went down like a Sopwith Camel in a dogfight."

Goodwin smiled. "I guess that makes you the Red Baron."

Dugan pointed at his head. "I've got the red part down. I don't know about the Baron."

"Listen," Goodwin said. "We've got to move quickly. Are you sure the man at the controls was Achak?"

Dugan took a deep breath. "Ninety-nine percent sure. I didn't see his face."

Goodwin waved his hand dismissively. "It doesn't matter. You were right about the importance of tying the eagle to Achak. That is essential. We know that he told Mrs. Brackenbury to come here tonight to have an encounter with the Thunderbird. Now we have the evidence of the crashed drone. Obviously, the drone isn't a spiritual entity. The FBI will thoroughly examine it. There'll be fingerprints and serial numbers to help connect the dots to Achak. Wherever he took this thing he terrorized people. Like you said, he may have even used it to set up the murder of Rowland Brackenbury. I think we have enough evidence now to put out an A.P.B. on him."

"I agree." Dugan reached for his cell phone. "Do you want me to make the call?"

"Yes. Time is of the essence. He may be planning an escape."

Dugan phoned the Sheriff's headquarters and instructed the dispatcher to put out an all-points-bulletin on Achak Rowtag and provide a detailed description of Achak's van. Hoping they might catch him at home, he ordered the patrol car in the Frisco vicinity to check Achak's house immediately. He wanted deputies at every bridge along the Outer Banks from Hatteras to Kitty Hawk to stop traffic and check vehicles. Knowing Achak owned a boat, he asked the dispatcher to contact the Coast Guard to give assistance by looking out for vessels crossing the Pamlico Sound. With the skeleton crew on the night shift, he gave orders to call in all available off-duty deputies.

"That should do it," Goodwin said.

Dugan asked, "Do you want me to stay here until the scene is secured?"

"No. I'll wait for the FBI to get here. Why don't you take Mrs. Brackenbury home and then head back up to Manteo to help manage the manhunt."

"Will do."

"But Dugan," Addy said, "my car is in the parking lot at the Ocracoke Bar and Grille."

"No problem," Dugan said. "I can run you back over tomorrow on my boat."

"That'll work. I'm exhausted, but I don't want to stay at my house alone with Achak on the loose. I guess you could drop me off at a hotel."

"You could stay at the detention center near the Sheriff's office. I'm sure there's an empty cell."

Addy laughed. "I'd certainly be safe there. Sure. Why not?" Addy turned and stared at the smoking wreckage of the drone.

To Dugan, she seemed to drift away. "Are you all right?"

She turned back to him and smiled. "I was just thinking. You said we'd have Thunderbird for Thanksgiving dinner. I'd say you overcooked it."

Chapter 28

On the boat ride back to Hatteras, Addy grew quiet. He knew the past week had to be one of the most trying weeks of her life. He decided to let her stir the stew of her thoughts without interruption. He sat back and enjoyed the breeze in his face and the gentle rhythm of his Scout Dorado as it skimmed across the water. He needed a few minutes of relaxation after the encounter with the haywire drone. Perhaps it was a bad decision to put Addy at risk. What's done is done, he thought. He couldn't turn back time. At least the Thunderbird mystery had been solved and Achak's culpability unveiled. He wondered how Addy was handling it all.

After about ten minutes she spoke up. "I've made a decision."

"About what?"

"Several things, really. First, I want to get away from here and all the things that have happened here. I'm going back to England."

"What about your development plans?"

"That's the second thing. I'm not going through with the plans. I know Achak crossed ethical lines to protect Ocracoke and convince me not to proceed . . ."

"That's putting it mildly. He killed your husband."

"Despite what he did, I'm basing my decision on my own intuition." She grasped her beaded necklace and rubbed the half-moon bone. "Kimi spoke to me tonight. I felt her presence so strongly. I'm convinced Ocracoke needs to remain protected and preserved. It's one of the most unspoiled and breathtaking places on earth."

"Wow." Dugan straightened and stretched his back as he gripped the steering wheel. "I'm pleasantly surprised. I thought you believed the spirits on the island wanted their stories told."

Addy shook her head. "I once believed that, but in these last few days I've discovered just the opposite. Those restless spirits deserve to dwell there in peace. They don't want bulldozers, cranes, and cement trucks scarring their beautiful seascape."

"Addy, I must say I'm glad you see it that way. I know there was a lot of money to be made there, but some things are much more important than money."

She reached and gently placed her hand on Dugan's forearm. "That brings me to the third thing."

"And what's that?"

"You"

"Me?"

"I want you to come to England with me."

Dugan didn't know how to say no without hurting her feelings. "Going to England with you would be . . . difficult in my circumstances."

She raised her hand. "Please don't make your decision tonight. Think about it for a day. Tell me tomorrow. You've done so much for me. I know how happy I could make you. You wouldn't have to worry about anything. We could become partners in new development adventures around the world."

I know the answer already, Dugan thought, but he said, "Okay. I'll think about it."

On the drive up to Manteo, Addy slept most of the way. Dugan yawned often and shook himself awake several times. It was 3:30 in the morning by the time they arrived at the Dare County Detention Center. Dugan managed to wake her up and escort her into the building. Then he arranged for her overnight stay in one of the cells. He promised to pick her up sometime before noon. However, he knew that promise may hinge on Achak's capture. Hopefully, one of his deputies would make the arrest before the sun came up.

He was dead tired, but he knew he had to head over to the Sheriff's office and supervise the manhunt. When this was over, he wanted to stretch out on his bed and snooze for twenty-four hours. However, he didn't foresee catching up on his sleep any time soon. It had been a long night and would be a long day before his head could hit the pillow. He pulled into his parking space with one thought occupying his mind—*I need a large, strong cup of coffee.*

When he entered the building, he noticed the receptionist's desk was empty. He checked his watch—3:50. Doris Bonner wouldn't be in for another four hours. He'd have to make his own coffee. First he headed to the dispatcher's office. Bill Nagel was working the night shift; the older man was one of the most dependable people he knew. A Vietnam vet, good ol' Bill enjoyed his work and had no plans of retiring.

"What's happening, Bill? Any news?"

"We're working on it." With his index finger Bill pressed his black-framed glasses to the bridge of his nose. Hel sat back in his swivel chair and clasped his hands behind his shaved head. He was a stout man and very strong for a seventy year old. "Deputy Dufresne reported in an hour ago. Rowtag wasn't at his house in Frisco."

"Didn't figure he would be. Hope he didn't get across one of the bridges before our people set up their check points." Dugan pointed to Bill's desktop. "Where'd you get that coffee?"

"Just made a pot. Go ahead and pour yourself a cup, and I'll catch you up on all that's happened."

Dugan found a tall mug on the shelf next to the coffee maker and filled it to the brim with the steaming brew. He noticed the Cape Hatteras Lighthouse imprinted on the side of the cup, its black and white stripes spiraling to the top. The image reminded him of the day the black SUV had tailed Addy. Then she had panicked, swerved, and turned the car over at the Frisco Campground. Who could have been following her? Did Achak have an accomplice? He thought of all the possibilities and wondered if someone from the Ocracoke Preservation Society had made a radical alliance with him. Then again, it may have been Addy's imagination.

Dugan sipped the coffee and sat down in the wooden chair across from Bill's desk. "That's good stuff. A little strong but good."

Bill raised his cup. "Keeps me going all night."

"So what's been happening?"

"Not much. All the deputies have reported in, and no one has spotted Rowtag. The bridges are all secure, and vehicles are being stopped and checked."

Dugan nodded. "Well, if he catches on to what we're up to, he'll find another way off the Outer Banks. Was his boat at the dock behind his house?"

"Yep. Deputy Dufresne is staying at the house just in case he returns. Marla Easton is cruising the streets in the vicinity, keeping an eye out for his van. She'll alert Dufresne if she sees him."

"Good. Hopefully we'll hear something soon. I've got a question for you."

"Shoot."

"Do you know any people in the Ocracoke Preservation Society?"

"A few."

"Do they seem radical?"

"Radical? No. I'd describe them more as passionate. They truly believe in the importance of keeping Ocracoke unspoiled."

"Can you think of any one in particular who may take his commitment of preservation too far?"

"No one comes to mind, but you never know." The phone rang, and Bill picked it up. "Dispatcher's office. Go ahead . . . okay . . . Did you contact Deputy Dufresne? Great. Let me hand you over to Sheriff Walton." Bill extended the phone. "It's Deputy Easton. She caught sight of Rowtag's van turning onto Timber

Trail."

Dugan took the phone. "Marla? Where are you?"

"I'm parked behind Floral Creations where no one can see the vehicle. Rowtag just turned onto Timber Trail. I alerted Deputy Dufresne. I'll hang back a ways and follow him to the house. He's probably heading to his boat. I told Dufresne to keep his car out of sight. Hopefully, he'll make the arrest, and I'll be there to back him up."

"Sounds like you've got it under control. Be careful."

* * *

Marla drove out from behind the flower shop into the parking lot and made a right turn onto Timber Trail. She kept her speed under twenty miles an hour. She didn't want to catch up to Achak until he turned into his driveway. If he caught a glimpse of a squad car in his rearview mirror, he may try to flee. By timing it right she could pull in behind him and block his vehicle.

Achak lived at the end of Timber Trail. The road curved toward the sound and then wound back around toward Route 12 but dead-ended on a peninsula created by a meandering creek. As she rounded the final turn, she spotted his van. She hit her brakes, and he drove out of view. She took a deep breath. *Hope he didn't catch sight of my headlights in his rear view mirror.*

She waited about thirty seconds and proceeded down the road. He had to have reached his driveway by now, she thought. She picked up speed. When she arrived at his house, she spotted Deputy Dufresne standing in front of the van with his gun drawn. Dufresne shouted, "Exit the vehicle with your hands up!"

Marla pulled in behind the van, her headlights helping to illuminate the scene from the rear. She slammed on her brakes, threw it into park, and sprang from the car. Staying low, she pulled her Magnum from her holster and trained the gun on the driver's side door.

The door popped open and two hands appeared pointing skyward. "I'm unarmed." Achak extended his legs out the door, scooted forward and stood. "What's all this? Why the guns? What crime have I committed?"

Dufresne yelled, "Shut up! Put both hands on the van and spread your legs!"

Achak complied.

Marla holstered her pistol and frisked him. "Just a wallet and keys. No weapons."

"Stand back from the van," Dufresne ordered." Put your hands behind your back. I'm cuffing you."

Marla read him his Miranda rights.

Deep lines formed on Achak's cheeks and forehead, and his brow knotted, making him resemble a wooden carving in the harsh light. "I demand to know why I'm being arrested."

"Fleeing an officer to start with," Marla said.

"When? Where?"

"Last night. Ocracoke Island," Marla said.

"I was here last night."

"And then there's a little matter of murder," Deputy Dufresne said.

"What proof do you have?"

Marla shrugged. "I don't know much at this juncture. I do know that your drone was recovered at Springer's Point last night."

Achak's shoulders drooped, and his head lowered. He closed his eyes.

Dufresne shoved him toward Marla's vehicle. "What's the matter, Rowtag? Did you think your bird was bulletproof?"

Marla opened the back of the squad car, and Dufresne placed his hand on the top of Achak's head and lowered him onto the seat. Marla slammed the door.

Dufresne slapped his hands together several times as if he were brushing off sawdust. "So much for that. Are you going to be okay taking him back alone?"

"I'll be fine. The news about the downed drone took the air right out of him."

Dufresne chuckled. "Yeah, like a kid who just got his favorite toy smashed by the neighborhood bully."

Good analogy, Marla thought. "I'll see you back at headquarters."

"Catch you later."

Marla opened the door to the Dodge Charger, climbed in, and buckled up. She glanced in the rear view mirror. Through the protective bars she noticed Achak's head was lowered. She backed out of the driveway and headed down Timber Trail to Route 12. She wondered if he would talk to her. Wouldn't hurt to try to get some information out of him, she thought.

"Are you okay?" Marla asked, taking the sympathetic angle.

"Everything's fine."

"Sorry about your drone."

"What happened to it?"

"It went berserk, so Sheriff Walton shot it out of the sky."

Achak grunted. "The end comes to all things."

"Why didn't it return to your house? Did you drop the remote when you fled?"

"It doesn't matter. My mission has come to an end also."

"I must confess I thought it was a real bird. A few nights ago in eastern Ohio it swooped down on us. Scared me to death. How in the world did you control it so effectively?" Marla glanced in the rearview mirror.

Achak looked up and met her gaze in the mirror's reflection. "I became one with the Animikii. To you, it was a sophisticated flying machine. To me, it was spirit. Together we brought disaster. Together we brought hope."

"What about death?"

"What about it?"

"Why did Rowland Brackenbury have to die?"

"Why do we all have to die?"

He's talking in circles, Marla thought. "Because we're flesh and blood, but we don't have to die before our time like Brackenbury did."

"From death comes life."

"In other words, because he died, life on Ocracoke will go on unmolested, unthreatened by development."

"Brackenbury is not the only one who died."

"There were others?"

"Many. In Pennsylvania, Ohio, West Virginia."

Wait a minute, Marla thought. Is he a serial killer about to confess to a string of murders? "Who else died?"

"You should know."

"How could I know?"

"You were there."

The face of the shooter from the Youngstown protest site flashed in her mind, her gun firing, and the flowering of crimson on his chest. The explosion at the house in Towanda, Pennsylvania, and the dead bodies along the shore of the Ohio River in Wheeling, West Virginia, burst into her vision. Marla had to shake her head to rid the images from her mind. "So you are claiming responsibility for the deaths associated with these tragedies?"

"My union with the Animikii has brought disaster and death to all of these places, but we have also brought hope and life."

A shiver went down Marla's spine. According to Achak's reasoning, she was part and parcel of his means to battle mankind's mismanagement of nature's bounty. Did he seriously believe he influenced her decision to shoot the shooter? Did he believe his union with the Thunderbird triggered the explosion and earthquake?

"Sorry, Achak. I don't believe you have that kind of power over me or nature. However, I do believe you have the power and motive to stick a knife in an innocent man's back."

"Believe what you want to believe."

Chapter 29

Dugan, Agent Russell Goodwin, and Deputy Jonathan Reed stood in front of the Dare County Detention Center waiting for Marla and the prisoner to arrive. The center was a sprawling, beige-block building with light blue accents on the corners and window trims, creating sleek lines and a modern design. When the squad car swung into the parking space in front of them, Agent Goodwin asked Dugan to brief Marla and then come to the interrogation room to question Rowtag. Reed, a husky deputy with butch-cut blond hair, opened the back door and pulled Achak from the Dodge Charger. Marla stepped out of the vehicle and stretched as the faint light of dawn tinged the eastern sky. It was almost 5:30. Agent Goodwin and Deputy Reed escorted Rowtag into the building.

Marla yawned and smiled. "You better show some appreciation after getting me up at three in the morning to chase down Achak."

"I'll bring two chocolate pies to dinner at your place next

week."

"That's a start. I'm sure you could come up with something more to add to the tally."

Dugan drew closer. Marla's beauty in the pale light entranced him. Her long dark brown hair rippled in the breeze, and her large blue eyes eyed teased him playfully. "Did he put up a fight?"

"No. Once we told him we impounded the drone, he became despondent."

"It won't be hard to tie the drone to him. We're still waiting on forensics to give us the results of the knife-point fragment. If it matches one of the bone knives we confiscated, a murder conviction will be clear-cut in a jury's eyes. Did he say anything to you that might be considered incriminating?"

Marla tilted her head, her lips tightening, head nodding slightly. "I would say he made an odd confession. He said that he and his Thunderbird were responsible for all the deaths and disasters that occurred at these threatened sites. To me, it sounded egotistical, as if he could control nature and people at will. Maybe he wanted to sound crazy to escape conviction on Brackenbury's murder charge."

Dugan fought off a yawn and arched his back. "That's possible."

"You look exhausted."

"I haven't slept for over thirty hours. But there's work to be done— interrogation time. I want to explore another possibility when I question him."

"What's that?"

"I'm convinced he had an accomplice, someone just as passionate as he is about protecting Ocracoke. Like I told you before, he was out of town when Addy Brackenbury was followed. It may have been a team effort that night in the woods when Brackenbury was stabbed."

Marla nodded. "You're probably right. But I don't think he'll squeal on anybody. I think he likes the idea of being recognized as the mastermind."

"We'll see."

Marla checked her watch. "My second shift starts in another hour. I think I'll get some breakfast."

Dugan gave a half salute and a large smile. "Have a great day, Deputy Easton."

Dugan pivoted and headed toward the detention center entrance.

"Dugan?" Marla's voice sounded a little jittery.

He stopped and stared at her.

"I . . . I love you."

Dugan's heart ramped up into another gear. He wasn't expecting those words. "I love you too, Marla. I'll see you some time later today."

She smiled and climbed into the Dodge Charger.

* * *

Dugan and Russell Goodwin entered the interrogation room, a cramped space with gray walls. A light hung over the middle a formica-topped table casting deep shadows on the walls and ceiling. Achak sat peacefully, hands folded in front of him. Goodwin slid into the chair on the left and scooted up to the table. Dugan pulled out the chair on the right and plopped down, leaning back.

Goodwin hunched forward on his elbows. "Mr. Rowtag, first I must inform you that our interrogation will be recorded and could be used as evidence in a court of law."

"I understand."

Goodwin templed his hands just below his chin. "We can make this interrogation easy or very difficult. It's up to you. "

Achak smiled an eerie smile that cut deep lines into his cheeks. "It won't be difficult for me."

"I hope you don't plan on denying ownership of the drone. It won't be hard for us to connect the dots to you," Goodwin said.

"The drone belongs to me."

"Okay." Goodwin glanced at Dugan, tilted his head, raised his eyebrows, and then shifted back to Achak. "Do you admit to flying that drone on Ocracoke last week when you met with the Brackenburys and the paranormal researchers?"

Achak nodded slowly. "Yes. I flew the Animikii that night and last night on Ocracoke. I also flew it in Ohio, Pennsylvania, and at other sites where people reported it."

Dugan scooted up to the table. "How did you control it in the presence of the ghost party? No one saw you with a remote."

"The remote was in my pocket. I preprogrammed its flight to come where I was standing and dive toward us. All I had to do was press a button to activate the flight pattern. I knew everyone would run toward the woods. I programmed it to screech and swoop down several times as it flew in our direction. It was tracking the remote. It appeared as if it was attacking all of us."

"Hmmmph." Goodwin rubbed his chin. "Sounds like you are extremely skilled with this kind of high tech equipment."

Achak smiled again. "The drone was very advanced and expensive, about $25,000, but worth every penny."

Goodwin said, "It also facilitated your plan to murder Rowland Brackenbury. You followed him deep into the woods and then stabbed him in the back three times with a bone knife. Correct?"

Achak's eyes narrowed, and his smile faded. "I take full responsibility for all death and destruction wherever the Animikii made its appearances."

Goodwin sat back. "You take responsibility? In other words, you murdered Rowland Brackenbury?"

"Call it what you want. I take full responsibility."

"Listen, Achak," Dugan said, "I don't believe you and your Thunderbird triggered natural disasters and accidental deaths. Neither do I believe you acted alone when you murdered Rowland Brackenbury. I think you had an accomplice. A black SUV followed Adelaide Brackenbury just south of Buxton a few days ago. She panicked and took off toward the Frisco Campgrounds. There she lost control and flipped her vehicle. At the time you were up north in Ohio. Who helped you?"

Achak's odd smile returned. "I take sole responsibility for all death and destruction wherever the Animikii appeared."

"You understand you are being recorded?" Goodwin asked. "And your words are tantamount to a murder confession."

"My words are my words and no one else's." Achak crossed his arms. "That is all I'm going to say."

Goodwin sat straight up in his seat, his brow knotting.

"You're not going to answer any more questions?"

Achak sat like a carved wooden statue, the odd smile frozen on his face.

Both Goodwin and Dugan asked several more questions and insisted this was the time to talk. They reminded him that his confession and the evidence provided by one of the bone knives confiscated from his house could put him in prison for life. A prosecutor may even call for the death penalty. Achak didn't seem to care. He sat stoically with his arms crossed and his mouth shut.

Finally, Goodwin called for Deputy Reed to come in, handcuff Achak, and take him back to a holding cell.

Goodwin glanced at Dugan. "Did you eat breakfast yet?"

"No. I'm starved."

"Let's get something to eat."

* * *

Dugan recommended the Front Porch Café along Route 64. He loved their potent coffee, blueberry muffins, and croissant breakfast sandwiches. The place had a farmhouse style front porch with a green metal roof. As soon as they entered, the smell of newly roasted coffee and the bubbling of the brewers ramped up his caffeine craving. He needed a recharge. They stepped up to the counter and gave their orders. With large coffees and muffins in hand, they sat down at a wooden table for two in the middle of the room. At seven o'clock in the morning the place buzzed with about twenty customers, several at the bar facing the front window and the rest scattered around the other tables. By the time the waitress delivered their breakfast sandwiches, Dugan had already downed a cup of coffee and devoured a muffin. He held up his cup and asked for a refill.

"Take it easy there, partner." Goodwin took a sip from his tall cup. "This is strong java."

"I need it. Been up all night. I'll have to crash sometime today."

"Yeah. Me too. What'd you think about the interrogation? Sounds like you're convinced Rowtag had an accomplice?"

"It's possible, but I have no idea who it could be."

"The FBI has interviewed most of the members of the Ocracoke Preservation Society. Those people seem fairly harmless—no criminal records, no shady backgrounds. They definitely are committed to keeping the island unscathed, but I don't think any of them would kill someone in order to preserve paradise. "

"So you're sure it was a one-man job?"

Goodwin nodded. "Ninety-five percent sure. Mrs. Brackenbury is a good looking woman. Some lech may have been tailing her. She went nuts and took off. Then she literally lost control and wrecked her Escalade. "

Dugan shook his head. "That's possible. Rowtag certainly wants us to believe it was a one-man job, but considering the circumstances, I have a hunch he had help."

"He glories in his misdeeds. To me, that's egomaniacal. I think he sees himself as some kind of martyr for nature."

"He blurs myth and reality. He's willing to take all the blame and endure all the consequences to become a part of the myth. He believes he'll become a legend."

"He's a legend all right," Goodwin said, "in his own mind."

"There may be another motive. If his goal is to take the rap himself and protect his accomplice, then he'll have someone on the outside to carry on his radical mission against anyone who threatens Ocracoke."

"I hate to break the news to you, but his confession is problematic."

"I know." Dugan took another swig of coffee. "He wouldn't go into detail. He kept saying, 'I take full responsibility for all death and destruction.' To me, that sounds like a football coach taking responsibility for the team's loss."

"If his confession is too ambiguous for a jury's ears, we still have the possibility of matching the knife point to one of his knives. The results should be in today."

"Good. Possession of the murder weapon seals conviction just about every time."

Goodwin agreed.

Both men decided they wanted another breakfast sandwich

and refills on their coffees. Goodwin updated Dugan on Mee Mee's health, not surprised at her ability to bounce back from a near drowning. Dugan reported about Addy's decision to return to England and not pursue the development of Ocracoke. Goodwin thought that was odd, knowing her late husband had all the politicians and investors lining up to make money on the venture.

Dugan shrugged. "She says she's convinced the spirits of Ocracoke want their privacy. I guess she had an epiphany last night when the drone almost fell on her. Now she thinks it would be a crime to develop the island."

"Good. Nowadays greed usually wins. I hope the island remains unmolested long after I'm dead and gone."

"She wants me to go with her to England." After the words escaped, Dugan had second thoughts about revealing Addy's offer.

"You're kidding. She must really be stuck on you."

"I guess." Dugan stared at the empty plate in front of him. "I like Addy. I tried to keep things on a professional level with her, but it was difficult. She's so good looking, so . . . sensual. You know what I mean?" Dugan glanced up.

Goodwin nodded. "I'm flesh and blood too. Be honest with me. Did you go to bed with her?"

Dugan shook his head. "No. The possibility of getting back together with Marla kept me from giving in to that temptation."

"Good. What's your status with Marla now?"

"Things are looking up. She told me she loved me this morning. I hope we'll eventually get married."

"Wow."

Dugan noticed a strange smile on Goodwin's face and an unusual questioning in his eyes.

Goodwin placed both hands on the edge of the table. "I . . . I . . . think I want to ask Mee Mee to marry me."

"No kidding?" Dugan sensed a new familiarity between them, a step of trust in their friendship. "When are you going to ask her?"

"I don't know. She's been an independent woman for a long time. The moment has to be right."

Dugan's cell phone erupted from his front shirt pocket. He quickly slid it out and answered. "Sheriff Walton here."

"It's Marla."

"What's up?"

"I'm back at headquarters. Guess what just came in."

"Uh . . . "

"It's in a sealed envelope from forensics."

"The results from the knife tip comparisons."

"You got it."

Dugan lowered the phone. "Marla's got the results from forensics."

Goodwin straightened. "Great."

Dugan put the phone back to his ear. "Could you bring them over to the detention center?"

"I'll have them there in about thirty minutes."

"See you then."

Chapter 30

Marla checked her watch—almost 8:30 in the morning. She'd been up since Bill Nagel had called at 3:30 to mobilize all available officers for the manhunt. Her regular shift didn't end until 3 p.m. That's another six and a half hours on four hours sleep. She knew she'd be dead by the end of the day.

Poor Dugan. He was going on no sleep. This morning after bringing in Achak, she finally realized how much she loved him. She felt foolish when it hit her. She'd been acting like a teenager. Mee Mee was right. True love was more than a rollercoaster ride of emotions. In Dugan she had found commitment, tenderness, and a willingness to sacrifice. He loved her son, Gabriel, nearly as much as she did. He was a very good man. What was she thinking? She missed her late husband but needed to let go. When the feelings overwhelmed her earlier that day, she couldn't help telling Dugan she loved him. She hoped it wasn't too late. Had Addy Brackenbury found a crack in his vulnerable state and exploited the opportunity? She definitely had the feminine assets to make a man feel alive. I need to trust Dugan, Marla thought. *Please God, don't let me lose him over this blonde bombshell.*

When she pulled into the parking lot of the Dare County Detention Center, she noticed Dugan and Special Agent Goodwin standing by the front doors. She grabbed the envelope off the front passenger seat, climbed out of the vehicle, and hurried in their direction.

She held up the envelope. "I thought you might be interested in seeing the results."

"I'd say we're even a little anxious," Dugan called back.

"Like a couple of long-tailed cats in a room full of rocking chairs," Goodwin said.

Marla handed Goodwin the manila envelope.

"Well . . ." Goodwin tore it across the top. "Hopefully, this will be the lock on Rowtag's birdcage." He reached in and extracted the documents. After about a minute he grunted.

"What's the matter?" Dugan asked.

"It's not a match."

"Dugan!"

All three turned to see Addy Brackenbury stepping away from the closing front door. Marla noticed how low-cut her flimsy white maxi dress was. She took a deep breath and held it for a few seconds, trying to relax.

Dugan waved and then faced them. "Mrs. Brackenbury stayed in a cell at the detention center last night. With Achak on the loose, she didn't want to be alone at her house."

"I see," Marla said.

Adelaide rushed up to the three of them, stepped in between Dugan and Marla, and linked onto Dugan's elbow with the crook of her arm. "This man's my hero. I lost count of the times he's been there for me this past week. Last night he saved my life."

"Very commendable," Goodwin said.

"We've got good news," Dugan said. "Achak has been apprehended. In fact . . ." Dugan pointed to Marla, "Deputy Easton played a major role in bringing him in."

Adelaide reached and patted Marla's arm. "Thank you so much. Now I won't have to stay in a detention cell tonight."

Marla felt like pulling away from her touch but managed to remain motionless.

Goodwin cleared his throat. "Mrs. Brackenbury, Sheriff Walton informed me that you will be leaving the Outer Banks soon, heading back to England."

Adelaide still clung to Dugan's arm. "That's right. I need to get away from here for a while, maybe for good."

"If there's a trial, you will need to testify," Goodwin said.

"I could always fly back if I'm needed." She tugged on Dugan's elbow. "Have you been thinking about my offer from yesterday?"

Dugan's face flushed. "Well . . . yeah, I've made a decision."

Adelaide raised her hand. "Don't tell me now. You can tell me on the boat ride over to Ocracoke when you drop me off to get my car."

"Before you leave here," Goodwin said, "both I and an FBI investigator will need to interview you."

Adelaide appeared flustered and released Dugan's arm. "How long will that take?"

"Maybe two hours."

"Ugh! I wanted to go home, get out of these grimy clothes, take a shower, and then go pick up my car."

Goodwin shrugged. "I'm sorry. You are a key witness. You need to answer a lot of questions about everything that happened, especially where Achak is concerned."

Adelaide nodded. "I understand. I just feel messy. I probably smell."

Dugan pointed to the building. "You can take a shower in the detention facility."

Her eyes widened and she raised her hands. "No, no, not here. I'll just wait until I get home." She faced Goodwin. "Can we get this interview started? I don't want to be here longer than I have to."

"Sure." Goodwin motioned toward the front door.

Adelaide clasped Dugan's hand between her hands and raised it waist high." Dugan, you'll pick me up and take me home after these interviews, won't you?"

"Of course. I promised I'd get you back to Ocracoke so you could pick up your car."

"Thanks." Adelaide gave Dugan an affectionate hug. "I'll see you in a couple of hours." She released him and headed toward the entrance.

Goodwin eyed Dugan and said, "We'll talk about the knife point results later." He turned and followed her.

Once Adelaide and Goodwin entered the building, Marla said, "You two seem quite familiar with each other."

Dugan stiffened up. "I was assigned to watch over her all week. Of course, we got to know each other better. I told you all about it already on the way home from West Virginia."

Marla closed her eyes. "I know. I know. I can't help it. I'm jealous."

Dugan smiled. "You must love me if you're jealous."

Marla opened her eyes. "I told you I loved you this morning, and I meant it. What was her offer to you from yesterday?"

"Believe me, nothing you have to worry about. If you want me, I'm all yours."

"I want you." Marla raised her finger. "And I'd give you a big hug and a kiss right now, but I'm not going to do it because we're on duty, and that wouldn't be professional."

Dugan smiled. "We'll take care of that later."

* * *

Dugan felt frustrated over the forensic results confirming the bone tip didn't match any of Achak's knives. Now more than ever he believed Achak had an accomplice. Perhaps he had a partner that helped him purchase the drone. The FBI would trace serial numbers and any paper trail left behind by the purchases. Dugan guessed the person shared the same passion about Native American relics and sacred lands, the same radical perspective on protecting Ocracoke. When the ghost party met at Springer's Point, the accomplice probably waited in the woods to kill Brackenbury while Achak orchestrated the Thunderbird attack. A few days later he followed Addy into the Frisco Campgrounds. The murder weapon was still out there. Identifying Achak's partner was the key to finding it.

After completing his paperwork at the sheriff's office, he

made several calls to local politicians over various concerns in the county. As sheriff he continually had to put out small fires of conflict and negotiate situations among various civic representatives and local boards when disagreements arose over ordinances and practices. It was part of the job, and he did what he could to keep the peace, always trying to exercise good judgment and fairness.

Around eleven o'clock he decided to head back over to the detention center to see if Addy was ready to go home. What a relief it would be when he could finally drop her off on Ocracoke. He enjoyed getting to know her and had almost succumbed to her beauty, but now that Marla had come around, he looked forward to saying adios to Addy. He hoped she'd take it well. He also hoped that Marla truly meant what she said about wanting him. Why was there still a shadow of a doubt?

Turning into the parking lot, he caught a glimpse of Addy's white dress rippling in the wind as she stood in the late morning sunshine near the entrance. The wind pressed the thin fabric against her body, clearly delineating her near perfect figure. Dugan took a deep breath and blew it out. *Easy, boy, take it easy.* Dugan eased to a stop.

Addy bounded up to the car and swung open the door. "I just called your office. They told me you'd be here any second. I'm ready to get out of here." She climbed in and buckled her seatbelt.

Dugan put the car into reverse and backed out of the parking space. "How was the interview?"

"Long and stressful. They wanted to know every single detail about everything that happened."

"I'm guessing this won't go to trial. Achak will work out some kind of plea bargain to avoid the electric chair."

Addy stretched her arms and arched her back. "I hope so. I don't want to come back here. I've decided to put the house up for sale."

"Clean break, huh?"

"Yep, and I hope you decide to come with me."

"Addy, I'm afraid . . ."

She raised her hand. "Don't tell me yet. If you're going to let me down, I'd rather it be out on the Pamlico Sound with the breeze in my face and the rhythm of the waves beneath me. I won't cry as much out there."

"Whatever you want."

Addy was chatty the whole way back to Hatteras. Dugan didn't have to say much to keep the conversation going. Her flood of words outlined her plans for the near future. Dugan figured she hoped to sway his decision by presenting all the wonderful possibilities—travel to exotic places; development projects in Spain, Germany, and Italy; the possibility of purchasing an island off the coast of Florida and building a fabulous estate. This was a new side of her Dugan hadn't seen: the material girl. She didn't realize Dugan could care less about extravagance and opulence. In fact, people who overindulged in their wealth never impressed him. He was happy with the simple things in life. He looked forward to getting back together with Marla,taking Gabriel fishing out on the sound, working around the house, going out to dinner with them at a local restaurant

As Addy rambled on, Dugan almost fell asleep at the wheel. She gasped, grabbed his arm, and shook him.

He jerked the wheel and swerved back to the center of the lane. "Sorry about that. I'm really tired."

"Oh my heart! You almost went off the road."

"It won't happen again. We only have a few miles to go."

"You need a nap. When I'm taking a shower and changing, you should take a half-hour nap in one of the downstairs bedrooms."

Dugan nodded. "That's not a bad idea. A good nap usually brings me back to life."

"Once I'm ready, I'll wake you up, and we'll head over to Ocracoke."

"That sounds like a good plan."

When Dugan pulled into the parking space at Addy's house, he had to shake himself awake again. Addy gripped his arm as they walked to the door. He wanted to tell her to let him go but figured she was only trying to steady him. Once they entered the elevator, he hit the button for the second floor.

When the door opened Addy said, "I won't be long. Thirty

minutes at the most. Get a good nap."

Dugan stepped out and glanced over his shoulder. "I will."

He found the bedroom he'd slept in a couple nighys ago. Quickly, he slipped off his shoes and crawled onto the king size bed. He flipped onto his back and spread his arms and legs. It felt so good to lie down. He closed his eyes and drifted off to sleep within seconds.

* * *

Marla's stomach growled; it was almost noon. The morning shift had passed slowly. The most interesting incident occurred when she chased down a souped-up Mustang going seventy-five in a fifty-five zone just south of Salvo. When she stepped up to the window, a gray-haired lady in her mid-seventies greeted her with a big smile. The old gal claimed she was late for a lunch date with her boyfriend at Dirty Dick's Crab House in Avon. Marla shook her head, somehow managed to stifle a giggle, and let her off with a warning.

Since she was heading in that direction, Marla decided to go to Avon too and stop at the Surf'n Pig BBQ to pick up a chicken sandwich for lunch. On the way she pondered her jealous flare-up over Adelaide Brackenbury's affectionate attachment to Dugan. *Good riddance to that woman. The sooner the hussy planted her feet on Great Britain's soil the better. The Pope could lose his virginity around her.* Marla felt a slight pang of guilt over her thoughts. *It's partly my fault. I did push Dugan out of my life and into the grieving widow's open arms. That was my mistake, but I'm going to make up for it.*

She decided she would head down to Frisco on her lunch break and stop in the gift shop at the Frisco Native American Museum to buy Dugan a gift—a peace offering. A year had passed since Dugan had asked her to marry him. Like a wishy-washy teenager, she had called off the engagement. Now it was her turn to pop the question. Perhaps she could find a neat present that would be appropriate for the proposal—maybe a ring, or artifact, or even a pipe. With all that had happened she believed Dugan would appreciate something well-crafted from the museum store. Then, hopefully, he'd say yes .

The museum was located along Route 12 just north of Frisco. The exterior of the building offered a Native American flavor: Adobe-tan siding with evenly spaced logs jutting slightly from the flat roof line presented a rustic, southwest appearance. Large boulders lined the edge of the property along the road. Marla had visited the gift shop several times to purchase toys for Gabriel. He especially loved a drum with a hand-painted picture of a stag on the leather head cover.

She entered the shop and drifted around the glass cases and shelves, admiring the incredible skill the artisans exercised to produce their work. She especially enjoyed the beauty of the original artworks—carvings, paintings, dreamcatchers, pottery, and baskets. The geometric designs, bright colors, and primitive style of the objects demonstrated a beauty and grace that could not be matched by mass produced items at the chain stores. When she arrived at the case with the jewelry, she knelt closer in hopes of finding a ring or necklace for Dugan. *There.* She spotted a necklace with blue turquoise beads and a black arrowhead for the drop. *That's perfect. Sixty-five dollars. Reasonably priced too.*

While the sales clerk, a thin man with a white goatee, looked for a gift box, Marla headed to the artifact case in hopes of finding an arrow head to add to Gabriel's collection. The first thing that caught her eye was a bone knife display. One of the knives was missing. She leaned closer to inspect the others. They were definitely old and expensive, the prices ranging from $900 to $1500. The more expensive ones had long, bone blades and decorated handles made out of painted wood with leather wrappings. The leather was worn and the paint faded.

"I found a box for your necklace, Ma'am," the clerk called from across the shop.

"Sir, could you come here a second."

"Sure thing."

He walked over and stood on the other side of the case. "You interested in one of those knives?"

"Yeah." Marla pointed to the empty space. "The missing one."

He nodded. "That was purchased about two weeks ago. Quite an ancient artifact, I'd say nearly two hundred years old. The buyer didn't blink at the $2000 price tag. Whipped out the VISA card like it was a switchblade."

"Hmmmm." Marla rubbed her chin. "You wouldn't happen to remember the person's name?"

The clerk shook his head. "No. But I do remember her face and figure. She was hard to forget."

"Why's that?"

"She reminded me of Marilyn Monroe."

A chill went through Marla's chest like a blade made of ice. She pulled out her cell phone, scrolled down her list of contacts, and tapped Dugan's number.

Chapter 31

The Thunderbird screeched above him. Dugan reached for his gun but something restricted his hand. The creature dipped lower and screeched again. He tried his other hand, but something restrained it. The talons swooped closer, but this time the bird's screech sounded more like a ring—his cell phone ring. *I'm dreaming.* Dugan forced his eyes open and blinked. The phone trilled again from his front shirt pocket. When he reached for it, his right hand yanked a chain attached to the bed post. *What the hell?* Both hands were handcuffed and chained, each to the opposite bedpost.

"I'll get that for you."

Dugan glanced up to see Addy wearing almost nothing—a necklace of faded beads with a half-moon pendant drooped over a skimpy tan bra tied together in front with a leather lace. A bone knife hung from a leather strap around her waist, and below the strap she wore a matching tan thong. A geometrically patterned headband circled her head with a tall white feather sticking up in the back.

"What's going on?" Dugan demanded as he shook the chains.

Addy pulled the phone from his pocket and glanced at the caller ID info. "It's your ex-girlfriend, Marla."

"I need to talk to her."

Addy placed the phone on the night stand. It rang twice more and stopped. "Once I do what I want to do, you won't want to talk to Marla anymore. Trust me."

"What are you talking about?"

"Remember what I said to you on Ocracoke the other night? I want to make love to you like no one has ever made love to you before. Then you'll forget Marla and all the trouble she's caused you. That's why I asked you to wait before you made your decision."

"Addy . . . please . . . you don't understand . . ."

"I understand perfectly. I know what a man wants." She crawled onto the bed, straddled him, reached for the headboard above him, and lowered her breasts in front of his face. "Do you see that string?"

How could I miss it? He nodded.

"Take it between your teeth. It won't be hard to untie."

Dugan opened his mouth. *Wait. Wait. Wait. You can't do this.* The temptation to release the tie strained the metal of his fortitude.

Ding!

Dugan turned his head away from her breasts and focused on the phone. "Marla just texted me. It has to do with the case against Achak."

Addy sat back. "Interruptions. Interruptions." She climbed off of him and picked up the phone. "*Dugan. Call me back. This is important.*" She placed the phone back on the stand. "Sorry, Marla. Dugan's busy." She crawled on top of him again. Sitting back, she reached for the knife. "Listen. I'm going to take this knife and tickle you until you untie my bra with your teeth."

"Please, Addy, this isn't right."

She held the knife blade to her lips. "Shhhhhhh."

She lowered the blade and drew the tip very gently down his cheek, under his chin, and across his neck.

Dugan stiffened, the bone tip sending chills through him.

She held the blade in front of his face. "I'll drive you crazy with this if you don't obey me."

Dugan stared at the tip of the knife. A small fraction of the point was missing.

"You are really focusing on that knife point. I'm not going to hurt you, Dugan. I want to give you pleasure. I want to make you happier than you've ever been in your life. Now are you going to untie my bra or not?"

Dugan shook his head.

"Playing hard to get, aren't you? Okay. More tickling." She gently drew the tip across his other cheek, down and across his neck.

Dugan sucked in a quick breath, the tingling on his skin sending surges through his body.

"It's getting hard, isn't it? Hard not to obey me."

Ding!

Dugan swallowed and glanced at the phone. "Listen. I know that text is important. It could make or break the case against Achak."

Addy grunted in disgust and slid the knife back into its slot on her leather waist strap. "Okay. I'll check the text. If it's not that important, I'm going to turn the phone off so you can focus on me." She slid off of him and reached for the phone. "Hmmmm. What's this? *Mrs. B. purchased a bone knife. We need to find it and compare it with the fragment.*" She turned and faced Dugan. "What fragment?"

Dugan shrugged.

"I remember you telling me you found the possible murder weapon at Achak's house. You said you had to match up the evidence."

"Right." Oh no, Dugan thought, she's figuring it out.

"What kind of evidence?" She pulled the knife from the belt and examined the knife tip. "A fragment." Her eyes grew wide. She held the knife in front of Dugan's face. "No wonder you were staring at the tip."

Dugan watched the warmth drain from Addy's face, her beauty turning to ice.

She paced around the bed and back, and then raised the knife chest high. "They found a fragment of this knife, didn't they?"

Dugan nodded. "Embedded in your husband's back."

"I knew I should have thrown it into the Pamlico Sound, but it's sacred, a Pamunkey Indian relic. It cost me $2000."

"Why'd you kill him?"

Addy lowered the knife. "Kimi insisted."

"Kimi?"

Addy nodded. "She wanted me to be independent and in control."

"The Indian girl that possesses you made you kill your husband?"

She nodded. "Kimi had been abused by men all her life. A man raped her and then murdered her."

"But your husband loved you."

"I was one of his possessions. He loved beautiful things. When he became impotent, I threatened to leave him. He didn't want to lose me, so he offered me partnership in his development projects. I agreed to stay with him and learn the business."

"That's not reason enough to kill him."

She stepped closer. "Even though we were partners, he tried to control me psychologically. He thought he was smarter than me. The ghost party was his last attempt. He offered the two paranormal researchers a small stake in the Ocracoke development. After his death, they brought in the medium, Darrin Brownstone, to seal the deal."

"Now you have control of his financial empire."

"*My* financial empire. I will make all the decisions from now on, but I'm not alone. Kimi will be my spirit guide."

If I can just keep her talking, Dugan reasoned, I'll increase my chances of getting out of here alive. "Why not Ocracoke? There's a lot of money to be made. You've got the investors and politicians lined up."

She shook her head. "I don't make all my decisions based on money. I truly wanted to respect the wishes of the departed on Ocracoke. Like I told you, I felt the confirmation to not develop the island when Kimi possessed me two nights ago, the night you shot down the drone."

Dugan shook the handcuffs. "These are uncomfortable. Could you please release me?"

Her eyes narrowed. "I don't think so. The question is . . . should I kill you?" She raised the knife, closed her eyes, and tilted her head upwards.

She's summoning Kimi, Dugan thought. "Wait! Stay with me! I want to ask you just two more questions."

She opened her eyes and took a deep breath. "Okay, since you've been so nice to me, go ahead."

"So you weren't in partnership with Achak?"

"No. He's another man who wanted to control me. Achak thought he was more powerful than me. He probably believes he somehow moved me to kill Rowland. He worshiped his Animikii, sent it out to wreak havoc, and then took credit for everything that happened. I admire his passion and sacrifice to protect sacred lands, but I have no ties to him." She extended the knife and touched Dugan's chin with the point. "One last question, and then I must make a decision."

Dugan backed his head away from the knife point. "Who tailed you in the black SUV?"

She chuckled. "No one. Wrecking my Escalade was the perfect ploy to insure no suspicions for my husband's murder fell on me. I knew rolling the vehicle over on that sharp turn in the campground was risky, but it was a chance I had to take."

Dugan nodded, the knife point still less than an inch away.

"No more questions." Addy brought the knife up to her chest with both hands, the blade pointing up between her breasts. She closed her eyes and raised her head.

Dugan swallowed. She's crazy enough to kill me, he thought, especially when she becomes Kimi.

Her mouth moved slowly, odd sounds softly escaping. The chanting became louder. She paced around the room, eyes half closed, as the queer language spewed out of her mouth faster and faster. Her face contorted, and she shook all over like an epileptic having a seizure. Suddenly, she stopped and turned, facing him. Silence. Her eyes widened. She raised the knife and plunged it again and again into an imaginary target.

She's envisioning me, Dugan thought. I'm the target.

Her breathing accelerated, and the stabbing slowed to a stop. Her chest heaved with each inhale. She blinked several times, her eyes refocusing on him. "I'm sorry Dugan. Kimi says you must die."

"Why?"

"She says you want to send me to my death."

"That's not true."

"The constable murdered her. She says you're the constable on this island now. You'll testify against me. I'll go to the electric chair."

Dugan's mind rambled for some logical defense. "If . . . if you kill me, they'll catch you. Marla knows about the knife."

"We're not worried about what Marla knows. I bought a bone knife at the Frisco museum. So what? Without the knife they can't prove anything. It's your knowledge that will insure the murder conviction. I've confessed everything to you. I'm sorry. You must die."

"But they'll find my body. They'll know you killed me."

Addy shook her head. "My assistant, Sebastian, will be here in about an hour. He'll land at the Billy Mitchell Airstrip down the road. I'll go pick him up, and we'll come back here. Together we'll clean up the mess and make sure there's no evidence left behind. We'll put your body into one of my large trunks, load it into the car and put you on the plane. Halfway across the Atlantic, we'll dump you into the ocean." She held out the knife. "This will go into the trunk with you, never to be found." She stepped toward him.

"Addy, please, you told me you loved me."

"I really did. I wanted to love you with my body, mind, and spirit. I was hoping you'd decide to come with me. It would have been wonderful. But now . . . but now I must kill you."

"If you love me, you can't kill me."

Addy nodded slowly. "You're right. I can't." Her features began to harden, eyes narrowing. "But Kimi can." She closed her eyes and tilted her head backwards. Her mouth moved and the odd words began to flow again.

* * *

Marla didn't understand why Dugan didn't call her back or at least text her. Something was wrong. It didn't take long to drive from Frisco to Hatteras, maybe five or six minutes. When she passed Charlie Cash's beach house, she glanced to the left and noticed Dugan's boat still tied to the dock. She shifted her focus to the Brackenbury house straight ahead. *Dugan is still there. Why didn't he return my call?*

If Adelaide Brackenbury murdered her husband for her own gain, she'd surely kill again to preserve her appearance of innocence in front of a judge and jury. Did she see the text Marla had sent? Her heart dropped into her stomach as she drove the squad car slowly along the side of the large beach house. She'd have to assume the worst. She opened the car door gently, trying not to make a sound. She slipped out of the vehicle and headed to the back of the property. There she managed to open a gate to the tall wooden fence that surrounded the back yard and swimming pool.

She remembered the great room and master bedroom were on the third floor. Wooden steps ascended from the patio to the second floor, where another flight rose to the third floor deck. Quickly, she scurried up the steps like a cat without making a sound. At the top she pressed herself against the wall and pulled out her Magnum pistol. Then she edged to the glass door. Peering in, she saw no one. The door had been slid half open with a screen allowing in the breeze. She reached to tug on the sliding screen. It was unlocked.

She stepped into the great room, her eyes adjusting quickly to the sudden change from sunlight to a darkened interior. She glanced around the kitchen and living room area. All was quiet. Then she noticed the bedroom door halfway open. She tiptoed over and peeked into the darkened room, hoping not to see Dugan in bed with the murderess. Relief! The bed was empty. She felt a twinge of guilt for considering the possibility. Where could they be? She walked back into the great room and stood at the top of the steps. She heard a woman's voice coming from the second floor, but the words were indecipherable like some kind

246

of weird chant.

* * *

Dugan watched as Addy paced around the room. She was working herself into frenzy. Her head shook, and her arms jerked uncontrollably. To Dugan, the words she growled, murmured, and bellowed sounded more and more like gibberish rather than a Native American dialect. She's completely lost it, Dugan thought, like some wacko who just fell off the schizo wagon. Finally, the gyrations stopped, and she caught her breath. She stood still at the foot of the bed, turned, and stared at him. Her expression reminded him of a hyped-up cocaine addict.

She raised the knife and edged around the corner of the bed. Her eyes widened.

He tried to shift his legs and plant them on the mattress so that he could kick up at her. If she stuck him in the femoral artery, he'd bleed out in minutes.

She lunged and plunged the knife, nicking the inside of his thigh. He managed to kick her back with his other foot. She regained her balance just out of his reach. He glanced down at the hole in his jeans but quickly refocused on her.

She charged and stabbed again, but he kicked her shoulder, causing the knife to glance off his knee. Rage distorted her face into an angry she-wolf. How much longer could his luck hold out? He yanked the chains, but there was no hope of breaking free from the cuffs and thick posts of the headboard.

She eyed the space between the bed and the wall. Slowly her head nodded, and a sinister smile cracked her icy demeanor.

Dugan could see she was forming a plan of attack. She had plenty of room to get around his legs and plunge the knife into his heart before he could adjust to kick her. Dugan swallowed. *This could be it.*

Taking her stance, she raised the knife and feinted to the left.

Dugan jerked in that direction by reflex. *No! She's going to come right.*

"Hold it, or I'll shoot!" Marla shouted from the doorway, aiming her Magnum straight at Addy.

Addy froze a step away from Dugan's chest. Slowly, she turned around and faced Marla.

"Drop the knife and walk toward me."

Addy's hands lowered to her side, but she held on to the knife. She advanced tentatively toward Marla.

"I said drop the knife."

Addy stopped, glanced over her shoulder at Dugan, and stepped to the right, keeping Dugan directly in the line of fire. "Shoot me, and you'll shoot him." She raised the knife and lunged at Marla.

Marla dropped to her knees and fired as Addy landed on top of her. The bullet struck the wall a few feet above Dugan's head.

The two women rolled on the floor. Dugan rose up as best he could. He saw Marla's hand gripping Addy's wrist, the knife thrashing the air. She must have dropped her gun, Dugan thought. They rolled over again and disappeared at the foot of the bed. Dugan could feel their bodies thrashing against the bedframe. He heard thuds and grunts.

They rolled into view to his left. Marla's hand still gripped Addy's wrist, but now Addy was on top of her. Marla's other hand broke free from Addy's grip. She reached and grabbed a thick lock of platinum blonde hair. Addy screamed. Marla yanked, and the tress ripped from the top of her scalp. Blood seeped from her forehead and into her eyes.

The pain seemed to inflame Addy to a new level of strength. She broke free from Marla's grasp and struggled to her feet. She raised the knife above her head, but Marla somersaulted backwards along the bed towards Dugan. Addy stepped forward and dove, the knife thrusting at Marla. Dugan shot his legs out and kicked Addy midair. She flew sideways, head ramming into the oak dresser. Marla struggled to her feet and backed into the lampstand. Addy didn't move.

"Where's your gun?" Dugan said.

Marla scanned the floor and spotted it next to the door. She leapt over Addy's body, retrieved her pistol, whirled, and pointed it at the immobile woman.

Dugan noticed a large lump forming on the back of Addy's head. "I think she's unconscious."

Marla unclipped handcuffs from her belt, dropped onto Addy's legs, and quickly clamped her hands behind her with the cuffs. Then she reached over Addy's shoulder, picked up the knife, and placed it on the dresser. Marla stood and peered at the unmoving body. "She's out cold." She looked at Dugan. "Nice kick."

"Thanks. I had the right angle from here."

She put her hands on her hips and eyed the cuffs and chains linking Dugan to the bedpost as if seeing them for the first time.

Dugan rattled the chains and tried to smile but could see Marla's eyes narrowing. "I . . . I know this looks bad."

She shook her head. "Sheriff Walton, all I can say is you better have a good explanation for your compromising situation."

Epilogue

The flight from the Billy Mitchell Airport to the airstrip on Ocracoke only took a few minutes. The unusually cool September morning with its bright sunshine and light breeze brought a freshness to the day. Mee Mee enjoyed flying with Russell. He was a good pilot, but most of all she enjoyed their conversations. He had a great sense of humor. Just being with him the last few days had put a bounce in her stride. She climbed out of the Beechcraft Baron and waited for him to circle around the plane. The steady wind winnowed her shoulder-length hair as she watched a formation of pelicans gliding above the surf. When Russell moseyed around the front of the plane, she noticed something bulging from inside his brown leather jacket.

"What do you have hidden in there?" She reached and patted his chest.

"It's my rapidly beating heart. It goes into overdrive whenever I'm with you."

Mee Mee laughed. "Right." She unzipped his jacket and noticed some kind of handle.

He grabbed the handle and pulled out a collapsible spade. "Today we are going to find Blackbeard's treasure."

"You know what they say?"

"What's that?"

"Hope springs eternal in the heart of a fool."

Russell chuckled. "This fool has something no other treasure-hunting fool possessed where Blackbeard's treasure is concerned."

"Oh yeah. What do you have that's so special?"

"Have you ever heard of Israel Hands?"

Easy question, Mee Mee thought. "He's one of the pirates from Robert Louis Stevenson's *Treasure Island*. I believe he was second in command to Long John Silver."

"Right. But that fictional character was based on a real person."

Mee Mee nodded. "Of course. If I recall correctly, Israel Hands was Blackbeard's right hand man."

Russell slid his hand inside his jacket. "I have a copy of a map of Ocracoke Island that Hands drew."

"Where did you get it?"

Russell pulled out a piece of folded white paper. "In the same restricted archives where I discovered the depositions of Blackbeard's crew—the men he abandoned at the Beaufort Inlet."

"You said that one crew member claimed he stumbled upon Blackbeard in the middle of the woods near here."

"That's right. Blackbeard was chiseling something onto a big, flat rock. He told the crewman he was about to open the gates of hell. I believe he was preparing a marker where he would someday bury his treasure."

"Finding a big rock in the woods would be unusual. Rocks don't occur naturally on the Outer Banks."

"Right. But Blackbeard was a big man. Ships carried rocks for ballast. He could have easily carried one into the woods and chiseled some kind identifying mark on it."

"And you found the map where 'X' marks the spot?"

"Not 'X'." He handed Mee Mee the map. "Can you read the word that Israel Hands wrote on the map?"

Mee Mee focused on the drawing. "There. Right in the middle of that clump of trees it says, 'HELL'."

Russell nodded." Hell is the key. When I discovered this document, I recognized the shape of the southern end of Ocracoke immediately. Then I saw the word 'HELL'. Like I told you before, Blackbeard told another crew member that nobody but he and the devil knew where his treasure was, and the longer liver shall take it all. If we find that rock, we'll find the treasure."

"Hopefully, it won't be under two feet of sand. If so, we won't find it."

"Maybe not. But we know approximately where it's located."

Mee Mee pointed to where the shore jutted out on the map. "That looks like Springer's Point to me. If that's the case, then the rock would be located in the woods about one hundred yards beyond the clearing."

"That's exactly what I figured. Let's go."

They cut across the marsh, trying to avoid the soggy footing until they came upon a path.

"I've walked along this trail before," Mee Mee said. "It winds through the woods and eventually comes out at Springer's Point."

Russell rubbed his hands together. "I can almost hear the clinking of gold doubloons."

"Don't get too anxious. Like I said, it may be buried several feet under the sand."

"That's true. Then again a few tropical storms have blown through here recently. You never know what they might have uncovered."

Marla had to agree with that possibility. Because the wind shifts the sand so much on the Outer Banks, the ribs of old wooden shipwrecks are often uncovered for months at a time. Then a storm will blow in from another direction and cover them right back up.

They followed the path through the woods. Only a week ago Mee Mee had taken cover there to escape Achak's Thunderbird drone. She'd never forget that night. Hearing that Adelaide Brackenbury had murdered her husband had shocked her. She knew the woman was kooky but didn't figure her to be a psychopath. Then again, money and power often drive people to commit illegal and sometimes lethal acts. She didn't have to worry about those kinds of temptations. Managing a bookstore in Buxton and writing an occasional article for the *Island Free Press* provided a fulfilling career but definitely not a bloated bank account.

They finally exited the shadows of the woods and stood in the sunshine of the clearing at Springer's Point. Russell unfolded the map, and they estimated the distance to the spot marked by the word 'HELL' by cross referencing other points on the map with the current landscape. Once they agreed on a direction, they paced back into the woods for about a hundred yards or so, taking into account the variations from a straight path caused by the many live oaks and thick undergrowth. Eventually, they reached the area that seemed most likely to be Israel Hands's location mark—the HELL spot. They decided to separate and carefully examine the ground in a forty yard circumference in hopes of finding a large, flat rock.

Mee Mee wasn't having much luck. All she could see was sand, roots, and weeds.

After about ten minutes, Russell called out, "Look here!"

Mee Mee rushed over. A corner of a flat rock stuck up out of the ground. It was hard to determine its size because most of it was under the sandy soil

"This could be it." Russell fell to his knees and began to brush the sand away with his hands. In less than a minute he uncovered a marking. "Do you see that?"

Mee Mee gasped. "It looks like the letter 'L'."

Russell continued clearing the sand. To the left of the L another L appeared and then an E.

Mee Mee's heart thumped like a wind-up toy drummer. She leaned on her knees and watched as Russell uncovered an H.

He glanced up. "We found it! The HELL rock." He stood and pulled the collapsible spade from his jacket. "I'll dig under the edge so we can get a handhold. Then we'll flip the rock over. I'm guessing the treasure chest is three or four feet below the surface." He stared at the small shovel and then back at Mee Mee. Back and forth he shifted his gaze between her and the spade several times.

"What are you waiting for?" Mee Mee asked.

"Well . . . you know digging for treasure on this part of the island is illegal."

"That's true. This is protected land, and you have sworn to uphold the law. But wouldn't finding Blackbeard's treasure be an exception?"

Russell shrugged. "It would be an incredible find but still unlawful. Then again, no one would have to know besides you and me. We'll dig it up, cover up the hole, and haul it back to my plane. We could sell it on the black market and make millions. What do you think?"

Mee Mee rubbed her chin. "It doesn't matter what I think. This is your life's work. It all goes to you."

"You're wrong about that. Everything you think matters to me. We started this journey more than thirty years ago.

Whatever we find is half yours."

Mee Mee straightened. *Half mine? Possibly millions of dollars? Oh, what I could do with that kind of money.* She took a deep breath. "Decisions, decisions."

"Should I start digging?"

"You know . . . my mother almost named me Eve. That would have made my decision easier. Instead, she went with Michelle, and everyone called me Mee Mee. Do you know what Michelle means?"

"I have no idea."

"It's a form of Michael which means a gift from God. If it's up to me, I'd have to say no. But it's not up to me. It's your decision."

"I'm glad you said that."

"Why? Do you think finding Blackbeard's treasure would make your life complete?"

"No, but I wanted to make sure you felt the same way I did." Dropping the spade, he got down on one knee. He stuck his hand into his jacket pocket, withdrew a small velvet box, and opened it. Inside was a dazzling diamond ring. "Mee Mee Roberts, you are a gift from God, and there's only one thing that would make my life complete."

Mee Mee felt suddenly dizzy. She gulped in a deep breath and steadied herself.

"Blackbeard's treasure couldn't make me nearly as happy as you. Will you marry me?"

Mee Mee reached and planted her hand on his shoulder to steady herself. "Whew! Decisions, decisions."

* * *

On the way back to the plane through the marsh, the wind rippled the grasses like currents on a green sea. They walked hand in hand as the sun warmed their smiling faces. A flock of seagulls flew overhead as the sound of the surf from beyond the airstrip rumbled and splashed.

"Whatever happened with Marla and Dugan?" Russell asked.

Mee Mee chuckled. "Poor Dugan. It took some talking, but somehow he convinced Marla that he was out cold when Addy

Brackenbury handcuffed him to the bedposts. Marla made him sweat a little but finally removed the cuffs. They're getting married in October at the Elizabethan Gardens in Manteo."

"I know the perfect song for their bridal dance."

"What would that be?"

"'Unchained Melody.'"

Mee Mee laughed so hard she had to stop and catch her breath. "You know something? I love your sense of humor."

"I could make you laugh for a lifetime. Why don't we make that a double wedding ceremony at the Elizabethan Gardens in October."

Mee Mee squeezed his hand and started walking again. "Decisions, decisions."

Books by Joe C. Ellis

Outer Banks Murder Series

Prequel – The Healing Place
Book 1 – Murder at Whalehead
Book 2 – Murder at Hatteras
Book 3 – Murder on the Outer Banks
Book 4 – Murder at Ocracoke

Other Books

The Old Man and the Marathon
A Running Novel

The First Shall Be Last
A World War II Novel

The Christmas Monkey
A Children's Book

About the Author

Joe C. Ellis, a big fan of the North Carolina's Outer Banks, grew up in the Ohio Valley. A native of Martins Ferry, Ohio, he attended West Liberty State College in West Virginia and went on to earn his Master's Degree in education from Muskingum College in New Concord, Ohio. After a thirty-six year career as an art teacher, he retired from the Martins Ferry City School District.

Currently, he is the pastor for the Scotch Ridge Presbyterian Church and the Colerain Presbyterian Church. His writing career began in 2001 with the publication of his first novel, *The Healing Place*. In 2007 he began the *Outer Banks Murder Series* with the publication of *Murder at Whalehead* (2010), *Murder at Hatteras* (2011), *Murder on the Outer Banks* (2012), and the latest installment, *Murder at Ocracoke* (2017).

Joe credits family vacations on the Outer Banks with the inspiration for these stories. Joe and his wife, Judy, have three children and five grandsons. Although the kids have flown the nest, they get together often and always make it a priority to vacation on the Outer Banks whenever possible. He comments, "It's a place on the edge of the world, a place of great beauty and sometimes danger—the ideal setting for murder mysteries."